Two letters beckoned him to Arizona:

My dear Jonathan: I want you to act as my agent in my new enterprise which will take your time for the next six months ... and which, if we pull it off, should net you at least $12,000. ... I have started a new town ... I need good people. ... You will be the one to recruit these key people. ...

TOBY LANE

Dere Mister Fontaine—The Injun which you wuz lookin' fur is back around these parts again. ...

A. J. BEESLEY

Then came the telegram:

NOW YOU MUST TAKE MY OFFER STOP
INDIAN IS HERE STOP WILL TRY TO SAVE
HIM FOR YOU SIGNED TOBY

THE IRON SHIRT
is an original *Pocket Book* edition.

Also by John Whitlatch

Gannon's Vendetta
Morgan's Rebellion
Tanner's Lemming

Published by Pocket Books

The
Iron Shirt

by John Whitlatch

PUBLISHED BY POCKET BOOKS NEW YORK

THE IRON SHIRT

Pocket Book edition published November, 1970

This original *Pocket Book* edition is printed from
brand-new plates made from newly set, clear, easy-to-read type.
Pocket Book editions are published by Pocket Books, a division of
Simon & Schuster, Inc., 630 Fifth Avenue, New York, N.Y. 10020.
Trademarks registered in the United States and other countries.

L

Standard Book Number: 671-75642-7.
Printed in the U.S.A.

In May of 1888 Arizona had been a territory for twenty-five years. The AT & SF had crossed the northern part of the territory five years before, and Geronimo had been stopped in 1886. The great blizzards of 1886 and 1887 had decimated the cattle industry. Some cattle barons had lost as many as 30,000 head. When they saw their fortunes standing in icy death on the range, or the survivors slowly starving and limping along without the hooves that had been frozen to the barren land, they knew they would have to change to survive.

North of the Mongollon Rim was a most beautiful land, wild and barren between the towns, and lonely, a land of green valleys and brush-covered plains, high mesas and cliffs and deep canyons, and a few Indians. It was a land of great promise, where a man could control his future; it was a land of death, where a man could be consumed by the scavengers without a trace. A man's enemies were equally divided between nature and his fellowman. Water, a horse, and a gun, in that order, were necessities for survival.

The towns were small and used for four things: commerce, fighting, drinking, and wenching. While law and propriety were slowly being felt, self-defense was still condoned on the most flimsy evidence and horse stealing brought a sure and quick rope. If a man wore a gun he had to be prepared to use it; if he wasn't quick he didn't wear Mr. Colt's product. As in most civilizations, the evil and weak were in the towns.

The people were a polyglot group, some looking for a new start, some escaping from a bad start; a very few had been born in the territory. They dressed in two ways: practical, as a rough country dictates, and, in the towns, stylishly in an attempt to follow the latest Eastern fashions, efforts that fluctuated wildly and were usually a year behind. Women were scarce, and an unattached female was a rare thing. There were two categories: wives and daughters in the first, and dance-hall girls and prostitutes in the second. The first were closely guarded. The latter were available from one dollar up. The men were usually braver than Easterners and certainly tougher, though not necessarily wiser. The Western man who was both brave and wise was the man who controlled the country and wrote its history.

To this country Jonathan Fontaine returned in his quest for the Iron Shirt.

Chapter One

ꖌꖌꖌꖌꖌꖌꖌꖌꖌꖌꖌꖌꖌꖌꖌꖌꖌꖌꖌꖌꖌꖌ

The driver pulled off the road and stopped the stage so that the horses were under the shade of a large cottonwood tree. He tied the reins securely and jumped down to stare at the boots of his only passenger, which were propped on the window ledge.

"What the hell you stopping for?" a deep voice inquired from within the stage.

"We stop and rest 'em here a bit, then they don't have to be hot-walked. We change horses in Pinyon anyway. . . . Thought you might like to get down and stretch."

The boots disappeared and in a moment the door opened and Jonathan Fontaine stepped down, smiled at the driver, stretched, and then unbuttoned the four buttons of his fashionable Eastern suit, pushed his gray homburg to the back of his head, and ran a finger around his stiff boiled collar. The driver, because it had occurred to him that Justin boots didn't go with the fancy Eastern clothes, started to remark on it, then changed his mind; it was none of his business. Instead he reached for the canteen and offered it to his passenger.

"Thank you," Fontaine said and took a long drink and returned the canteen. "How long will you be stopped?"

"Long enough for me to go behind that tree," the driver grinned.

Fontaine nodded and reached into his inside coat pocket and took out a wallet that contained a narrow, fifty-page notebook and pencil and several letters; then he took off the coat and tossed it into the stage, revealing that the shoulders were his and not the coat's, as well as a pair of slim hips that indicated a great familiarity with a saddle. He leaned against the stage and opened the notebook to the middle, where he had carefully printed the last entry in ink:

YOU THINK YOU KNOW . . . SO PROVE IT!

After that were four underlined words in a column:

1

OPPORTUNITY, ESCAPE, PROOF, RETRIBUTION

Fontaine studied his message to himself for a while and then put the wallet back in the coat as the driver returned.

"Wanna ride up top and see the sights? Pinyon's just over the next rise."

"All right."

Fontaine put his coat on again, pulled the homburg down to his eyes, and climbed up beside the driver as the man shook the reins and the team started forward.

"I understand they've got a maverick Indian around here who's been killing beef. I thought that went out when they shipped Geronimo to Florida."

"Yeah, I heard about it, but I ain't seen 'im," the driver replied. "Heard lotta stories, all different, but they agree on one thing: He ain't no Apache, or no local Injun of any sort, for that matter. Some says he's a Kiowa, some says he's a Comanche."

"A Comanche?" Fontaine replied. "I understand most of 'em are dead."

"Yeah? How'd you know that?"

"I read it in a book."

"Do tell," the driver remarked with a raised eyebrow. Then he pointed down the road as they topped the hill. "There's Pinyon."

Fontaine nodded at his first look at Pinyon in almost two years. The wide spot on the trail which had become the main street now ran between some twenty buildings on each side. It had taken over twenty years to get from a shack in front of a well, and for the well to be pumped into a trough, but it wasn't until the first saloon had been opened that Pinyon was really born. Now there were several saloons, a general store which doubled as the U.S. Post Office, the marshal's office and jail, Mrs. O'Bannion's boardinghouse, a combination hotel, saloon, and dining room named the Pinyon Hotel, a saddle shop, a barber shop (with baths), the Territory Bank, a feed and fuel store, two cattle brokerages, the telegraph office, sundry businesses which opened and closed, and a livery stable and a blacksmith at the end of town. Pinyon had lengthened considerably and Fontaine noticed that it now sported boardwalks for a block on either side of the trough, which was across the street from the hotel, the center of local commerce.

"Son of a bitch!" the driver said, pointing to the other end of town.

Fontaine turned from looking at the general store and saw the buck trot toward them on his spotted pony. His eyes widened and then his face quickly became a blank mask as he took in the details of the Indian. He wore his hair in braids and had two eagle feathers tied in the back like a Plains warrior. He wore fringed buckskins, jacket, and leggings and had a huge chest, bigger than any Fontaine had ever seen on an Indian. Most were either slim and lithe, or fat from eating white man's food, but few Indian bucks were heavily muscled because they simply didn't work that hard. Tied under this one's thigh, on top of the pony blanket, was a long buffalo lance; over his shoulder was a quiver and in his left hand he held a bow.

"That's a bit too much," Fontaine said dryly.

"Huh?"

"The coincidence is too much. I came out here to see an Indian, and here's an Indian."

The driver nodded as he pulled the team to a halt just short of the hotel steps. Both men jumped down and Fontaine climbed the steps to the hotel porch to watch the Indian. The driver reached in the stage and brought out Fontaine's carpetbag and saddlebags and put them on the steps. The two men exchanged nods and grins, and the driver went inside to have a beer. The Indian stopped his pony at the trough and slid off, holding the animal loosely by the chin strap; he let it drink while he stared across the street at Fontaine. At that moment a young boy of no more than twenty, a Mexican vaquero by his clothes and dark skin, burst out of the swinging doors, bumped drunkenly into Fontaine, and dropped down the steps to stare at the Indian with his hand close to his gun.

"Sorry," Fontaine said indulgently, but the boy didn't appear to notice.

"*Bastardo!*" the boy shouted at the Indian.

The Indian ignored him and reached for the dipper hanging on a post, and the boy fumbled for his gun.

"No, you mustn't," Fontaine said and started for the drunken boy, but there was nothing drunken about the gun that was suddenly shoved into his back.

Fontaine froze, then slowly turned his head to see a fat cowboy next to him, grinning like the whole thing was a big joke. The man was much bigger than Fontaine and his fat belly hung over his big belt and, though his shirt was dirty and he hadn't shaved for a week and his tan Stetson was filthy, his gun was well oiled and the gunbelt was tied very low. One word flashed through Fontaine's mind, "Pig," but with the gun in his ribs he thought it better to keep his opinion to himself. Another cowboy had followed his friend from the saloon, but when he saw Fontaine's pale face and eastern clothes he didn't bother to finish pulling his gun, he just grinned.

"Let 'em be," the fat one said. "That drunken Mexican ain't gonna do nothin'. Watch," he added, putting his gun away.

But the Mexican did. As the Indian completed his two steps to the post and reached out, the boy put a slug in the post and the Indian turned, reaching over his shoulder for an arrow. The boy, trying to steady his weaving gun with both hands, took a moment to aim and put his next shot into the center of the Indian's chest. Fontaine saw the buckskin tear, and the Indian staggered back against his horse for a moment but then he recovered and finished nocking his arrow. While the onlookers watched in disbelief the Indian pulled the arrow before the boy could steady his aim again and put the shaft into the boy's chest. The boy dropped in his tracks and the body rolled onto its back as Fontaine stepped out onto the dirt and started slowly toward the Indian, his hands away from his sides to show that he was unarmed. The other cowboy started to pull his gun but the fat one stopped him.

The Indian quickly pulled another arrow and Fontaine said, "Wait. I want to talk to you."

"I do not," the Indian said in passable English. "I will leave now."

"I will follow you."

"You cannot track me, unless I let you."

"You'd better ride far."

"I cannot be killed. You saw it."

"I saw. And I can see your face. I could put a bullet between your eyes before you could pull that bow."

"You have no gun. If you had one you would not use it." The Indian's stoic face almost broke into the barest of grins and he added, "Because then you would never know."

Suddenly the Indian turned, grunted to the pony, and mounted as the animal bolted and was quickly running flat out for the edge of town. Fontaine turned and sprinted for the nearest horse, at the rack in front of the hotel. As he tried to untie the reins he was backhanded on the side of the head by the fat cowboy and pushed into the horse, which shied, kicked the other horse, and then both animals pulled free and trotted erratically down the street, away from the Indian. As Fontaine recovered he turned back to his assailant and the fat one pushed him in the chest and into the outstretched boot of the other cowboy, tripping him onto his back in the dust.

"Stay out of it, you son of a bitch!" the fat one shouted and the two cowboys ran for their horses. As Fontaine picked himself up and began to brush the dust from his suit the animals were quickly caught and the two men raced down the street after the Indian who was already out of sight. He finished dusting his clothes and joined the crowd that had gathered around the corpse.

"Did he miss?" a man shouted.

"No," Fontaine answered. "I saw the buckskin rip."

"Maybe he was using bad charges," another said.

Fontaine shrugged and knelt by the body; he gently eased the gun from the dead hand and began to shake the shells into his hand. Two were empty but the rest looked good. Fontaine palmed a bullet, put the rest back in the gun and got to his feet.

"You got an undertaker?"

"Naw," a man said. "The barber. He's got a deal with the town council."

"Uh huh," Fontaine replied. "If those two fellers come back, tell 'em to wait out here in the street for me, I'll be down."

A couple of citizens nodded quickly and exchanged glances. Fontaine climbed the steps to the hotel, grabbed a young man who was obviously the clerk and pulled him inside with one hand while he picked up his gear with the other. Fontaine spun the register, signed his name and held out his hand. The clerk handed him a key and said, "Upstairs, second on the right, on the street side."

Fontaine nodded and went to his room. He locked the door and threw his bag on the bed. Then he took off his hat, coat, vest, tie and collar, rolled up his sleeves and poured water from the tin pitcher into the basin. After he'd sloshed water over his face and the back of his neck he carefully washed his hands and dried himself while he looked down onto the street. It was empty. He opened his carpetbag and took out a carbine that had six inches of the twenty-inch barrel sawed off and checked it carefully, making sure the lever action worked smoothly and that there was no dust in the barrel or chamber. Then he reached into a saddlebag and began to slip the shiny bullets into the magazine. When it was full he put one more into the chamber, making thirteen. Then he went to the window and saw the two cowboys sitting insolently on their horses, facing the front door. Fontaine grinned, put his hat low on his head and, holding his carbine down by his right leg, went out of his room, locked the door and stomped down the steps to make sure the clerk heard him.

He did. "They're . . . they're outside," the young man stammered.

Fontaine nodded and continued out onto the porch, down the steps and stopped in the street.

"Where the hell you think you're going?" the slim one demanded.

Fontaine saw that some fifty people were gathered at a goodly distance on each side of the street but he gave no notice and looked up at the cowboy and grinned:

"Why, I thought I'd borrow one of your horses and track that Indian."

"You son of a bitch!" the fat one shouted. "What the god-dam hell makes you think you're better'n we are? That goddam redskin ran to the forks so fast he was outa sight before we even got there. And there's no way to track 'im in that dust, not with so many people comin' in and outa town. Besides, that Injun ain't fer shootin'. He's Mr. Lane's private property, he wants 'im alive. . . . Come on, answer me! What makes you think you can do better?"

"I may not," Fontaine answered evenly, "but you shouldn't call a visitor a son of a bitch, a man could get shot that way."

"Ha! Listen to him, Alfred!" the slim one laughed. "You can't git us both!"

Fontaine grinned widely. "You want to try it? The first one moves get shot. And the other one better not miss, 'cause he'll only get one chance!"

Alfred, to Fontaine's right, exchanged glances with his friend; they couldn't back down now, the whole town would see it, so Alfred started to sidestep his horse to get a bigger spread and instantly the carbine raised up, a shot was fired into the dirt next to the animal and it shied the other way.

Fontaine's right hand flicked and the lever flashed out, ejecting the shell and inserting another, then the lever was closed and the gun was ready, and nothing had moved but Fontaine's right hand.

"What's the matter?" Fontaine said. "You running out of guts already? Or maybe you're too far away with six-guns, and me with a rifle, it's not fair. . . . Tell you what. Both of you dismount and walk toward me. Either one of you want to draw, fine, we'll have at it. But make no mistake, don't stop walking or the town's going to laugh at you."

There was a silence while each man tried to make a decision without looking at his friend.

"Well!" Fontaine demanded good-humoredly. "Come on, step down!"

Still they hesitated. Fontaine shrugged and for emphasis he suddenly raised the carbine at arm's length with both hands and shot as the gun seemed to be still moving; as it dropped another shell was levered into place and Alfred's hat was sailing into the dirt. That did it; both men quickly dismounted, their hands well away from their guns, and started walking toward Fontaine with slow, careful steps. At ten feet Fontaine spoke again.

"Last chance. Either of you want to apologize for calling me a son of a bitch and knocking me into the dirt?"

Both men grinned now, thinking that at this distance they had more than an even chance; the carbine couldn't be raised before one of them could get off a shot.

"All right," Fontaine shrugged casually, then moved forward with a deceptive speed and rammed the barrel into the sternum of the slim one, withdrew in one fast motion and cracked Alfred's wrist with the butt of his carbine, momentarily halting the draw. He continued forward, spinning the butt up in a tight arc, striking the man to his left on the side of the head. As the man dropped in his shadow Fontaine continued to spin back toward Alfred who was still trying to draw his gun. A shot into the dirt next to his boot stopped his hand and the fight was over.

"All right," Fontaine said, stepping back. "Take your friend and get out of town so I can get after that Indian."

"Gawd damn," Alfred said. "I don't understand you; I do not. But you'd better not chase that Injun. Mr. Lane, he don't take kindly to people disruptin' his plans."

"Well, you tell your Mr. Lane that I intend to go after that Indian and if he intends to stop me he'd better hurry. Where is he?"

"At his ranch."

"Uh huh. If you ride fast, how long?"

"Uhh, half hour, maybe more. Both ways."

"Well, get at it. Tell him I'll wait one hour, no more. If he's not here by then I'll come looking for him!"

"You're crazy, I think," Alfred said, wide-eyed.

"Maybe. Tell him I'll be in that saloon over there."

Alfred nodded in some wonderment, picked up his friend like a sack of flour and threw him across the saddle, picked up his hat while keeping an eye on Fontaine, then mounted and pulled his friend's horse behind him as he headed out of town, toward the northwest and away from the Indian. At the end of the block he slowly pulled his horse to a halt; then Alfred changed his mind again and turned away and gigged his animal.

Fontaine entered Willard's saloon and walked up to the bar, wondering if Willard would remember him. Willard said "Howdy" in such an almost friendly manner that Fontaine was sure he was remembered. Fontaine returned the nod, smiled and said, "Beer, please." Willard nodded and that ended the opening amenities, even after two years.

No one in Pinyon actually knew if Willard was his first or last name. Local protocol dictated that it was up to him to elaborate. He never did. He had arrived in Pinyon five or six years before, bought the saloon from a man who was incapable of running it, and had run it ever since with a minimum of fights, much to the appreciation of the few wives and the local law. He sold good beer and passable whiskey at fair prices. He did not interfere in fist fights as long as the furniture or fixtures were not involved and neither participant drew gun or knife. In the rare event that someone did get carried away to the point where they might use a weapon Willard had several scatterguns under the bar which had always been the final arbitrator. He was a brute of a man, less than six feet by an inch or two, but he weighed well over two fifty and no one had been known to try him personally. He had two fancy gamblers running his tables but he had such a reputation for honesty that he was often the holder of wagers.

Fontaine put a dime on the bar and looked over his shoulder as several bar flies entered to watch him. As he took the beer Willard said:

"Would you rather have whiskey? It's on the house."

"No thanks, I'm thirsty. But why the offer?"

"You'll be good for business. These loafers will buy while you're in here."

Fontaine grinned and shook his head and took a long drink of beer. "Does Beesley still run the livery stable?"

"Yes, he does."

"Thank you." Fontaine reached into his hip pocket and took out his notebook. From it he took a piece of cheap paper upon which a letter had been written in a crude scrawl:

Dere Mr. Fontaine—The Injun which you wuz lookin' fur is back around these parts agin. He ben here awhile feedin' off local beef. I think he will stay abit. You wuz kind to me and I jest thot you wood like to no.

It was signed, "Yr. obdt. svt., A. J. Beesley."

Fontaine nodded to Willard, finished his beer, and went outside.

As he entered the stable a tall, leathery old man came out of a stall with a big, tobacco-stained grin, his hand held out. They shook hands and the old man said:

"Mr. Fontaine! It shore is good to see ya."

"Hello, Beesley, how are you? I got your letter, thank you."

"I'm fine, jest fine. . . . How long will you stay?"

"Long enough to see about that Indian."

"Yeah, I wuz watchin' from the door. My, that's a fancy weapon you got there, you use it nicely."

"Thank you."

"Kin I see it?"

Fontaine nodded and presented the gun sideways. Beesley wiped his hands on his pants before taking the carbine. He hefted it, raised and lowered it with one hand, tried the lever partway, then said:

"My! Ain't that fancy? Forty-four Winchester, center fire, ain't it?"

"Yes."

"How many does it hold? Eleven?"

"Twelve, and one in the chamber."

"Oh yeah. . . . Say, how come no six-gun? I would've thought you'da got real good with one . . . you know, after your trouble."

"No, not me," Fontaine grinned. "That Mexican gave me a real good cut in the shoulder. It healed all right but it slowed me a bit on lifting my arm. I was never fast anyway. . . . Half the drunks in town could beat me," he added, not telling the old man the real reason. "Say, how's business?"

"Good, good. I may open a second place when the new town opens up."

"Yeah, I heard about that. Think it'll go?"

"Sure. Though there's lots in town who's agin it. They think the new town will put Pinyon right offen the map."

"Hell!" Fontaine laughed. "It's only on the biggest maps anyway."

"Yeah, but they got their life's work tied up in the land and buildings and to move they'd have to have Lane's backin'. There's some who ain't too keen on goin' into debt like that."

"Uh huh," Fontaine replied. Then, changing the subject, "What about the Indian?"

"Cain't add but what I put in the letter. And you seen him your ownself, big as life."

"Yes," Fontaine said dryly, "I certainly did. . . . A.J., you think the Indian will stay?"

"Seems so. He's been around a few months now, killin' off some of Lane's beef. And Lane, he don't like that and he put out the word that nobody is to shoot at the Injun, 'cept in self-defense. Seems he wants to git him his ownself."

"Then why hasn't he done it before this?"

"Yeah," Beesley nodded sagaciously, "that is a thing to ponder."

"It certainly is," Fontaine grinned, and added, "And doesn't it seem pretty coincidental, the Indian meeting my stage?"

"Mebbe. But he's been meetin' several stages of late, mebbe lookin' to steal a horse or somethin'. But this is his first time in town, though I gotta admit, it's been pretty hot the last couple days, mebbe come in jest fer water."

"Yeah," Fontaine said, allowing that it was possible.

"But," Beesley added, "you cain't git that Injun without help. You need men, and horses, and supplies. Anyone chases him he runs to the Rim and hides in the woods. Ain't a white man alive can track 'im alone."

"Maybe," Fontaine replied slowly. "I'll figure that one out this afternoon. . . . Well, I'll be around for a while. See you in a day or two."

They shook hands again and the old man said:

"Glad to see ya back. You always had a nice face."

Fontaine grinned and returned to the saloon.

Though the patrons tried not to notice him there was a momentary hush when he entered. He put down a dime, nodded to Willard, and took his schooner of beer to a table against the wall where he could see out the window. He put his carbine on the table by his right hand, facing the door, and sipped his beer. When he felt the patrons wouldn't bother him with questions he took another letter from his notebook. This one was several sheets of good paper covered with a flowing script in a bold, masculine hand which read:

My dear Jonathan:

I hope this finds you recovered from your many wounds with no lasting effects. But though I am concerned with your health the real reason for this letter is to enlist your aid; no, it is really to hire you. I want to offer you a position with me . . . no, that's not quite right, either; I want you to act as my agent in my new enterprise which will take your time for the next six months, perhaps more, and which, if we pull it off, should net you at least $12,000 in the first year. From then on, your fortune should be made.

Because you are the only man I know whom I can trust without question, and the only one I know who is qualified to handle the task, I feel I owe you a full explanation. As you know, I was almost wiped out by the last two winters. Jonathan, almost my entire herd on the New Mexico range was lost. Twenty thousand head, give or take a thousand, frozen in its tracks. The only thing that profited from the last two winters were the buzzards.

That left me with lots of hands to feed and not enough money in the bank. And it showed me that the day of the big cattleman is over. Oh, we'll always needs lots of beef to feed the East, but it'll be done by small outfits with quality beef, running their stock directly to the nearest railroad. And the RR is all the way across the Territory now and will start to send off trunk lines to those places that will make the RR a profit . . . but that profit will have to consist of something more than beef. When I realized this, it came to me that I had the necessary tools (land, water, men) to make a fortune, only I was going about it the wrong way. That's when I decided to build such a town that the RR would come to me!

Jonathan, it is already under way, I have started a new town! Pinyon is too old, and does not have enough water, and is poorly located. The new site is up toward the Rim. There is plenty of water, and good, high mesas, where we can raise the best quality beef (the Longhorn's day is over, too), and have enough fruit trees to feed Chicago. And there's enough timber farther back where we can build a sawmill and ship lumber to New Mexico and West Texas where they have nothing but mesquite.

Now, old friend, comes the part that I'm sure you will keep in the utmost confidence. I have a commitment from the RR that if I build my town they'll go in with me on a trunk line! Obviously this news must not get out, speculators would ruin it, but I have no doubts as to your discretion.

Now, to your part. . . . I need good people. Not the type that came out in the 50s and 60s because they were losers in their own towns, or mere adventurers, but selected men with professions and skills we can put to good use. . . . You will be the one to recruit these key people. I already have enough who work with their hands. What we need are teachers, and a lawyer, and a minister (though I don't think that's too important, the wives of the others will), and a good timberman, and a doctor, and a man good with figures to keep the books and maybe be the banker (I'll own the bank, of course), and a good cabinet-maker (I have in mind to build furniture, also), and several other professions, though the women will be clean and the gambling honest.

I have gathered the names of several of these people and have located some, but I need your talent to persuade them to join us. I do not propose to invite good men with a story of wild dreams, I plan to offer them a great opportunity to get in at the beginning and I intend to back up my offer with whatever amount is right to get them off to a proper start. I will loan them money, at a small rate of interest, of course, build them houses, guarantee them an income greater than they're now making; whatever would seem right to my agent. That's why I must have you; I trust you, and your intelligence. I know of no other man I would want for the job, and I cannot do it myself, I must stay here to see that all goes well during the first critical months.

Again, I give you my personal guarantee that you will make enough money so that you will never regret it. Of course, I would hope that you would stay on with me and be one of the leading citizens of our new city. Please let me know by return post.

My best personal regards,

TOBY

Fontaine put the letter away and smiled when he remembered his answer. He had replied that he was flattered, and interested, but that he would have to pass up the more than generous offer, as he had, as Toby well knew, the certain matter to take care of before anything else.

Then, a month after he'd replied, he had received Beesley's scribbled note. That Beesley had written out of friendship, and no inducement offered by Toby, Fontaine had no doubt. Beesley was too full of stubborn honesty to be swayed by anything like money. That same afternoon Toby's wire arrived. It read:

NOW YOU MUST TAKE MY OFFER STOP INDIAN IS HERE STOP WILL TRY TO SAVE HIM FOR YOU SIGNED TOBY

Fontaine had taken the next train west.

He waved for another beer and Willard nodded and brought it to the table. As he picked up the dime he looked out the window and said, "Lane's coming," and returned to his place behind the bar to watch. Down the street rode four men, walking their horses in slow unison, their eyes watching the doors and windows and the tops of buildings as they passed. There were two men in front and a magnificent black horse with a black saddle between the two men in the rear. The fat cowboy, Alfred, was one of the men in front. The other was a sturdy, barrel-chested man in his early fifties, wearing a corduroy coat and a fawn-colored Stetson. The gray at his temples and the lines around the mouth and eyes added to the image of a leader of men. All four wore tied-down six-guns.

Two men seated at a table near the door got up quickly and went to the bar. Fontaine smiled a little and moved the beer glass to his far right, leaving the carbine on its side, pointing at the door.

The muffled sound of the horses' hooves was the only thing to break the silence. Then high-heeled boots stomped across the boardwalk, the batwing doors were flung open and Lane scanned the room and said in a loud voice:

"I'm looking for a man who calls himself Fontaine!"

Fontaine got to his feet, his hand resting lightly on the carbine. "You found him."

"You gonna use that thing?" Lane demanded, his eyes flicking from the carbine to Fontaine's face.

"No . . . no, I don't think so," Fontaine replied. "Somebody could get shot."

Lane advanced slowly, his coat out of the way of his gun hand which hovered over the walnut stock of the .45.

"You going to draw that?" Fontaine asked.

"No. Like you said, somebody could get shot."

The two men stared at each other for a long moment in the complete silence, each man frozen and taut. Then Lane's craggy face broke into a bare smile. Fontaine smiled a little in return, and they broke into gales of laughter and pounded each other on the back and then they broke away and shook hands.

"Hello, Toby," Fontaine said.

"Jonathan, you came. I'm very, very glad. Now the whole thing will work." Lane turned to the crowd and said in a loud voice, "If you expected a gunfight at someone else's expense you picked the wrong day."

Over Lane's shoulder Fontaine saw the look of disgust on Alfred's face as he and the others went to the bar.

"Let me look at you," Lane said, stepping back. "You look good. You got your weight back, but you look awfully pale."

"Well, I was in bed most of last summer and there hasn't been much sunshine in New Orleans for a while. . . . But, first things first. I want to talk about the Indian. Your men told you what happened?"

"Yes." Lane waved to Willard for a beer and they sat at Fontaine's table. "I hear you put on quite a show. But it must be a coincidence. You think he knew you were returning?"

"Looks like it. I was just talking to old Beesley. He says Indians just know such things, but I don't put much stock in that. Indians aren't very smart anyway, much less clairvoyant."

"Uh huh," Lane took a sip of beer. "I agree. I hear he's been watching the stage of late, maybe looking for a driver alone so he can rob him. Maybe he spotted you on the way in and came around from the other side just to see if the war is still on. But, whatever, you can't track the son of a bitch, he's like a ghost."

"Yeah," Fontaine smiled coldly, "but I'd sure like to try."

"Well, you did for goddam near a year. How close did you get?"

Fontaine laughed ruefully and finished his beer. "You're right there. I never even saw him. Not once, Toby."

"Well," Lane said, slapping the table in an air of jovial finality, "you just made my point. I need you to get my men and you need me to get that Indian. Looks like we're in business." At Fontaine's nod Lane added, "Come on, let's go out to the house. I got lots to show you."

Lane's ranchhouse was the biggest structure within two hundred miles. It rose out of the center of his valley with a magnificence that reflected the pride and financial status of its owner. It was made entirely of hand-hewn lumber hauled down from the Rim, except for the two huge local stone fireplaces at either end of the long, two-story house. It had a gabled, shingled roof with dormer windows at each of the six upstairs bedrooms. There was a long, covered porch running the length of the front of the house which was finished off with lots of gingerbread scrollwork imported from the East and painted white every spring to contrast with the natural dark brown of the bat and board siding.

Lane had spared neither time nor money to have the latest in conveniences and expensive furniture. The tapestry-covered horsehair furniture in the sitting room was imported from Massachusetts and the rugs over the pegged hardwood floors were Orientals, imported through New Orleans. The kitchen, as big as an ordinary house, had a big brick oven built into one wall and, to the wonder of every local woman who had seen it, porcelain sinks with built-in running water from a two-and-a-half-story water tank standing a hundred feet away. Four of the six upstairs bedrooms had private baths each with its own tub and watercloset and running water brought through iron pipe which Lane had shipped in from Chicago at a cost of three thousand dollars.

There were also three barns, two for animals, one for hay and grass. There was a huge warehouse, dark and cool, where no one was allowed to smoke on pain of instant dismissal; it was usually full of hundred-pound sacks of salt and flour and dried beans and coffee beans and coarse sugar, and barbed wire by the two-man roll, and gunpowder by the barrel, and lead by the hundred-pound bar, and coal oil by the fifty-gallon drum. And there was a place for tools, and all kinds of tack, and great yellow blocks of sulfur for the cattle, and blocks of salt for licks, and all of the many necessary things for running an enterprise so big that many of the hands had yet to ride over half of Lane's holdings.

And there were three separate bunkhouses at the ranch headquarters in addition to numerous line shacks scattered throughout eastern Arizona and western New Mexico. While one big bunkhouse might have sufficed, Lane found three more practical; one for white men, one for his vaqueros (with its own *cocina* run by Mexican women), and one for the several varieties of Indians who lived in the area and worked off and on for the TL outfit. It was not that Toby Lane had any prejudices that were particularly strange to his time and area, it was just that he'd found that the use of three bunkhouses cut down on the number of knife fights and the resultant loss of men. Farther to the rear of the ranch were the holding pens and corrals for the great number of animals, both working stock and cattle, that were equally vital to the survival of Toby Lane.

Fontaine knew that the ranch was also local headquarters for all visiting drifters, cowpokes without a job, those down and out, and those on the run. Friends and strangers alike, all were welcome to eat and spend the night. A man on the run was welcome as long as he didn't draw his gun or do anything to offend the hospitality of the house. He was welcome to one night's lodging, a meal, and feed for his horse. Those who violated Lane's hospitality were never welcomed into the area again. The story of the gunman who was given a night's sanctuary and repaid the hospitality by raping one of Lane's Mexican women had been told and retold, until it became legend. Toby had caught him in the act and had put a crease in his buttock with his six-gun while the man was, as the phrase goes, still in the saddle. He was then summarily hanged from the hay pulley on the front of the barn. The body was left swaying in the breeze for a week, the trousers at half mast, as a warning to all, until the cook complained that the corpse was bringing too many flies to the house a hundred feet away.

When they rode in, Lane circled the main buildings to show the progress that had been made, despite the last two winters, since Fontaine had been gone. Everything looked orderly and prosperous and the riders nodded respectfully as their boss passed by. While he was most complimentary, as befitted his momentary status as a guest, the thought again occurred to Fontaine that Toby's letter had entrusted him with some dangerous information. Despite their friendship, he was realist enough to know that it would never do to cross Toby Lane. Fontaine made a mental note not to muddy his tracks.

When they stopped at the hitching rack their horses were taken by a Navajo groom, and another Indian silently took Fontaine's bags into the house. They were met on the front steps by Leroy Starrett, Lane's foreman, who had been sitting on the porch reading a dime Western entitled *Six-Gun Law*. Fontaine had known the grizzled, leathery foreman two years ago and remembered that Starrett was never known to have taken his hat off, even while shaving or bathing, with one exception: when he entered Lane's house—although only then when ladies were present. And he never came into the main house unless he had on clean boots. He was a reformed gunman who'd passed through, spent the night, and stayed on to become foreman. Fontaine had heard that he was as fast as anyone with a six-gun and, though well over fifty, he was probably the best foreman in Arizona. Starrett smiled broadly at the sight of Fontaine and came down the steps to take his hand, in itself a singular sign of respect.

"Glad to see ya back," Starrett said. "That was a helluva fight you had in skinnin' that Mex. You recovered?"

"Yes, thank you."

"Well, it was a helluva fight. Been meanin' to tell ya."

"But that was a year ago," Fontaine said with a grin.

"Yeah, but I ain't seen ya since. I'll likely see ya fer supper."

"Most likely," Fontaine replied.

Starrett nodded to his boss and followed the grooms around the side of the house. Lane turned to Fontaine with an apologetic grin and said:

"I've got something else new to show you. My little orphaned niece came out to live with me." He raised his voice as they entered the entry hall and called upstairs, almost sweetly, "Oh, Mary Kaye. Come down, please."

"What the goddam hell!" a deep, yet female voice yelled down the stairs. "I'm busy making curtains, trying to make a home out of this cowboy whorehouse you've been running! I don't have time to jump every time you . . ."

The voice trailed off as a busty, robust young woman almost as tall as Fontaine, and with bright red hair, came to the head of the stairs with a length of white dotted swiss in her hands. When she saw Fontaine she blushed profusely, cleared her throat, and then came down the stairs.

"Good morning," Fontaine said politely, removing his homburg.

She stared openly at her visitor, and rather coldly, for a moment. Then her face softened and broke into a grin.

"I didn't mean to be impolite," she said in her husky voice, "but the way Toby talked I expected a gunfighter ten feet tall."

"I'm neither, as you can see," Fontaine replied, looking into her green eyes which were only lower than his by the height of his boot heels.

"Oh sure!" she said in some disbelief, "you come into town and rough up two of his best hands and we're supposed to think you're a missionary! Well, there'll be no goddam gun-fighting in this house!"

"No, ma'am, I'm here on business."

"Uh huh," she replied, the doubt still in her voice.

Lane smiled and picked up Fontaine's bags. "Come on," he said, breaking up the impasse, "I'll show you to your room. You need some trail clothes?"

"No, I've got some. Picked 'em up in El Paso."

"I'll bet!" Mary Kaye said under her breath as she stepped aside.

Fontaine nodded with a brief smile and followed Lane upstairs. He was shown to the center room in the back, one with a bath. Lane put the bags on the bed and said:

"Cold lunch'll be ready time you change. Then I want you to see Lane City."

The ranch was out of sight and they were on a wide wagon road that climbed slowly into the hills before Lane said:

"Jonathan, you'll be gone many times for a month or more but there are telegraphs, so we can keep in touch. Granted, they may be a day's ride or more from wherever the hell you are but if I have some news, any news, I'll wire each station. . . . I'll have my men keep a lookout for the Indian and no one is to kill him 'cause I know you want to talk to him."

"I certainly do," was the flat reply.

"If we can get him to hole up anywhere I'll keep as many men as it takes to stay on him and I'll send for you. If I can capture him, I will. If I hear that he's anywhere else I'll wire you."

"Thank you, Toby," Fontaine grinned, almost pleasantly. "I appreciate it."

Lane nodded and waved his hand at the green foothills as though Fontaine hadn't seen them. Fontaine nodded silently and they rode another half mile before Lane spoke again.

"Too bad about the Mexican. He didn't say anything at all?"

"Nothing you could print," Fontaine lied.

"He musta been a tough one," Lane said.

"Uh huh. He figured I would torture him or kill him anyway, and he already had a bullet in his side."

"Did you?"

"Yes," was the casual reply, "both. Maybe I shouldn't have, but he flung that machete at me and I shot him without thinking. But I hurried my shot and got 'im in the right side. . . . My, we were a sight, there was blood all over that cabin."

"I heard that," Toby grinned. "And I've heard about nailing a man's hide to the wall but they say you actually did it."

"They say rightly. I was sort of out of my head. I'd been after those bastards for so long, and then they split up and the Indian just melted. But that fool Mexican laid a track like an elephant with crappy feet across your sitting-room rug. . . . And then I got dizzy from the loss of blood and I just kept at it."

"But did you actually nail him to the wall?" Lane persisted.

Fontaine nodded. "There was an old bucket of rusty nails there, and a hammer. I cut his clothes off and tied his feet and stood him against a wall and run a couple of nails through his shoulder skin to hold him up and then I nailed his thumbs up and brought him to with some water and you know that son of a bitch still wouldn't talk? He just began cussing me in two languages, so I began to peel strips off his belly and nailed 'em to the wall. I was about to cut his navel out and the bastard died on me."

"And you were such a mild fellow, too," Lane said, shaking his head. "I don't think you ever killed anybody before in your life, much less cut 'em up. Did you?"

"No, I didn't. But that mild fellow you mentioned ceased the day I walked in and saw what they were doing."

"Uh huh," Lane nodded in sympathy. "You still have that dream?"

"Once in a while."

"Well, come on," Lane said, gigging his horse. "I've got lots to show you and we have to be back in time to clean up for the party."

"What party?"

"Why, Jonathan, you're the guest of honor at my dinner party. I've got to show you off as the sophisticated man of intelligence who returned all the way from New Orleans just to get in on the new town. All the best people of Pinyon will be there, those who are going to move to Lane City, that is."

Lane's dream of a real estate development was in a high, green meadow, just below the timber line and the area of intense cold, yet close enough for easy logging. A gushing stream ran through the middle of the meadow and dropped down to a series of lower meadows and disappeared on the flats twenty miles away. The road entered the meadow from below and to one side, made a right angle in the middle, crossed the stream on a log bridge, and wound up into the mountains.

"This is the main street," Lane said as their horses' hooves echoed on the bridge. "The business district will be here, with homes farther back, on the next street up, and the warehouse and sawmill and things like that toward the far end of town."

Fontaine nodded in appreciation. Several log and plank houses were being erected at the edge of the meadow. The main street was already staked out, a hundred feet wide and a mile long, with room for another mile after that; the business lots were also staked, a hundred feet square, with alleys at the back on either side of the street. In the center of "town" a sturdy log building was the only structure standing, though several others were in various stages of completion.

"That's the warehouse and bank, right now," Lane said. "As soon as we get enough people I plan to build a brick one. There's a clay flat farther on where I can make enough bricks to pave the whole town street. And there's more than enough water, no matter how many people come. There's enough for tens of thousands of people, and all the animals the land will hold! As people come in, I'll build some check dams farther up. There's one spot that's a natural, it's the place that gave me the idea for the rest of it . . . high rock walls on either side. Blast 'em down and we'll have a lake more than a mile long, and year round! First I'll build water tanks for the town's storage, fill 'em, and then blast the dam and put in a big pipe with a floodgate. That way we'll be able to control our water and have places to set up waterwheels for the sawmill and furniture factory. . . . Jonathan, do you realize that over half the cost of furniture out here is in freighting it from the East?"

"No," Fontaine smiled, though he was impressed by Lane's eagerness, "as a matter of fact I hadn't thought too much about that lately."

"Smart aleck! Goddam smart! That's what you are!" Lane grinned.

"Maybe," Fontaine nodded, serious now, "but I'm truly impressed. Looks like you've planned it well. . . . What about the railroad?"

"The depot will be there," Lane pointed to the end of the main street, then to the curve of the meadow. "It will run along there and wind around to the north a bit, because it's not so steep, and then it drops downhill, there, and runs all the way to the mainline, probably northwest to Flagstaff, but the route's not picked yet."

Fontaine frowned for a moment, then said: "Toby? What about those who won't move?"

"That's a problem, too," Lane grinned. "Those who have

decided not to come already hate me, they think I'm stealing the bread from their mouths."

"Well, aren't you?"

"Progress, my dear boy, progress."

"Uh huh," Fontaine nodded noncommittally.

Fontaine came down the wide stairway adjusting the lapels of his freshly ironed suit and stretching his neck inside the freshly starched, boiled collar. His clothes had been cleaned by a stately, handsome Indian woman who had asked him, as he was about to take a bath, if he needed a fresh shirt. She had spoken in surprisingly good, though terse, English, and Fontaine correctly surmised two things: that she was Toby's woman and that she somehow knew that he was after the Indian and therefore he was the enemy of all Indians. As to her being Toby's woman, this was not surprising, considering that Fontaine knew Toby's young wife had left him after their first two winters in Arizona and returned to the hometown beau. After that Lane was no longer concerned with building a dynasty for any reason other than wealth and power and therefore had no interest in women other than sexual.

When Fontaine entered the big living room only Toby and Leroy Starrett were there, standing near the sideboard, and the whiskey. Starrett was resplendent in a twenty-year-old suit and a higher and stiffer collar than Fontaine's. His only concession to practicality was the fact that he still wore boots, though they were bright red and highly polished. Lane smiled at Fontaine and poured two fingers of Scotch whiskey into a cut glass and held up the bottle.

"I bought six cases for you so you can take some with you. I wouldn't want you to die of thirst on the trail."

Fontaine exchanged smiles and nods with Starrett and examined the bottle of twenty-year-old whiskey. "My compliments, sir."

"A little spring water?" Lane said, holding a pitcher over the glass.

Fontaine nodded, took the drink, and they raised their glasses.

"To a pleasant journey," Lane smiled.

"When do I leave?"

"As soon as possible. Tomorrow, if it's all right."

"Fine. Where to?" Fontaine said, noting that Starrett had

politely gone to the other end of the room to look at the stereoscope while they talked business.

"Your first assignment is not people. It's to bring back four blooded bulls that I bought. In fact, it's so important that there's a twenty-five-hundred-dollar bonus in it if you can deliver 'em. . . . Oh, don't worry about Leroy. I pay him twice what any other foreman in the Territory gets. Besides, he knows I'm paying you well, but it's none of his business how much."

"I understand, partly," Fontaine said, taking another sip of the wonderfully smooth Scotch. "But if you've already made the arrangements, why me? Not that I mind, especially for the price. So, obviously, there must be a teeny weeny mite more to it."

Lane smiled, chuckled once, and said, "As a matter of fact, there is. All the directions are written down, I've got 'em in an envelope in the safe, together with the bank draft you're to deliver. The hitch is the fact that some of the locals in the area didn't like the idea of an outsider buying them. They bid eight thousand for the bulls, and I bid ten, all according to the rules. I put up fifty percent with the rest on delivery. The local boys could only come up with a thousand dollars and a note against the stud fees and the threat that the animals would never reach me."

"Oh fine!" Fontaine said cynically. "How many men do you suppose I'll need to start this war?"

"That's just it. The major, the man I bought 'em from, said to bring a lot of good guns. Well, listen, I've stayed out of the Pleasant Valley War so far, and that's a lot closer to home than these stud bulls, and I don't aim to get involved."

"Pleasant Valley? I didn't know you had any holdings around Young?"

"Yeah, I've got a few thousand acres, but it's completely fallow. But until those idiots finish killin' each other off I can't use the land. Jonathan, war's too expensive, especially if you can get what you want another way. You watch, time they get through, Young, Arizona, will be nothing but a ghost town. . . . But about the bulls. I could go in there with a lot of men and do a lot of killing, but that might give me a bad name and hurt the new town. And I might not get 'em out. With those bulls, in that high meadow country I could raise beef that would put the longhorn in a class with the buffalo. That's why I need you; to pay the rest of the bill and assess our chances of getting them out."

"Sort of an advance scouting party?"

"Yes, sort of. You can decide what we need: how many men, what route to take, how many wagons we'll need. . . ."

"Wagons?"

"For the bulls. Hey, Leroy! Tell him about the bulls."

"Fattest things you ever seen," Starrett grinned. "Walkin' beefsteak . . . and a big whang!"

"All right," Fontaine grinned. "What do I do, get word back to you or return when I've figured it out?"

"I thought I'd hedge my bet," Lane said. "Leroy will send one of our best riders with you . . . Charlie Moss, he's a good wrangler and has a way with horses. Besides, he only weighs a hundred and thirty pounds and if maybe you couldn't get to a telegraph you could send Charlie with a message."

"Uh huh," Fontaine said slowly. Then, "I'll need trail gear and supplies."

"I'll see to that," Starrett said. "What about ammunition?"

"I've got enough of my own," Fontaine answered.

Starrett nodded. Many men preferred to use their own reloads, so the answer didn't surprise him. "You particular to a Texas double-rigged saddle, or a single cinch?"

"No matter, whatever your animals are used to."

Starrett nodded again and then Mary Kaye came down the stairs and the foreman opened his mouth to speak, then shut it and tossed off his drink. Starrett's restraint was most admirable. His employer's niece, though as foul-mouthed as any wrangler, had never been seen in anything but a floor-length gingham. Tonight, and by the look on her uncle's face it was also of some wonder to him, she was wearing a full-skirted, obviously eastern ballgown of bright green taffeta. It was gathered tightly at the waist and had leg-of-mutton sleeves. But in between the sleeves the maker seemed to have run out of material. The bodice was cut square and very low, and her more than ample breasts had been cranked up by a whalebone corset to the point where Fontaine smilingly assured himself that should she bend over even slightly one or both would come surging forth for all to enjoy.

As she came forward she smiled sweetly, almost too much so, to Fontaine and Starrett and kissed her uncle on the cheek. Starrett managed to nod woodenly, but Fontaine bowed grandly and smiled cynically. The gesture was not lost on Mary Kaye, but she chose to ignore it and joined her uncle in going to the door to greet their first guests.

Starrett quickly poured himself a shot of bourbon, then added some Scotch to Fontaine's glass, and tossed off his drink. "Whoo-eee! Ain't that a sight?"

"It surely is," Fontaine replied. "And in addition to being one of the world's most beautiful sights, it also indicates that the young lady could, if she doesn't watch her weight, end up looking like a brood mare."

Starrett almost choked on that one, and had to pour himself another shot. "Maybe. But I got an idea she's just like her uncle. Feathers is a little more brighter, maybe, but she strikes me as a gal what knows what she wants. And, seems to me, you don't think too highly of women."

"Oh, not exactly, Mr. Starrett," Fontaine said. "As to Miss Mary Kaye, I agree with your opinion, she's what one might call a strong-willed young lady. As to my liking of women, let me say that, generally, they're good for two things, one of which is cooking."

"Oh ho!" Starrett grinned. "This should be good!"

Fontaine nodded, put his glass down and went forward to be introduced to Toby's guests. Within five minutes the last of the twelve couples had arrived. This indicated a signal honor, in that the local, and leading, citizens dared not be late when invited by Mr. Lane. The men were dressed in black suits (in many cases probably their *only* suits), and the ladies all wore their best, though none could come close to matching the hostess as to finery or nakedness. The men were the most affluent and influential in the area. The banker was there, hoping to be the banker in Lane City, the local Methodist minister was there, hoping Lane would build him a church in Lane City, and all the rest of the men either wanted to be taken along or, in the case of several fairly well-to-do ranchers, hoped to be allowed to purchase some of the prime land that Toby had managed to tie up before he announced his plan.

The conversation was friendly and the guests tried their best to make it sparkling though most of the provincial ladies could only talk in platitudes and clichés. Fontaine was accepted politely, and when it was learned that he had traveled to New York in the last year he faced the usual questions asked by small-town people of world travelers. Was the Statue of Liberty really as imposing as they'd read? (Yes.) Did the new electric lights installed in New York really make a street so light that one could read a newspaper? (Yes, if one stood directly underneath.) Was Benjamin Harrison as great a man as they'd read in the papers? (Yes, if one believed the papers.) To all the inane questions put to him Fontaine replied with an answer that would offend no one. Toby was pleased, Starrett was amazed at Fontaine's knowledge and use of words, Mary Kaye huffed in the background but remained quiet.

After dinner was a different story. As was the custom, the men retired to the study to have cigars and brandy while the ladies went upstairs to ease their corsets and their bladders, and to chatter. When the ladies returned to the living room the men rejoined them and, within moments, the temperature dropped drastically. At first, Fontaine, while aware of the coolness, didn't know why. Then he picked up a word here and there as he made his way across the room to join Lane at the buffet and it began to come into focus.

"Toby," Fontaine whispered, "you hear what these dumb bitches are saying?"

"Yes, Jonathan, I heard, and . . ."

He was interrupted by Leroy Starrett who joined them and whispered, "Boss, these crazy hens has been tellin' their men that Mr. Fontaine is a hired killer, here to kill the Injun, and to kill anybody else what gets in your way."

"Yes, Leroy," Lane said quietly.

Lane had talked to but one couple when the banker's fat, pompous wife got to her feet, signaling that the evening was over. The banker quickly shook Toby's hand with something less than zeal, nodded to Mary Kaye, mumbled his thanks and took his wife to the door. The rest of the men quickly followed with their wives, though no man risked the wrath of Mr. Lane by failing to go through the ceremony of a quick good-bye. When the door had closed behind the last one Toby went to the sideboard and poured himself a stiff shot of brandy, tossed it off, and marched across the room to have a few words with the faintly smiling Mary Kaye who was seated on a couch. When he got to the center of the room there was a knock at the front door and Leroy Starrett waved off the Indian woman, opened the door and stepped outside for a moment. When he returned he said:

"Seems they've left their women in the buggies down the

road and they would like a word with you about hiring a gun hand."

"Christ!" Fontaine exclaimed. "Why those pompous sons of bitches!"

"I'll talk to them," Lane said through clenched teeth.

Fontaine, his eyes narrowed in anger, nodded to Lane's right to handle it and turned to stare at a grinning Mary Kaye. Fontaine pulled off his coat, slipped his tie off, undid his boiled collar and started up the stairs.

"Where you going?" Mary Kaye asked mockingly. "They're out front."

Fontaine ignored her and went to his room and closed the door. He dropped the coat and tie and collar on the bed, took his carbine out of the carpetbag, went to the open window and climbed outside, reached to a standpipe a few feet away and using it as a handhold dropped to the ground. He circled the house from a distance of a hundred feet, on the side away from the main road, then started to work his way to the front door. Lane's male guests were standing at the foot of the steps talking to Toby as he approached. He stopped some twenty feet past the hitching rack and said in a loud, flat voice:

"I think it's me you wanted to talk to."

Two of the younger men turned and reached for the guns which they were now wearing and Fontaine put a shot into the dirt near each man's feet, then pumped two more, so rapidly that the four shots sounded like one long explosion, one into each end of the porch, on either side of the group.

"Hold it!" he shouted, and they did, frozen in momentary fear. "Now, listen to me! I am no gunman or I would have shot several of you as an example to keep the rest in line! In case any of you are wondering, this gun holds thirteen shots. I've used four."

The group remained silent and immobile, all except Toby Lane, who was smiling broadly. Fontaine nodded cynically, almost like a schoolmaster who now had the attention of the class.

"That's better," he said distinctly. "Before you gentlemen listen to a lot of wild rumors I think you should hear my side. You've heard a lot of half truths and rumors tonight and that, on top of what happened in town today, has made you think that Toby hired a gunman and you don't want any part of it. Well, I am no gun sharp. Half the men here could outdraw me.

Now I picked on those two idiots today, knowing full well that they worked for Toby, in hopes that people would let me alone and I could avoid what's happening right now. . . .

"I returned for only two reasons; to find the Indian some of you saw today, and to work for Toby Lane. . . . Steiner, you were living here then. Am I right?"

A white-haired rancher nodded, an embarrassed look on his face. "Yes."

Fontaine lowered his gun and walked to the porch and stood behind Lane. The men mumbled a bit and one said, "Sorry, Toby."

Another said, "Come on, we've made big enough fools of ourselves tonight."

A fat man made the remark to which all the men grumbled their assent, "Goddam women, always startin' rumors."

They walked quickly to their buggies and Lane and Fontaine entered the house. Leroy, gun in hand, was standing behind the door grinning. Mary Kaye came forward, a contrite look on her face, and was about to speak when her uncle said, "Don't apologize now, you did enough tonight!"

Mary Kaye's face flushed and she turned and ran up the stairs as Toby laughed. Leroy stuck his gun in his belt, nodded pleasantly, and left through the kitchen. In a moment they heard the back door close and Toby nodded Fontaine to the sideboard where he poured each a stiff shot of brandy.

"You're, uh, pretty goddam fast with that thing," Toby said, indicating the carbine. He raised his glass in a toast of appreciation and took a sip.

"Thank you," Fontaine grinned coldly over the rim of his glass. "I've been practicing. I thought I might need it if I found me an Indian."

"Uh huh, I thought so. You checked on the legend of the Iron Shirt, too, didn't you, after you found you couldn't kill him?"

Fontaine's eyes widened a moment, then he regained his composure and said, "You know his name? You never said. How did you find out?"

"Oh, probably the same way you did," Toby smiled, "and I kept quiet for pretty much the same reason. . . . The less the locals know about him and the more they wonder, the more likely they are to leave him be. . . . The way I found out was real simple. After you told me you put two shots in his chest, and I knew you couldn't miss from so close, I got to wondering. Of course, this was a week or two after you started after him. . . . Goddam, you were a sight, skinned head half bandaged, one hand wrapped, looking like something dug out of a cemetery. . . . Anyway, the way you'd described him he sounded like a Plains Indian of some sort; he was too big for an Apache and certainly he wasn't a Navajo or a Hopi. So I wrote a friend in Washington and had him check with the Bureau of Indian Affairs and he wrote back with the Legend of the Iron Shirt. That had to be it, or him, whichever."

"That's him," Fontaine said curtly. "But tell me what your friend said, see if we have the same story."

"All right," Lane nodded, picking up the brandy bottle and nodding Fontaine into the study. When they were seated at opposite sides of the big, hand-carved desk Lane continued. "I guess it was about three hundred years ago, some Spanish explorers, maybe some of Coronado's men, had reached the edge of the Great Plains, looking for the legendary Seven Cities of Cibola, when they got into a fight with a Cheyenne war party; seems the Cheyenne were one of the biggest tribes in those days. Anyway, one of the Spaniards fell in battle and the war chief who slew him stripped him of his jacket of chain mail and wore it as an emblem of superiority in battle because the Cheyenne arrows hadn't been able to penetrate it. . . . Since then it's been worn by a succession of war chiefs who took the name of Iron Shirt."

"That's it, all right," Fontaine said, nodding and taking the cheroot which was offered by his host. "Seems you found out the easy way. I couldn't get anything from several local Indian Agents, half the bastards can't even read. . . . So last winter when I was well enough to travel again, I stopped in Washington and paid a clerk five dollars and he let me go through the records. I had a clue that you didn't, the Mexican once referred to the Indian by name, so I had something to go on. And I got a bit more, though it's more of a conclusion than a straight fact. The son of a bitch had a goddam broad chest, and the more I thought on it the more I came to think he was wearing something else. In a diary from a historian who traveled with the Cheyenne back in the forties I got the rest of it. The Iron Shirt at that time was shot, the chain mail wasn't that good, so the next chief added an underlayer of buffalo body armor, you know, like they made their shields; layers of first-cut back leather held together with hoof glue and lacquered with the same stuff. It's the combination of the two that turns a bullet."

Lane nodded, got to his feet and pulled aside a big leather couch and began to twirl the dial on a safe which was built into the floor. He took out an oilskin packet and tossed it to Fontaine. "In there is the draft for the bulls, a letter of introduction which the major will expect, and some expense money."

"All right, Toby. I'm flattered at your trust."

"If I didn't trust you I'd never've mentioned the railroad. . . . Jon, while we're on the subject, I'd like to ask you a question. I know you wouldn't 've come back if it wasn't for the Indian, but will you stay after you find him?"

"Yes, Toby," Fontaine nodded, finishing his brandy, "at least until I recruit all the men."

"I shouldn't 've asked," Toby grinned, "I'm sorry. . . . Come on, let's get you to bed, you'll be outa here come sunup."

Fontaine picked up the packet and his carbine and Toby saw him to the stairs. They exchanged nods and smiles and Fontaine ascended the stairs while Lane returned to his study and closed the door. As he reached the top of the stairs he saw Mary Kaye's door open and she peered out, trying to catch his eye. He ignored her and went into his room and closed the door. He started to lock it, then grinned and changed his mind. He pulled the drapes, turned up the lamp and took out his notebook; he sat on the edge of the bed and wrote:

I saw him today. . . . He wasn't as big as I'd remembered. I was unarmed so I couldn't make him talk to me. But he knows I'll track him some more. . . . The coincidence stretches my credulity. . . . He's gone again but Toby has offered every help . . . in order to get me to line up the men he wants . . . and plenty of money. . . .

He put the wallet and notebook in his bag, stood the carbine against the wall by the head of the bed and sat down, realizing that it had been a long trip on the stage, and a long day, and he was tired. He pulled off his boots, raised up from the bed and slipped off his pants and long johns, got his shirt off and tossed it on the foot of the bed on top of his pants, stretched out and closed his eyes and was asleep almost at once. But it wasn't a quiet, restful sleep; he had the dream again. . . .

It was almost dark when he topped the last rise in the trail from town and his eyes widened in horror. His barn was on fire and the stock had been scattered. He heard her scream and he pulled the mules to a mouth-tearing halt, jumped from the wagon and ran toward the house. When he was halfway there she screamed again for a good five seconds and then stopped abruptly. He shivered, though he was sweating, and ran faster. When he was fifty feet away he forced himself to slow to a trot and take in great lungsful of air. He could see no one, and no horses. He approached the closed front door and paused for a moment to listen. She was moaning in anguish and there was a strange scuffling sound. He put his hand on the door latch, pulled his .45 and flung the door all the way open.

He had had the dream so many times in the last few years that his mind had begun to play a trick on him. The scene that he'd originally absorbed in a flash of anger, and horror, and hatred, came back to him slowly, painfully, the characters reacting with jerky motions, like life-size puppets. She was on her back on the big round table, stripped naked except for her cotton stockings. Her eyes were wide and she was biting on the knuckle of her forefinger; her right breast was torn and bleeding profusely, her face a mass of cuts and welts, and she was being raped by a tall Mexican. He was fully clothed, even to his sombrero hanging down his back, but his pants were down to his knees and he was in her, with his big, dirty hands digging into her soft waist.

Standing in the back doorway was an Indian in buckskins holding a lance. His hair hung down in a braid on either side; there were two eagle feathers in his hair and around his neck was a necklace of human fingers. Fontaine pumped two shots into the Indian's chest and his eyes flashed back to the Mexican who had turned his head, the dirty grin still on his face. But the Indian came toward him, and then something hit him on the side of the head and the scene exploded into bright lights.

When he came to it was night and he was outside. His head hurt and he was sick to his stomach. Then the smell of smoke made him raise up on his elbows and he forced his eyes to focus on the fire. He shook his head and staggered to his feet.

His house was burning fiercely and flames had already consumed the roof. He staggered to his feet and shouted "No!"
and ran toward the house. The front was intact, and the front
door was ajar. He staggered to it and pushed it open and a
great blast of smoke forced him back for a moment. Then he
entered and tried to get to her body, though it was no longer a
body; it was on the floor but it was seared like charcoal and
only the shape remained and before the heat forced him back
he could see that the head had almost been severed. . . . They
found him the next morning lying by the hitching rack, the
only living thing on the property, his hair burned off and his
face and hands badly blistered.

What was left of her was put into a small trunk and buried
in the Pinyon cemetery and Fontaine decided there was only
one way he'd ever return to the burying ground. . . .

He awoke in a sweat and was sure he had cried out. He took
a deep breath and got up and went to the window and opened
the drapes. It was dark and quiet. He paced the room for a few
moments, then took the big towel from the bureau and wiped
his face and neck.

As he heard the footsteps near his door he wrapped the towel
around his waist, tied a quick knot in the side and went silently to his gun. He was pointing it at the door when the knob
turned in the moonlight. The door opened and Mary Kaye
stuck her head in. When she saw him she put her finger to her
lips and quickly stepped inside, closing and bolting the door
behind her. Fontaine put the gun down and came toward her
with a cynical grin.

"I didn't think virtuous young ladies came to men's room in
the middle of the night."

"Oh shut up!" she whispered. "I came to apologize, if you'll
keep that goddam nasty tongue of yours silent for a bit."

"All right," he smiled. She was wearing a cotton nightgown
and by the way her breasts jiggled he could see that she had
nothing on underneath it. "Won't your uncle be upset?"

"He's asleep, I heard him snoring."

"What about the Indian woman?"

"She only sleeps in the house when she's told to," she replied. "I said I want to apologize. I was as much to blame as
any of those old biddies tonight in spreading that story. I don't
usually do things like that. But I'd had a bit too much to drink

and I wanted to set you down a peg. I'm sorry, I truly am. I didn't know about you and the Indian, and your place being burned . . . and. . . . Well, I am very sorry, I apologize."

"Why, thank you, ma'am," he said without being cynical, and smiled.

She smiled back and sighed, relieved that he wouldn't hold a grudge. Then she added, "I guess you loved her very much?"

"Yes," he replied quietly. "She was so young, and happy. . . ."

"How old was she?"

"Fifteen."

"Fif—!" She exclaimed in confusion, then lowered her voice. "Why you filthy old son of a bitch! You were over forty! Why couldn't you get a grown woman?"

He chuckled at her confusion, which added to her anger, and backed against the bureau. "There you go off half cocked again! I've got a good notion to let you think what you will, but I'll be patient and try to keep you from making an ass out of yourself again. . . . She was my daughter."

"Oh!" Mary Kaye said meekly. Then her anger rose up again and she added, "You son of a bitch! You could've told me instead of letting me. . . ."

"Wait," he smiled. "What's changed? You said you were sorry."

"That's still right. But you deceived me."

"I did not!" His voice started to rise in irritation. "You never asked. And right now I think maybe I should not have told you. Maybe I should've let you go on making a big fool of yourself!"

Her right hand shot out, but he caught her wrist before she could slap him and forced her arm down. Then his teeth flashed in the moonlight as both his hands caught her bodice; he ripped the gown open and pulled it to her waist.

"I just wanted to make sure they're real," he grinned, staring at her big breasts.

Her mouth opened, then closed, but she made no move to cover herself. Then she grinned a little and moved her shoulders so that her breasts quivered.

"Well, they are," she said in a whisper.

He continued to stare at her and then her hand flashed out again and again he caught it but this time he held it. Then he pulled her to him and kissed her, forcing her head back. He

held her for a long moment, then pushed her gently away.
She took a deep breath, stared at him a moment, then dropped
the nightgown to the floor and came forward, holding up her
breasts for him to suck. After a few moments he raised up and
started to push her toward the bed but she put her hands on
his chest to stay him. Then she pulled the towel away and
looked at him, her mouth open. Slowly she dropped to her
knees in front of him and he could feel her mouth working on
him. When he could stand it no longer he pulled her to her feet
and pushed her to the bed and was quickly in her. As she
wrapped her legs around him she began to quiver in her orgasm
and whisper hoarsely:

"Fuck me! Fuck me. . . . Fuck me till I can't stand it. . . ."

When she'd returned to her own room he took out the notebook and added:

"Toby's niece, Miss Mary Kaye Bartlett, is a beauty!
And a hellion! Has big bosoms . . . and tasty, too!"

Chapter Two

They left before sunup the next morning. Each rider had
two of Toby's best horses and they also had a pack mule. Toby
and Starrett were at the stables to see them off. While Charlie
Moss, a slim, sloppy-looking fellow with dirty clothes and a
scraggly beard, checked his cinch Toby had a last word with
Fontaine.

"You've got the packet?"

"Yes."

"And I'll wire Major Tischner to meet you at the depot on
Wednesday. . . . Will you stop by your place?"

"I thought I might," Fontaine said with a faint smile. "It's
sorta on the way. But it's your place now."

"Yeah. But I haven't done a thing with it since the day I
bought it. . . . Been too busy with other things."

Fontaine nodded and the faint smile vanished; that was not
like Toby Lane. Then he grinned widely, shook Toby's hand,
exchanged friendly nods with Leroy Starrett and mounted his

horse. As they rode away from the barn he turned and looked back and saw Mary Kaye waving from the window. Fontaine stood in his stirrups and waved back; then Toby and Leroy waved, they thought he was waving at them. Fontaine shrugged.

When they stopped at what had once been his ranch Fontaine forced himself to keep an expressionless face, though his stomach was churning. Charlie Moss was politely silent, having heard the story. Fontaine climbed down, gave Moss his reins and wandered through the ruins. The only thing standing was half of the front wall of his house. The rest, and the barn, had been burned to the ground. Large tumbleweeds were growing through what had been his living-room floor and one would have to ride close by to see that anyone had tried to make a life at this place. But it wasn't particularly unusual, Fontaine thought, it merely indicated that another man had tried and hadn't quite succeeded. Fontaine returned to his horse with a clenched jaw and Charlie Moss looked the other way.

When they camped that night Charlie offered to tend the animals and set up camp if Fontaine would scrounge the firewood. When Fontaine returned a few minutes later with an armload of kindling he saw Charlie quickly jump to his feet from near Fontaine's saddlebag and turn with a big smile to help with the wood. Fontaine slept with his carbine that night, but there was no need. Charlie snored loudly all night long, thanks to six shots of Fontaine's Scotch whiskey.

The next morning Fontaine was up first and had a fire going and a teakettle and the coffee water on. As Fontaine gathered his things in a towel Charlie awoke.

"What the hell you gonna do, Mr. Fontaine?" Charlie asked from his bedroll.

"Shave."

"Out here? What the hell for? Ain't a white woman for fifty miles."

"Certainly," Fontaine smiled. "I try to shave every day. And brush my teeth."

"Yeah?" Charlie said in some wonder, and sat up. "What with?"

Fontaine held up a pig-bristle brush and a small, cylindrical can with a lid.

"What's that?"

"Salt and soda. Keeps your teeth clean and keeps you from getting a toothache."

"Do tell!" Charlie was amazed at the eastern ways. "Say, that's a pretty fine-lookin' razor. Pearl handle?"

"Uh huh. Sheffield steel. Sharp as a razor."

Charlie grinned at the joke, showing that he understood it right off. "Take yore time, Mr. Fontaine. I'll fix the whole breakfast, get the wood, tend the animals and all. Jest enjoy yoreself."

"Thank you," Fontaine grinned. That was unusual; Charlie Moss didn't strike him as being the type who would gratuitously do more than his share. He picked up the teakettle and strolled toward the stream. He shaved as fast as he could, brushed his teeth quickly, and then sprinted downstream a hundred feet; he circled the camp and came in by the uphill side, to peer through some bushes. Charlie was going through his notebook and making notes of his own on a small piece of paper with a pencil stub. Charlie was only partially dressed, but the first things he had put on were his boots and his gun, tied down and ready for use. Fontaine shrugged—he could never make it to his carbine—and silently withdrew. He ran back to the stream, gathered his things and made lots of noise returning to camp. Charlie had bacon and corncakes cooking.

When they had broken camp and were about to mount, Fontaine quietly pulled his carbine and stepped away from his horse. Charlie had his back to him, tying his cinch.

"Charlie?" Fontaine said in a conversational tone.

"Yeah?"

"Why did you read my notebook, Charlie"

Charlie's back tensed and his right hand started to drop.

"Don't do that, Charlie, just turn around."

Charlie turned slowly to see that Fontaine held the gun at his left side, pointing to the ground. Charlie grinned and side-stepped away from his animal. "It ain't none of yore business."

"Why do you want to know what's in the notebook, Charlie?" Fontaine said in the same quiet voice. "Or was it the letters? Now don't let the gun fool you, I can get into position before you can possibly clear."

"Yeah?" Charlie sneered. "I'm one of the fastest guns you ever seen."

"Tell me, Charlie," Fontaine persisted. "I don't want to have to kill you."

"Ha! A dude like you! You ain't got a prayer of me talkin', mister!"

"Oh?" Fontaine said mildly. "You heard the story about me skinning that Mexican? Well, that razor you saw is good for lots of things. . . . Tell me, Charlie, or I'll skin you, starting at the balls. . . . Charlie, you can't beat me."

Charlie's shoulders slumped, as if giving up, but Fontaine knew he was relaxing for a split second before starting his draw. As Charlie's hand moved an inch, Fontaine twisted his left hand and put a bullet through Charlie's sternum. The impact knocked him flat on his back, the gun flying from his hand. Fontaine shook his head and advanced to kneel by his target. Charlie's eyes were already glazed in shock.

"Why, Charlie?"

"But you never even changed hands," Charlie said in wonder.

"Maybe I should've told you," Fontaine said, shaking his head. "All you gunslicks are so conceited. To think that you can draw, cock, and fire, while I merely raise my weapon and touch the trigger. . . ."

"But I'm so fast," Charlie said in an amazed whisper as if to explain why he shouldn't die. But he did.

"You son of a bitch!" Fontaine said mildly to the body. "Goddam, Charlie, now I've got to bury you."

When the body was in a shallow grave Fontaine took out his notebook and wrote as he said the only words that would be spoken over the grave of Charles Moss:

Charlie Moss, a no-good cowhand, tried to go through my stuff. Seems to me somebody figured that Toby wrote me a letter. If news about the RR got out, somebody could grab up a lot of good land and make a lot of money. . . . Gave Charlie a passable burying, even left his boots on.

Fontaine gathered up the animals, put Charlie's gun in his saddlebag with the rest of his gear: a bowie knife, a spare bandana, two plugs of tobacco, and two hundred and fifty dollars. Then Fontaine took the money out and put it in his pocket, noting that it was more than six months' pay for a bronc peeler. Then he had a second thought and took out Charlie's gun, emptied the bullets into the saddlebag, and put in the bullet he'd taken from the Mexican boy who'd been killed. Turning to a nearby tree some ten inches in diameter he pulled the trigger. Then he raised his carbine with his left hand and shot a foot above the .45 slug. He walked up to the tree and compared the two with a cold nod; the .45 slug had gone in maybe halfway, but his carbine bullet had left a big hole on the way out. He allowed himself a cold, self-satisfied grin.

As he rode out, pulling the four animals behind him, he looked once at the shallow grave, shook his head and said:

"Stupid ass!"

He made good time that day and camped in the bottom of a big valley for the night. The next morning he got up early and stirred up the fire, put the water on, and went down to the stream to shave. It was a beautiful day and he was glad he was alone for a while. He put the coffee on and sliced three thick pieces of bacon and put them into the skillet. Then he stood up and watched the sun begin to rise and he smiled, merely because it was such a beautiful sight. To try and capture the moment he took a writing tablet from his saddlebag and a pencil and sat against his saddle and wrote:

The loneliness and beauty of the trail is so overpoweringly impressive that it prompts me to write more than my usual brief lines with which I hope to jog my memory at some future date when I might set down the whole of the affair at length.

Once off the stage roads the way from here to there is only sometimes marked. In open country a man will take whatever way seems best at the time; the straight line, if he's in a hurry, the soft way if he wants to save his animals, the bottom lands if he may need water, or perhaps the way just under the skyline if he's either the hunted, or the hunter.

Today I will head northeast by the arrow because I am neither. I have water, and there is water ahead. The land will be easy on the animals and I will take my time and do something that we seldom do anymore, enjoy the trip. In this day and age of hurry to get somewhere faster than the other fellow in order to get something done in a hurry we seldom take time to enjoy what's between here and there. Today I will.

I awoke just before dawn because the animals were shaking at their hobbles, knowing that they would soon have to go to work, and knowing the time better than man. I am in the middle of a large, unnamed valley. To the east are some low hills that I will skirt. To the west and south are some mountains that I reckon to be sixty miles or more behind me. To the north the land rolls on until it disappears beyond the tips of some purple mountains.

But what has prompted these words more than anything is the fact that I am probably the only living man as far as my eye can see and that, in itself, is a pity, 'cause there is so much beauty for the eye to behold, and so much quiet to hear, and the air is so clear that one can smell all kinds of wonderful things that cannot be noticed in the city.

Quiet, of course, just can't be described, at least by me; it has to be enjoyed and appreciated, and if a man could find a woman who could appreciate it with him, why, it would be the eighth wonder of the world.

The trail brings out the smells that we take for granted when we're with people. When I awoke I smelled the old leather smell of my saddle, which makes a fine pillow, and much better than a rock or a rolled-up horse blanket. Then I raised up and smelled the morning air, cool (though there's no dew hereabouts) and sort of grassy (though there's not much of that, either), but most of all clean. Now, as I write this, I smell the most wonderful smells a hungry man can endure, frying slab bacon slightly touched by a campfire of dry wood, and boiling coffee. But most of all it's the colors on the trail that make a man shiver (and I know if the wrong person gets this before I'm ready I got a fight on my hands!). The night sky, of course, is pure black, and the stars hang about only a hundred feet in the air. But about dawn the sky gets what my teacher used to call "diffused," and the east gets just a glimmer of the deepest purple. From there it goes on to a dark blue, then a light blue, then pink. Then the real true glory of Nature tells you what a little nothin' you really are and she dumps all this orange onto the skyline and the day begins.

I always thought that if you can look forward to another one of these that you got a good chance of makin' the day. And, of course, the odds are with me, 'cause no matter if it isn't a day like this one, there's only one you won't make.

Fontaine had stopped at the crossroads just out of town to rest the animals. He was a good hour early, and not knowing what he might meet in a town hostile to Toby he preferred not to ride in on a tired horse. He was just tightening the cinch when he heard a wagon approach the junction from his right. He mounted quickly, checked to make sure the carbine was loose in the boot, and rode forward a bit, leading the rest of the animals with his left hand. When he was about to enter the crosstrail he stopped and turned to watch, leaving room for the wagon to pass. There were two men in it, both watching him. The one with the rifle was old, with white hair showing under his hat and large, drooping moustaches. Though it was a warm morning he wore a gray cape over his shoulders. The rifle was steadied by his left hand on his lap. The hand was completely bandaged.

The driver was a large, rangy man with broad shoulders. He was dressed in worn levis and wore a tattered, wide-brimmed hat. As they drew closer he smiled through his full beard and Fontaine could see that he had a large, aquiline nose which lent a certain dignity to his dark brown face.

"Good morning," Fontaine smiled.

"Good morning," the old man replied civilly, and the driver nodded. The team slowed and the rifle dropped a bit, though it was still pointed at Fontaine.

"It would seem to me," Fontaine said, "that I am in luck. Would you, by any chance, sir, happen to be Major Tischner?"

"I am, sir. And what can I do for you?"

"My name is Fontaine, and I have a letter for you."

"Excellent timing, sir!" the major said in a booming voice for so old a man. "Yes indeed! And may I have the letter?"

"Yes, sir. If you'll answer me a question. . . . Do you know the writer of the letter?"

"I do, indeed. It is from Mr. Tobias Lane."

"Yes, sir, it is," Fontaine nodded, making no move to reach

for the wallet. "If you'll pardon my caution, sir, one more question. When and where were we to meet?"

"Caution is not unmanly, sir," the old man smiled and nodded. "Mr. Lane's wire said to meet Mr. J. Fontaine, his duly authorized agent, at the depot on Wednesday at ten in the morning. I believe we're both early, Mr. Fontaine."

"We are, sir," Fontaine nodded, urged his horse forward a few feet, extracted the letter and leaned forward.

The major took the letter, put it on his lap and extended his hand. Fontaine stood in the stirrups and his hand was covered by a large, gnarled, weatherbeaten hand which had a firm grip.

"I am pleased to meet you, Mr. Fontaine."

"Major."

"And this," the major said, indicating his driver, "is Linus Gonzalez. You might call him my foreman."

"Mr. Gonzalez." Fontaine nodded and started to put his hand out, but his horse pulled away and the two settled for friendly nods.

"Well, sir," the major said, "it's a good day for traveling. Would you care to ride the wagon with us into town?"

"Yes, thank you," Fontaine grinned. "I'm a mite rump-sprung after four days."

He let the wagon pass, tied his animals to the tailgate and climbed to the seat to sit between the two men.

"If you don't mind, Mr. Fontaine," the major said, "we'll go on into town; we need some supplies. Then we'll head directly for my place. I'm sure you're eager to see what your principal paid ten thousand dollars for. . . . Uh, you do have the bank draft?"

"Yes, sir, it's in the letter," Fontaine said.

It was a quiet little town which owed its meager existence to a spur line, a narrow-gauge railroad that ran farther back into the hills to several silver mines which were almost played out. Linus stopped the wagon in front of the general store and Fontaine jumped down and untied his animals while Linus went to the back, threw back a tarp, uncovered a wicker wheelchair and took it to the wagon seat. Fontaine raised an eyebrow and started to help but Linus shook his head. With ease he lifted the major down from the wagon and put him in the chair, then lifted both to the boardwalk.

"We'll be a while, Mr. Fontaine," the major said. "Join us,

or go have yourself a beer. Might be the last one you'll get in a while. Once the Fords find out who you are—and comin' in with us won't help—you might not have time for another. Anyway, soon's you get the lay of the land I expect you'll be goin' back for some help."

"Yes, sir. I'll have a beer. Where'll I meet you?"

"At the depot. It's on your way. And you'll be sending a wire, no doubt?"

Fontaine nodded and pulled his animals across the street, tied them to the rack and went into the dim, stale, beer- and cigar-smelling saloon. There was no one there but a drowsy barkeep. The sign said nickel beer so Fontaine had two big glasses, just to make sure he didn't get thirsty for a while. It took him ten minutes and when he came out the major's wagon was gone. He gathered up his animals and walked them to the town trough for a long drink. Then he rode down to the little, gray-painted depot. There were but a few people on the streets and no horses tied at the passenger side of the depot. As he dismounted and tied the animals he saw that the other side of the depot had a big storage shed and several loading shutes for livestock and several holding corrals. He left his horse, went up the steps and entered the office. The agent nodded but said nothing. Fontaine returned the nod and took a telegram pad and addressed it to Toby. It read:

MET MAJOR THINGS QUIET GOING TO SEE PURCHASE
STOP CHARLIE TRIED TO DRYGULCH ME STOP HE LOST.

He paid the dollar, which he knew was too much, and as he turned to go he heard the unmistakable sounds of a fight. With a frown he went outside and turned the corner to look to the other side of the platform. His eyes widened in anger when he saw Linus in the grip of two men. But what had made him almost rush forward was the sight of two more cowboys who were just pushing the major in his wheelchair down one of the loading ramps. The chair rumbled to the bottom, almost tipped over, then continued on until it crashed into a pile of hay bales and the major was dumped off into the dirt. With a roar Linus ignored the two men holding him, and two vaqueros who were standing by laughing, pulled free and dove headlong into the vaqueros, knocking them out of the way, and began to run down the ramp after the other two.

Fontaine started to join the fray but his common sense told him that they all had guns. He watched a moment longer while one of the men at the bottom of the ramp snaked out a rope and caught Linus by the ankles, dumping him on his back. Fontaine turned and ran for his horse, and the carbine. As he sprinted back up the steps he cocked the rifle and ran to the corner, stopped a second, turned the corner and shouted: "Hold it!"

One of the men to his right already had his gun out and had been aiming at Linus, who was squirming at the end of the rope. At Fontaine's shout he spun, his gun at waist height. As the six-gun came up, Fontaine shot him in the chest. The man was jerked backward as if on a wire and landed on the platform with a thud. A slug plowed its way into the wood next to Fontaine's left shoulder and he swung the gun, still level with his belt, and pumped two slugs into a startled vaquero. The man was dead before he fell off the platform.

Then Linus was standing, jerking the man at the other end of the rope off his feet. He headed toward the other one as Fontaine stepped forward, waiting for one of the men on each side of him and some twenty feet away to make a move. Fontaine felt something wide and hard poke into his back and a voice said:

"Drop it."

Fontaine's eyes darted to each man, but they made no move and the carbine barrel slowly pointed at the platform. Then the town peace officer, a small, wizened man with a small badge and a large twelve-guage shotgun, appeared to Fontaine's right.

"What's goin' on here?" the constable demanded.

The last man, the one on his feet near Linus, turned and grinned through his dirty gray, tobacco-stained beard and said:

"Don't let 'im get away, Harry! He's a mean one! They jumped us and when we fought back that one ran for his rifle and kilt poor Joey! Then . . ."

"That's a goddam lie!" Fontaine said. "I came around the corner and saw—"

The constable poked Fontaine in the back again and said, "Shut up! Go on, Mr. Ford. Speak your piece."

"It's like I tolt ya, Harry," Ford said. "Him and that big nigger jumped us and when we got the best of the nigger he got nasty and hauled out that sawed-off—"

"Liar!" the major screamed, pulling himself to a sitting position against a hay bale. "You're a bastardly liar, Cletus Ford, and you know it!"

"I know it," the constable said, grinning as he stepped away from Fontaine, much to Fontaine's relief. "I just wanted to see how far Ford would go. I seen the whole thing from the other side of the pens; it took me a bit to run around to the high side. And I seen poor dear Joey with his gun out, about to cut down on this here man. . . . He got what he deserved fer being a bad shot."

The constable pointed his shotgun at the two bodies and added, "Cletus, git these two outa here."

While Fontaine casually backed against the wall, the carbine down but cocked, Ford and his three survivors loaded the bodies onto their horses, moving warily, with an eye on the scattergun. Linus righted the wheelchair and lifted the major into it, and then slowly backed it up the ramp. By the time Ford had mounted, a small crowd had come forward to watch. Ford turned in the saddle and said to Fontaine:

"I'll see you again."

"I hope not," Fontaine replied.

With a quick glance of hatred at the major, a small nod to his men, Ford turned and slowly rode up the street.

"You all right, Major?" Fontaine asked.

"Yes, thanks to you."

"And my thanks, Mr. Fontaine," Linus grinned. "They might not have killed us but they surely had a crippling look in their eyes."

"Uh huh," Fontaine nodded. "I take it that Mr. Ford was the losing bidder?"

"He's the one," the major said. "He's nothing but a revolving bastard. No matter which way you turn him, he's still one. . . . You see, Mr. Fontaine, he's got a bad case of landitis. My little valley controls all the water for a bigger valley, which Ford has a chunk of, but he wants it all. . . . And he thought the bulls would be a fine addition to his holdings."

"You got yourself some real trouble now, Major," the constable said.

"Not much more than I had. If I can get home I don't think Ford'll try anything; I've got good neighbors, if they'll help."

Fontaine raised a cynical eyebrow. "Will they?"

"I think so, Mr. Fontaine."

"Well," the constable said, "Ford's best chance at you is on the trail. He'll take Joey and that Mexican to the buryin' ground first. That'll take a coupla hours. Then he'll come back and git likkered up and, if you're lucky, he'll spend the night. If you ain't, you got no more'n two hours start. You'd best git."

"Your logic, sir, is a paragon of clarity," the major said.

Linus and Fontaine exchanged quick grins and set about tying the animals to the wagon and putting the major in his wheelchair in the back of the wagon. They lashed it securely with ropes and put the rifle across his lap.

The road was wide and good and Linus kept the team at a steady canter for almost an hour until they stopped at a small stream for water. When they climbed down, the major was wan and pale, and took but a small sip of water. When they were in front of the horses Linus shook his head and tapped his chest with both hands; it would be a long trip for the old man.

"The consumption," Linus whispered. "That's why we came out here."

Fontaine shook his head. "How long before we get there?"

"We'll have to camp out tonight, we left too late, be there in the morning."

Fontaine nodded and scanned the hills. The country was fairly open, with small chance of an ambush; if they tried it, it would be after dark.

"How many more miles in those horses?"

"Enough to get us a good long ways before dark, Mr. Fontaine."

They exchanged easy nods and got back in the wagon.

The sun was down but it was still light. As they rounded a bend, the hills turned to rocks and there was little open land on either side of the trail. They made a few hundred yards and Linus stopped near a big boulder for a rest. They got down to stretch and saw that the major was asleep again. Fontaine walked a few paces forward with his carbine and Linus joined him. Linus stared at the trail ahead and his eyes widened; he pointed to a spot of grass along the trail and twenty yards ahead. Fontaine followed the finger with his eyes but saw nothing. Linus sprinted forward, off the trail, and knelt in the grass. In a moment he waved to Fontaine.

He ran forward and looked at the spot. Almost on top of it Fontaine could see where the grass had been trampled by several horses. Linus ran forward at a crouch, studying the ground. When he stood erect he held up four fingers. He waited until he was close to Fontaine to speak in a low voice:

"They were in a hurry, Mr. Fontaine. And they came from town."

"Could it be anybody else?"

"I doubt it. I'm only a quarter Indian, but I'd bet on it."

"Why?"

"Well, four horses, in a hurry, and staying off the trail. With fresh animals they could've run even with the trail, but a few miles to the north, and made better time than we did. But now that the land gets rougher, they had to come close to the road. I admit that it could be four others who happened to join the trail from the north, but it's just not reasonable that anyone would run their horses that fast this close to dark when there's nothing past here except our valley."

"Uh huh," Fontaine nodded. "So they wanted to get ahead of us by dark."

"Seems that way."

"It surely does," Fontaine said with a note of finality in his voice. "I'll ride on ahead and look for a place to camp. You follow with the wagon."

"Yes, sir."

Fontaine mounted quickly and loped past the wagon, his carbine across the saddle. When he was a hundred yards in front of the wagon he realized that his stomach was getting jumpy and he began to watch the long shadows at every bush and rock. As he moved cautiously down the road a part of his mind, acting almost independently, considered the situation again. He certainly had no desire to be ambushed, or shoot it out with Ford. They could turn and make a dash back toward town, but the long shadows told him even that was too late. Besides, they'd just have to turn around tomorrow, or the next day, and try it again. He concluded with an inescapable logic that they couldn't run and they couldn't hide; they would go on until he could find a place to make a stand and there they would make camp.

A half mile down the road he found it; a small draw with

steep sides that would hide the animals, with a nest of rocks in front of it, fifty yards off the road. He turned and waved his carbine and Linus urged the animals forward. When the wagon stopped, Fontaine jumped down and hurried to the major.

"Linus told me," the major said. "I'll guard while you make camp."

Fontaine grinned briefly and began to pull the team off the road. When he got the wagon where he wanted it, he set about undoing the harness and putting all the animals on a picket line inside the small box canyon. As he was running in the mule, Linus picked up the wheelchair with the major in it and climbed to the top of the nest of rocks.

Then Linus joined Fontaine to make a quick camp. They gathered plenty of firewood, mostly dried cholla and mesquite, and brought it to the wagon at a trot. While Linus watered the animals from the big keg on the side of the wagon, Fontaine built a fire, made a big pot of coffee and scrounged in the back of the wagon to find the bean pot. It was a big one and the beans had been cooked the day before, or maybe the day before that. He also found a slab of smoked bacon and several bunches of carrots. He poured a bit of water into the pot and set it into the fire, making sure he had the carrying rod. He found the big ladle and stirred the beans and then pulled his knife from the back of his belt and sliced chunks of bacon into the pot, gave the carrots a quick scrape to get off the biggest chunks of dirt, then sliced them into the pot, green tops and all.

"That's a fancy knife, Mr. Fontaine," Linus said in a low voice.

Fontaine jumped and looked over his shoulder; he hadn't heard the big man come up to him. "Damn! You scared me. You move mighty quiet for so big a man."

"Sorry, didn't mean to startle you."

"That's all right, I'm a bit jumpy. And the knife is a present from my dear Aunt Antoinette. No French gentleman from New Orleans should carry such a base weapon as a bowie knife. You know, the old dear would faint if she knew what this fancy-handled thing had been used for."

"Yes," Gonzalez said, almost sadly, "civilized ladies just don't seem to understand us, especially me."

"Why you? You're a handsome fellow," Fontaine grinned.

"Cleaned up maybe, but my skin's too dark for most. . . . But we're wasting time. What about the wagon?"

"Have to leave it here, but make it look like three men in the back."

Linus nodded and made up three beds by lining up the supplies and covering them with blankets. Then he took off his hat to put it on one and decided it would pass in the dark. They took all the canteens—Fontaine had four, the major six—filled them and took all the ammunition, three more blankets and Linus's rifle, three tin cups and plates and spoons to the hill. They came back and ran the rod through the steaming pot, Linus picked up the big coffee pot with his bandana, and they carried both to the major. Then they quickly dug a small hole with their knives and half buried the pot to keep it warm as long as possible. It was now full dark and Fontaine motioned for Linus to take the major from his chair and prop him against a boulder and cover him with a blanket. Linus nodded and Fontaine took his carbine and ran down for a last look. He stopped just out of the light for a moment and listened. Then he quickly ran to the fire, added the rest of the wood and turned and ran back up the hill. Linus and the major were already eating.

"Dig in, Fontaine," the major grinned, looking better than he had all day. "You made enough for six men, but it's mighty good."

"Let's hope it tastes that good in the morning," Fontaine said.

They ate in silence for a while and, when he was through, the major said:

"May I make a suggestion, Fontaine?"

"Certainly, sir."

"Well, Linus has the best ears, that part of him's Indian for sure, and I think he oughta stand guard tonight, or as long as he can without falling asleep. Then he can sleep in the wagon tomorrow."

"Fine by me, Major," Linus said. "I doubt that I could sleep anyway."

The other two nodded in agreement, and Fontaine and Linus finished eating. Then they each had a big cup of coffee and Linus gathered up the plates, cleaned them with sand, stacked them near the pot and took his rifle and went to the edge of the rocks to watch. At the old man's wave Fontaine sat next to him so they could converse in a whisper. They were silent for a while, Fontaine waiting for the major to speak.

"Wait until you see my place, Fontaine, it's one of the prettiest spots on earth. From what Toby told me in his letter you're a world traveler, says you've been to England and Europe, spent some time in France; even so, I think you'll be impressed with my valley. Now, I've traveled all over the eastern states, but this is the best. It's only five miles long, and half as wide, but to me it's the most beautiful spot on earth. It's hotter'n hell in the summer, but dry, warm in the winter, and the air is so clear you can see for seventy miles. We're ringed, but at a distance, by all kinds of mountains, and I tapped into an underground river. Most people think I've only got a spring, or a deep well, but that son of a bitch, Ford, he knows better. I've found enough water to make this whole goddam territory as green as Virginia, if I had enough pumps and pipes. . . . You know about soil?"

"A little. I had a ranch once."

"Well, you'll appreciate my land, and that Linus, he's got a way with growing things, and animals for that matter. He grows melons you can hardly lift. If I could work it another five years, with enough hands, I could make a fortune. But that's why I bought the bulls. Then I realized I didn't have enough time for that. So I sold them, just to keep me for what time I've got left. . . ."

Fontaine was polite enough to remain silent. The major coughed quietly and then pulled the blanket around him; in a few moments he was asleep again.

An hour later Linus crawled close to him, put his mouth to his ear and whispered:

"They're stopped out there, getting ready."

Fontaine nodded, nudged the major, and whispered, "They're here."

The old man was awake at once, nodding his head. He motioned to Linus, who spread out a blanket at the front of the rocks, picked up the major, and laid him carefully on his stomach, propped up on his elbows with the rifle. Fontaine could hear the horses now; they were in a group, just out of the glow of the dying fire. Then one started, then the next, in single file, and at a dead run. The first one ran into the light, shooting into the wagon, followed by the next one, until all four had made a run at it. Then they stopped in the darkness to regroup.

"Cover me," Fontaine whispered to Linus. The big man nodded and Fontaine carefully worked his way out of the rocks, wanting to make sure they didn't come for their horses. He found himself a boulder between the wagon and the animals and waited. In a few moments one rode in and poked at the blankets with his rifle. As the ruse was about to be discovered, Fontaine snapped off a quick shot, but his aim was bad in the flickering light and he only grazed the man's horse. The animal reared in fright and bolted toward the south. In a moment he heard the others run after him. He fired a spread of six but he didn't hear anything that sounded encouraging. In a few moments the hoofbeats of the fearless bushwhackers were out of hearing. Fontaine waited five minutes, then worked his way back to the rocks. As he was about to climb them he whispered, "It's me."

"Yes, sir," Linus whispered back, "I know."

Linus had been asleep in the back of the wagon since five thirty; it was now something after nine o'clock. Ford had not returned and Linus had stayed awake all night. Fontaine had managed to close his eyes around one and it seemed but an instant when Linus had nudged his shoulder and pointed to the faint light in the eastern sky.

Fontaine kept the team at a steady pace for another hour until he came to the top of a small hill at the end of a narrow valley where the road twisted around lots of large boulders. He couldn't see the road in the valley but he could see where it came out at the other end. He stopped the team for a rest while he studied the terrain.

"Ever been married, Fontaine?" the major asked.

"Yes."

"Well . . . I won't pry."

"That's all right. I've been a widower for a long time."

"Really? What brings you out here? There must be something besides doing nasty jobs for Toby Lane."

Fontaine raised an eyebrow at the major's perception and said, "I'm looking for a Cheyenne."

"A Cheyenne? This far south?"

"Yes, just one. Haven't seen any strays, have you?"

"Of course not. You're in the wrong direction. What's left of the Cheyenne should be far north; especially after the 'Reverend' Chivington butchered a good two hundred at Sand Creek."

"I heard; that's called progress, Major," Fontaine said dryly.

"Bullshit!" was the succinct reply. Then, "You've got a snowball's chance finding a particular Indian, you know that?"

"Yes. But I've been at it a while, I'm used to it."

"Uh huh. . . . It's obvious that you're no saddle bum, discounting the fact that Toby went to great pains to tell me what a gentleman you are. . . . When you find this Indian, will you stop traveling . . . I presume that's why you're working for Lane."

"Yes, on both counts."

"Well, on the other side is the best spot in—What's the matter?"

Fontaine had held up his hand and was listening. "Linus?"

"Yes, sir," Linus said from over Fontaine's shoulder. "I heard."

"Thunder?" Fontaine asked.

"No . . . no, I don't think so," Linus replied.

"Me neither," Fontaine said.

He lashed the team with the reins and ran them down into the rock-strewn valley, wanting to get to the far end to see, but hoping it wasn't what he expected. When he was fifty yards from the crest he pulled the team to a halt, jumped down, and tied them to a mesquite bush. "Come on, Linus, let's look for tracks."

They trotted twenty yards, checking each side of the road. Then Linus said:

"There're no tracks out here, Mr. Fontaine. What did you want to say?"

"You're right," Fontaine replied. "Is your valley on the other side of that hill?"

"Yes."

"And that wasn't thunder. Now what do you suppose it was?"

A horrified look crossed the big man's face and he said, "Oh no! God, no! Dynamite?"

Fontaine nodded and turned to look at the wagon. Then he heard the pounding hooves at the same time as Linus and turned back to see a vaquero with a pistol in his hand bearing down on them from over the crest.

"Get the major out of the wagon!" Fontaine shouted. "I'll get this one."

Linus turned and sprinted down the road, his long legs eating up the distance as Fontaine followed, gauging the ap-

proaching hoofbeats. When the first shot hit the dirt near him
Fontaine threw himself forward in a somersault, landed on his
back, rolled over on his elbows and faced the rider down the
sights of his carbine. His first shot hit the horse in the chest
and the rider was thrown forward onto the road. As he came
up on his knees and started to raise his pistol, Fontaine shot
him in the face and the body was thrown on its back.

Without waiting to dispatch the screaming horse Fontaine
scrambled to his feet and turned to see Linus carefully put the
major down with his back against a boulder, across the road
from the wagon, his rifle across his lap. As Fontaine ran toward
them, two more men, one of Ford's cowboys and a vaquero,
pounded up the road from the other direction. The major tried
to raise the rifle, but he was so close to the boulder that he
was unable to lift the weapon to aim to his right. Linus started
to dash across the road to the wagon, but it was obvious he
wouldn't make it. Without a moment's hesitation the major
shouted, "Linus!" and tried to throw the rifle to him.

He wasn't strong enough and the weapon landed halfway
between them. Linus hesitated a moment, and he was trapped.

Without pausing, Fontaine shouted, "Drop, Linus!" and continued to run toward them. Now both riders were firing their
six-guns. But from a distance of forty yards, and on horseback,
their aim wasn't effective. Fontaine continued until he was just
behind Linus and the two riders were but twenty yards away.
Then Fontaine dug his boot heels into the dirt and came to a
fast halt, raised his gun and quickly killed the horse to his
right, while a shot tugged at the shirt under his arm. As he saw
the horse go down he forced himself to turn carefully, lever
another shell into the chamber, take a half breath, and shoot
the man to his left. The shot caught him at the belt and the
man was thrown backward in the saddle as his horse thundered
by. Fontaine took a quick step to his right to avoid the horse
and turned as it passed. The rider's hand on the reins brought
the animals to a rearing halt and the rider tried to shoot Fontaine from over his shoulder. Fontaine raised his rifle again
and put two shots into the man's back, knocking him out of
the saddle.

Fontaine turned to see that Linus had closed with the other
rider; they were grappling with the man's gun for a moment
and then it went flying. In the next moment Linus had the
man by the neck with both hands and was shaking him like

a dog with a bone. As the man grabbed those powerful wrists and tried to stay alive Fontaine saw Ford ride from the rocks behind them and up to the major. Fontaine tried to raise his carbine but Linus was in the way.

In the instant it took him to get to one side he heard a loud snap and the man Linus was holding went limp, his neck broken. Linus tossed him aside and started for Ford but it was too late. For a terrible moment Fontaine saw Ford and the major in a macabre tableau: Ford slowing his horse and pointing his six-gun at the major from no more than twenty feet while the major pointed his bandaged left hand at his enemy as if to ward off the impending shot. Ford's bullet caught the major full in the chest and the old man was thrown back against the boulder. Then, as Ford advanced, the major's left hand raised again and the bandages erupted as the two shots from the major's derringer ripped open Ford's face and he was thrown onto his back in the dirt, screaming and tearing at what was left of his face.

Linus ignored him and ran to the major. Fontaine came forward, his nostrils flared in hate, and put the carbine a foot from Ford's temple and pulled the trigger. The screaming ceased and Fontaine turned quickly to check the other three. They were dead. The first horse was still kicking and Fontaine raised his rifle again and shot the animal in the forehead. Then he turned to Linus and the major.

Linus had the old man propped against the boulder, his coat and shirt open. It was no use, there was a gaping hole in his chest which bubbled as he breathed.

The major smiled wanly, his face gray with approaching death, and looked from Linus to Fontaine.

"Pretty clever, wasn't it?" he whispered. "I thought that son of a bitch might come close enough. . ." He held up his left hand. "Take it off, Fontaine, I want to stretch my fingers."

Fontaine pulled his knife and cut the bandages, and slowly took the small gun from the stiff fingers. The old man flexed his hand and sighed.

"Whew! That's better. They were so stiff I didn't know if I could pull the trigger."

"Major," Linus said, tears running down his cheeks, "we've got to get you to a doctor."

"Don't be silly, Linus," the old man smiled. "You know

there's no doctor for a hundred miles. Besides, looky there, I'm breathin' out of it."

The two men stood there, helpless for a moment, then the major looked up at Fontaine and said:

"I want you to do something for me."

"Yes, sir."

"The draft . . . in this pocket."

Fontaine nodded and pulled the envelope from the major's right pocket and opened the envelope.

"You got a pencil?"

"Yes, sir."

Fontaine fished his pencil out of his wallet and Linus knelt beside them. The old man took the draft out, put it on Linus's big arm and slowly endorsed it. Then he gave the draft to the big man.

"Linus," he whispered, "see that Fontaine gets his bulls . . . and the money and ranch is yours. . . . But, and I'm not so far gone that I don't know that was dynamite we heard . . . in case he doesn't get the bulls, that they run 'em off, give the man his money back . . . a deal's a deal. . . . You hear?"

"Yes, sir. But don't worry, you're not dying. We get you home and I'll dig that slug out. . . ."

"You goddam fool black bastard, or Indian, or Mex, whatever the hell you are, I forget . . . I'm dying and you know it. And if you don't get off your big ass and get me there I won't even get to die at home. . . ."

Fontaine shook his head, got to his feet and stacked the blankets in the back of the wagon while Linus lifted the major in his big arms and carefully put him in place. Then Linus got up on the seat to drive while Fontaine sat with the major. As the wagon moved out the old man opened his eyes and said:

"Fontaine, I want you to witness; Linus Gonzalez is my heir. I have no blood kin. And what I leave is his . . . you hear?"

"Yes, sir, I'll see to it."

"Good. Linus, he's part nigger, and Indian, and white, so some folks might not believe him, but you bear witness. . . . I'm charging you on my deathbed."

"It will be done, Major," Fontaine promised. "I'll see that it's legal."

"Listen, you might find out who those Mexicans are . . .

might be trouble . . . they don't work for Ford. . . . Check 'em,
I don't want Linus to get into trouble. . . ."

"No, sir."

As they neared the crest of the hill the road got bumpy
and before Fontaine could stop him, the major raised up and
said, "Stop, Linus!"

"But we're almost home, Major," Linus said.

"Stop, goddam, I don't want to die in this stinkin' wagon!
I want to die on the ground!"

His face was very pale and his eyes were out of focus. Linus
exchanged glances with Fontaine and Fontaine nodded. Linus
jumped down and carefully lifted the major in his arms and
started up the road, tears running down his cheeks again.

"We're almost home, Major. Just over the top of the hill."

"Get me there, Linus, so I can see it."

Fontaine stayed by the team, not wanting to intrude. It was
very quiet and a small breeze blew the major's faint words
back to him.

"I can't see, Linus . . . I can't see my valley. Can you see
it?"

Linus stopped at the crest of the hill, laid the major in the
spring grass, and held him cradled in his arms, pointing toward
home.

"Yes, sir, I can see it," Linus sobbed.

"How's it look, Linus?"

"Green, Major, greener than I've ever seen it . . . just beautiful."

"Tell me what you see. . . ."

"I . . . I see the house, just as snug as a painted picture . . .
and I see our little stream with the sun on it . . . and the berry
bushes . . . and most of all I see the grass. Major, clear to the
other end, it's so green, and it's wavin'. . . . Oh, Major!"

Then Linus broke down and cried, gently rocking his dead
friend in his arms.

Fontaine walked to the crest then, and stood a long moment
looking down at the valley, and tears came to his eyes. It was
dynamite. And Ford had done a thorough job. The house was
blown apart and burning, the barn was a column of smoke,
and the grass was green no longer, just the remains of a range
fire. It was a scene of utter desolation. . . .

Chapter Three

Linus had dug the hole but he couldn't bring himself to fill it. Fontaine picked up the shovel and said, "Go down to the barn and lash a couple of sticks together for a cross; I'll fill it in. Later we'll do a proper job, carved headstone and all."

"Thank you, Mr. Fontaine," the big man said quietly and trotted down the hill.

He waited until Linus couldn't hear, then he threw the first shovelful of dirt on top of the Army blanket and the sword. He worked slowly in the mid-afternoon heat, pausing every few moments to scan the horizon. He was on a small hill overlooking the ranch from several hundred yards. What was left of the house and barn still smoldered. The thick-walled adobe house had been dynamited, and the beams from the ceiling had caught fire but were now pretty well out. Of course the bulls were gone, as well as the rest of the major's livestock, a milk cow and a dozen head of horses. The pump to the underground water supply had been blasted and one side of the house was a mass of mud and oozing water.

Fontaine had yet to discuss the possibility of going after the bulls with Gonzalez; he thought it more proper to bury the major first. But it was obvious that a number of men had carried off the bulls. A set of partly filled-in, heavy wagon tracks and the prints of at least four, maybe six, horses led south, indicating to Fontaine that the affair had been well organized and the attack at the top of the hill had been a delaying action.

In a few minutes Linus returned with a wooden cross. He silently stuck it into the ground at the head of the grave and then stood back while Fontaine patted the dirt into place.

"He was a fairly religious man," Gonzalez said. "Would you say a few words?"

"Well, I . . . uh . . . wouldn't you rather say them?"

"I don't think I could do it properly," Linus said in a low voice. "I'd appreciate it if you'd say something brief. You seem to have a way with words."

"Well, all right," Fontaine said, taking off his hat. Though he was an agnostic he thought it fitting that he ignore the point at the moment. "Lord. . . ." He motioned for Gonzalez to take off his hat and put his rifle on the rock next to his. The big man swallowed hard and hurried to comply.

"Lord, we are here to say a few words over the body of Major. . . ?"

"Llewellyn," Linus said.

". . . We are here to say a few words over the body of Major Llewellyn Tischner, born . . . ?"

Linus shrugged. "He was about sixty-five, I think. . . ."

". . . Born sixty-five years ago and died this day, May the . . . May the twenty-ninth, eighteen hundred and eighty-eight, by the foul hand of one whose name we will not mention in Your presence. Suffice to say, Lord, he died a brave man, in defense of his home. He leaves his good friend, here, Linus Gonzalez. And he leaves many other good friends in this area who will weep for him, as soon as they know of his demise.

"Lord, we ask that You take this good man in, and see that he has a good place in the order of things, and please know that those who did him in are, right now, en route to the other place, if they aren't there already. . . . He lived a good, long life; he had happiness and sorrow; he worked hard; and he was a good neighbor. And, most of all, he left a good friend here, who grieves for him. So You know he was a good man. Amen."

"Amen," Linus said and replaced his hat and looked at Fontaine. "Thank you."

"I wish I could've said more."

"It was fine," Linus added sincerely. After a short silence he added, "What will you do now? Will you go after the bulls? If you don't, of course, you're not out anything. I'll return the draft."

"Thank you. I haven't quite decided yet. What will you do?"

"I'll run them down," was the quiet reply.

"Alone?"

"If I have to."

"Well," Fontaine said slowly, as they walked down the hill, "I've been thinking on it. If I go back now, my employer has broken even. But I'll be the loser. No one will say anything, of course, but it won't do much for me. On the other hand, if I run 'em down, and get the bulls back, it will do considerable

for me. . . . Now, don't get me wrong. I'm no gunslick, and
I don't need that kind of reputation. But I do need a certain
standing, for something I want to do. . . . And I wouldn't want
you to try it alone. . . . I'll go with you."

Fontaine stuck his hand out and Linus grinned and gripped
it hard and said, "I'm glad I waited to tell you, Mr. Fontaine."

"Tell me what?"

"That those two vaqueros today, and the one you killed at
the depot, are all from the Acosta family. I recognized the
one today as a son of Don Guillermo himself."

"So? And what does that mean?"

"It means, Mr. Fontaine, that if you continue you must kill
them all, the other three sons and the father, lest they kill
you; or else you must run and never come back to this area
again, and always look over your shoulder at every vaquero
while you are in Arizona, or Sonora. . . . It means that you
cannot simply get the bulls back. To get them back you will
have to get all the males of the family."

"Well now!" Fontaine said in some irritation, though he was
smiling coldly. "You mean that if one of the boys was a back-
shooting bastard, I've got to kill 'em all?"

"Something like that."

"Uh huh. Well we'll just see about that. . . . Now I'm going
for damn sure! Should we start now?"

"No, sir," Linus said. "They've got a real good start. I think
we should spend the night, get a good meal, rest the animals,
and start out early in the morning; the tracks should be easy
to follow."

"All right," Fontaine said. "Let's see to the animals."

"Yes, sir!" Linus grinned.

Though it was almost sundown, it was very bright. That fact
saved Fontaine's life. The water trough had escaped destruction
and Fontaine had flushed it out and was taking what he knew
would be his last bath for many days; they were headed for
southern New Mexico, a land not noted for its overabundance
of water. He was leisurely soaking himself in the tepid water
up to his neck. His head, with his hat still on, was resting
against the spout. The vaquero had made the mistake of
coming in from the east, so that Fontaine's head and the spout
blended into one dark spot. Fontaine had heard the quiet
jingle of a rowel and had frozen, one hand outside the trough

on the carbine. In a moment the vaquero passed fifty feet to his left, headed toward the main house. As he got close, Linus backed out of the front door, pulling a desk that somehow had not been completely burned. As Fontaine slowly raised up in the water the vaquero flipped his gun over and stepped forward and started to bring the butt down on Linus's unsuspecting head.

"*Halto!*" Fontaine shouted, but the gun butt descended and Linus dropped in his tracks. The vaquero flipped his gun back into his hand, turned and ran, not knowing from where the sound came. Fontaine was standing now, naked except for his hat and carbine, and he began pumping shots on either side of the man's heels. The vaquero came to a halt, his gun in the air.

"Drop it!"

The gun dropped and the man turned slowly to see a nude apparition step out of the trough and walk carefully across the dirt toward him. The man even managed a brief smile before the carbine whipped out and the butt crashed into his left temple.

In a few minutes Gonzalez shook his head and staggered to his feet as he heard Fontaine call; "Hey, Linus! How about a towel or a blanket?"

Linus shook his head again and turned to see the vaquero. He ran to him, picked up the gun, and turned to Fontaine, who was again sitting in the trough, but holding his carbine, and said:

"What happened?"

"He must have fainted."

Linus laughed heartily, felt the lump on his head, and went inside the house. In a moment he came out with a scorched but serviceable cotton comforter, which he tossed to Fontaine.

When he again had on his long johns, his socks, his Levis, and his boots, Fontaine stood up and said, "How's your Spanish?"

"I'm also a quarter Mexican, Mr. Fontaine. . . . If I may talk to him?"

"By all means," Fontaine grinned and sat on the remains of the front steps.

Linus shook the vaquero to his senses and the man got groggily to his feet. He saw Fontaine with the carbine nonchalantly pointing at him and his face grew sullen. He was big for a Mexican, almost as big as Linus, and dressed in bell-bottomed pants, a vaquero jacket, and a large sombrero. He was a young man, perhaps no more than twenty-five.

"Find out who he is, Linus, what he's doing here, and where they went. I got an idea he came back here to see about the others."

Linus nodded and began firing questions at his prisoner in rapid-fire Spanish that was far too fast for Fontaine to follow. The young man answered, but carefully and sullenly.

"He says he's Rudolpho, the youngest son of Don Guillermo, and we'd better let him go, that four bulls are not worth our lives. Other than that, he won't say."

"I see," Fontaine said. "Well, I won't torture him. If he won't talk, he won't. But now we've got us some trading material. Give him a drink of water, some food if he's hungry, and tie him up. We'll take him with us."

"Good," Linus smiled. "A sort of a pass through the lines."

"Yes," Fontaine grinned, "you might say that."

They were on their way at sunup the next morning. Their animals were fit, and they had two spares each, plus Fontaine's pack mule and another horse. The Mexican was tied to his horse, his feet lashed to the stirrups and his hands behind him. The wagon tracks were easy to follow, easy for Linus, that is, and they headed due south.

"How far is their place?" Fontaine asked.

"Two hundred miles, more or less. Almost to the Mexican border."

"You mean his father's place is in the States?"

"Partly," Linus allowed. "Depends on who you are."

Fontaine nodded and resumed watching the horizon while Linus followed the tracks. They made good time until noon, when they stopped for food. Linus untied the prisoner, who ate sullenly, and then he was tied on his horse again. As they were about to move out, Linus said:

"Mr. Fontaine, I wasn't asleep yesterday when you told the major about lookin' for an Indian and when we return I'd like to offer my help . . . by way of thanks."

"And my thanks to you," Fontaine said. "I accept."

They followed the wagon tracks for four more days without seeing anyone. They led due south without deviation, taking the easiest and most direct route, as if no one dared to follow them. After breakfast that morning Linus said:

"Today we will come to their country. By this afternoon we will reach Prado Verde. It is a small town, and it is in the States, but it is controlled by the Acostas."

"Do we dare go in?"

"With the boy here as hostage we are all right. But I would rather have help."

"Any ideas?"

"None of any value. Darkness only."

"Oh, good," Fontaine said cynically.

Just before noon help came in the form of a strapping blond young man on a big horse. He rode over the skyline and waited for them, his rifle across the saddle and his right hand in the peace sign. Fontaine raised his hand and rode forward.

"Good morning. My name's Eric Anderson."

"Jonathan Fontaine."

The two men exchanged nods and grins and then Anderson saw the Mexican.

"My," young Anderson grinned. "You got a bobcat by the tail. Ain't that young Acosta?"

"It is. You know him?"

"Sure, we know 'im!" Anderson said in disgust. "Hey! I think you'd like to meet Pa. In fact, let me invite you over fer dinner. We're only a few miles west of here."

"Thank you kindly," Fontaine said. "Five days and the trail pot gets old."

"Yeah, I figger," Eric smiled. "It's this away."

They rode into a large, flat valley with a big adobe house and several out-buildings. They were seen several miles away and a burly, blond man with several younger ones behind him met them at the hitching rack.

"I'm Axel Anderson," the big man said in a Swedish accent.

"Jonathan Fontaine. And this is Linus Gonzalez."

"Howdy!" Anderson boomed and Linus nodded, pulling his prisoner off the horse. "Hey! Don't you work for Major Tischner? And ain't that one of the Acostas?"

"I did," Linus said. "And his name's Acosta."

"The major's dead," Fontaine said, "and the Acostas were part of it."

"Aw, God rest his soul! I only met him twice or so, but

he was a good man. . . . Well, come in and eat and tell me 'bout it. . . . Boys! See to the animals!"

Acosta was tied to the hitching rack and they were taken inside and introduced to Mrs. Anderson, a husky, taciturn woman, and to Greta, Anderson's oldest daughter, a husky young woman with a ready smile and her family's blond hair. They were taken out back to wash, brought back in and fed a big meal, served in silence by the two women. Only when the dishes were being cleared did Anderson ask what had happened. Fontaine told him the story without interruption, except for a gasp from the women at the sink when they heard of the major's demise. Then Anderson leaned back in his chair and said:

"If them bulls has been taken into Prado Verde it'd take a small army to get 'em out. You got papers on 'em?"

"Yes, sir," Linus said, "blood-line papers, registration papers, everything."

"Uh huh," the old man said, his brows knitted in thought. Then he got up from the table and said, "Greta, fix me another plate fer the Mex, and a tin of water. If you gentlemen would kindly step outside, I'd like to talk to your prisoner."

Anderson shot some questions at the prisoner but he would only reply that his name was Acosta. Anderson nodded heavily, went to the door and took the plate and cup from his daughter and gave it to the man. He nodded and started eating. Anderson indicated the other end of the long porch and Fontaine and Linus followed him. When he was sure the prisoner couldn't hear him he said:

"Way I see it, you're damned if you do, and damned if you don't. You can't ride into town and demand the bulls, that would be accusing Don Guillermo of rustling. Though the town's half American he runs it, you'd never get out. . . . I suppose this thought has come to you?"

Fontaine nodded. "That's why we brought the boy, we'll use him for tradin'. If the old man won't go for it we'll take him back to stand trial for armed assault and anything else we can think of."

"They'd bushwhack you on the trail; you've got little chance."

Fontaine nodded and looked around the corner of the house at some holding corrals that were full of cattle, ready for market. They were typical longhorned range cattle. Suddenly the longhorns gave Fontaine an idea. He smiled and said to his host:

"Now I know you're running a risk, just having us and the Acosta boy here, and I'm most grateful. And what I propose will add to your risk, but in exchange I have something to offer that should make it interesting to you. . . ."

"I would always listen to an offer," Anderson said cautiously.

"Well," Fontaine said, "the risk comes in leaving Acosta here; for you, that is. We couldn't ride into town with him. They'd get him back and we'd be out the bulls."

"If that's all you'd be out," Anderson said dryly.

"But I do propose leaving him here with you. They don't know us. With the exception of the Acosta boy the ones that've seen us are dead. I thought we might circle around and come into town from the west, get a message to the old man that we'll exchange his boy for the bulls, and meet 'em somewhere out of town."

"You . . . you said somethin' about bein' interesting?" Anderson asked.

"You help me get 'em back, Mr. Anderson, and I'll give you all the stud service you can get out of those bulls in two days. That should start you a strain of cattle you could never buy."

"Huh!" Anderson was impressed. "Herefords, ya say? Yeah, we could ship earlier 'cause I hear that they fatten 'em at Kansas City before sendin' 'em on. . . . 'Course it's a couple months early fer breedin', we'd have to nurse the calves in close. . . . But then again, we're far enough south that the winters don't git all that cold. . . . My, my! You do turn my head, Mr. Fontaine. Lemme see, four bulls, two days, and me and the boys could help with the breedin' and git a good thutty or more shots. . . ."

"You'd have to, Mr. Anderson," Linus said, throwing in the clincher. "These bulls are so heavy and short-legged that they couldn't mount your heifers without help."

"By God! That does it!" Anderson grinned and pumped Fontaine's hand. "Fer a deal like that we'll ride right into Prado Verde and shoot up the town!"

"Whoa!" Fontaine grinned. "That may not be necessary. But we will need help."

"Jest tell me what you want, you got it."

"First you get Acosta out of sight, keep him tied up and fed while we're gone. Then give us a couple of fresh horses, good ones, and ones that aren't likely to be recognized. W'll go in late this afternoon and deliver the message and be back here late tonight. And keep our animals out of sight, just in case."

"That's easy. Got plenty of real good horses. You're welcome to pick."

"Thank you. And some clothes. . . Linus, is your Spanish good enough that you could pass for a Mexican?"

"My Spanish is, yes. But don't you think I'm a little dark?" The three men grinned at the easy joke and Fontaine said: "Well, you couldn't exactly pass for a Swede. . . ."

"Ha!" Anderson laughed again.

"But if we cut off the beard, leave you a big moustache, and dress you as a vaquero, you'll pass."

"Oh, that's easy," Anderson said. "My boy Axel, the big 'un, you seen 'im? He fancies Mexican clothes, he can fix you up real good."

"Why, Mr. Fontaine?" Linus asked.

"Because Ford's probably the one who blew the place up; the Mexicans would have no reason to, they just bought the bulls. So he probably talked to them and mentioned me and a big black man. Now if a gringo and a vaquero ride in from the west, we may cause some talk, but maybe not as much."

Gonzalez raised an eyebrow and nodded.

Late that afternoon two riders entered Prado Verde from the Bisbee road. One was a medium-sized gringo, dressed in black: boots, pants, shirt, and flat-crowned Spanish hat with a leather head strap down the back. The other was a big, dark Mexican dressed in tight brown vaquero pants, a short, piped jacket and a huge sombrero pulled to his eyebrows. The fierce look on his face was accentuated by his drooping mustachios.

They rode the length of the town, slowly and carefully. There were a few gringos, but mostly Mexicans; it was a typical border town. They got a few stares, but no one said anything. There was one little saloon, with two horses in front of it. At the other end of town was the cantina, with the watering trough across the street, and half a dozen horses tied on either side of the street. Fontaine nodded to the trough and they stopped their horses and let them drink.

"Ever have the feeling you're being watched?" Linus said to his horse.

"Several times," Fontaine said to his. "I guess the cantina's the place."

Linus nodded and they walked their horses across the street and tied them loosely to the rack. As they mounted the steps the rowels from Linus's Mexican spurs jingled noisily.

"Christ, you sound like a coffee can full of dimes!"

"But it's stylish," Linus protested with a grin. "One must dress properly."

They entered the cantina and saw a girl dancing near the bar to the beat of a third-rate trio, a bartender carefully wiping the bar, showing both hands, and four vaqueros sitting in a corner drinking beer, their hands conspicuously on the table. "Tequila," Linus said and they took a seat at a table against the back wall. The girl danced by and grinned, eyeing Linus as one might a stallion.

"See what clothes do for the man?" Fontaine grinned.

"Had I know thees, señor," Linus said in a Mexican accent with a big grin.

The bartender put two glasses of tequila on the table, two slices of lime, and a salt shaker. Linus nodded and tossed him a coin as Fontaine carefully put the carbine on the table, cocked. They licked the back of their hands, poured on the salt, tasted the salt, tossed off the tequila, then sucked the limes.

"Good boy," Fontaine grinned sourly. "Ask the girl about Acosta."

Linus nodded and waited a moment, then the music stopped and the girl pranced by. Linus had a rapid conversation with her, then tossed a coin to the bartender and the girl grinned and went to the bar. She whispered to the man, who poured her a drink, then went to the end of the bar and whispered to another man. This one nodded and went out the door.

"What the hell's that all about?"

"If I'd buy her a drink she'd get word to Acosta's *segundo*, who's in town." Linus tossed another coin to the barman and they were brought a second round. "Now, we wait. Drink slowly."

"Are you makin' a joke?" Fontaine demanded. "We might have to shoot our way outa here, and you think I might take more than two? No . . . thank you."

In a few moments the *segundo* pranced in; a proud Mexican, dressed much like Linus, though his skin was much lighter. In his left hand he carried a braided *latigo,* as though it were the emblem of his office. He approached their table with jingling spurs, pushed his hat back on his shoulders and paused, a faintly arrogant smile on his face. His eyes quickly took in the carbine and Fontaine smiled disarmingly and started to rise. The Mexican's hand quickly went to his gun butt.

"Whoa!" Fontaine grinned. "I was merely going to rise as a sign of respect from one caballero to another."

"Gunslinger, you mean!" the Mexican said in good English.

"No, I have no quarrel," Fontaine said quietly. "I merely have a message for your patron. I would like to talk to him."

"Anything that can be said can be said to me."

"All right." Fontaine got to his feet and the Mexican's hand went for his gun again, his eyes covering both men.

"Whoa!" Fontaine said. "I don't carry a handgun."

"Do you think, señor, that you're so fast with that one?"

"No, it's just that I'm very slow with a pistol.'

"I see," the *segundo* said sarcastically. "What is the message? Or would you prefer your *mestizo* to deliver it in his alleged Spanish?"

Linus stiffened and Fontaine said quickly, "Easy."

"What message?" the *segundo* demanded in a shout.

"I was sent to pick up four bulls," Fontaine said in the same quiet voice, his hand resting on the table near the carbine. "Don Guillermo will know. In exchange I will return his son, Rudolpho."

"Idiota!" the *segundo* roared. "You would threaten us? Do you know that you cannot get out of town alive, unless I approve it?"

"Maybe," Fontaine said. "But you might go with us."

The Mexican backed away from the table, grinning widely, and held out his left hand in an inviting gesture. Fontaine sighed loudly and said in an almost sad voice:

"Now, you shouldnt try to provoke me into a fight."

The Mexican chuckled, backed up another step and motioned them on. Linus got carefully to his feet, his hands out in front of him. Fontaine shook his head and held his left hand in front of him, then slowly reached for the grip of his carbine. The barrel was pointed away from the Mexican, and he kept it pointed in the same direction as he slowly pulled it off the table. The room was now absolutely silent, the spectators holding their breaths in anticipation. Linus turned to his right to cover the four men at the table and the Mexican took another step backward, stopping next to ▓▓ ently vacated table with two beer bottles on it. The carbine dropped to Fontaine's left side, pointed at the floor.

"We intend to go out of here very peacefully," Fontaine said, "so I suggest you do not go for your gun."

"As you gringos say," the Mexican chuckled, "you may go out of here, over my dead body."

"Maybe, but you do not have to prove your *machismo* to me."

"Do not take another step," the Mexican said. The smile was gone now.

"You goddam Mexican studs," Fontaine said with a slight shake of his head. "You always have to prove something. I don't even have my rifle in my right hand."

"Good! Then you will not dare take another step and force me to draw."

Fontaine shook his head again, with a slight smile. Then his eyes narrowed, the smile disappeared and he said, "Fuck you!"

The Mexican's gun hand quivered, moved a fraction of an inch, and the carbine came up in a blur. The sound of the shot was a roar in the quiet room and the beer bottle next to the Mexican's hand shattered; in the same fluid motion Fontaine's left hand flicked out, the gun was recocked and continued to point at the Mexican's belt.

"Gonzalez," Fontaine said without moving his eyes, "get his guns."

Linus carefully moved behind the Mexican, slipped his guns out and dropped them under the table. Then Linus quickly ran to the door, saw that the street was clear and nodded. Fontaine backed to the door, his eyes never leaving the big Mexican. He heard Linus get the horses and when Linus whispered "Ready," Fontaine said to the *segundo*:

"Tell your *jefe;* tomorrow, on the plains east of town at dawn, with the bulls. We will exchange them for his son."

The doors swung closed and they were on their horses, running flat out, and a hundred feet down the street before the Mexican reached the door.

They were in place at five the next morning. Fontaine was standing by a cutting horse that Mr. Anderson assured him would turn and twist with knee movements. Before he had accepted the cup of coffee he was sipping he had let out the right stirrup as fa~~r as it~~ would go. Linus had watched with interest and had nodded ~~his~~ head at Fontaine's caution. Linus was standing by his horse with his rifle. A few feet behind them Anderson and his four sons waited by their mounts: big Eric, the twins who were about twenty, and Gunnar, aged sixteen, but with a man's rifle. Acosta, his hands tied behind him, was sitting in the grass by a horse, guarded by Eric.

As it became lighter the coffee tins were put into Gunnar's saddlebag and from their place on a small hill a quarter mile from town they heard a heavy wagon slowly creak forward, followed by the sound of a number of horses. In a few moments it grew lighter as a wayward cloud floated away from the eastern horizon and they could see the four bulls in the wagon, being driven by a very old man. Riding four abreast in front of the wagon was a young vaquero, a *haciendado* who was obviously Don Guillermo, another young man and the *segundo*. A number of men had ridden out from town to see the festivities, but they kept a good two hundred yards to the rear. The old man was holding up a white flag.

Fontaine went to the Acosta boy, cut his hands free and nodded to his horse. Then he said to Linus, "Tell him to follow me by fifty feet, and fifty feet to my left. And tell him you will have your rifle on him."

Linus delivered the message and the young Acosta mounted silently. Fontaine nodded to the Andersons, then to Gonzalez, and mounted his horse. They rode silently down the slope, Fontaine approaching the horsemen from his left. When they were thirty yards away Fontaine held up his hand and young Acosta stopped. Then his father held up his hand and they were all still in the blue light of early morning. Fontaine sat his horse, the carbine across the top of the saddlehorn, the reins tied to it.

"What of my other sons, señor?" Don Guillermo called.

"They are dead, señor," Fontaine said in a loud voice. "They followed the Señor Ford, a cowardly gringo who put them to stealing another man's property . . . and they were shot in a fight . . . all mounted . . . all from the front."

"I paid well for those bulls!" the old man shouted.

"They were not his to sell!" Fontaine replied, his eyes on the *segundo*.

"Though I give them to you in exchange for my son, you will not get to your home with them!"

"No!" young Acosta screamed and spurred his horse toward his family, leaning low in the saddle and yelling in Spanish.

The *segundo* pulled his pistol and the rest took this as a signal and began to draw their weapons. Fontaine turned his horse at an angle and headed past the big Mexican at a gallop. When he was sure his animal was running true he slipped over the side onto the long stirrup, hooking his left toe under the saddle fender on the left side and raised his carbine toward the big Mexican. The Mexican fired twice, both shots falling short. before Fontaine got the man in his sights. He shot him in the chest and then began to shoot at each man as shots fell all around him. His animal screamed once as a slug grazed its flank but it recovered and held to its course. He hit the next vaquero in line in the face, then the old man fell with a bullet in the chest. Then the last man was shot in the side as Fontaine pumped the lever. When the fourth man fell he sat erect and turned the horse to his left to come in behind them.

As he came about he saw young Acosta whipping his horse in fear, away from his family. A shot rang out and he pitched out of the saddle. Fontaine risked a quick glance to his left and saw Linus bearing down on them. Fontaine's eyes went back to the fallen men in time to see one of the sons raise up and try to point his gun. Fontaine shot him in the chest. Then he pulled his horse to a walk and came in cautiously. They were all dead. He shook his head sorrowfully and pulled his horse to a halt and waited as Linus and the Andersons joined him.

"Damn!" Fontaine said. "You were right, Linus. The things men die for." He turned to the old man in the wagon. "You saw it all?"

"*Sì*, señor," the old man's voice quavered.

"Get down." Fontaine said. "Go tell them how it was. The truth; that the *segundo* shot first. . . . And tell them not to follow. The war is over. *Entiende?*"

"*Sì*, señor! I will tell the truth."

Fontaine nodded and waved toward the town and the old man scurried away, his eyes wide in the wonderment of what he had just seen. "Gunnar?"

"Sir?"

"Take the bulls to your ranch."

"Yes, sir!" the boy said, honored to be so trusted.

As Gunnar moved out with the wagon the rest waited to give him a start, but there was no movement from the town. In a few moments they followed slowly.

The Andersons worked all that day and the next on their version of artificial insemination. The old man would wrap the hind legs of the bulls in leather, chain them to a snubbing post and bring in a heifer. Then Mr. Anderson would finish the job, using an oilskin bag and impregnating at least three heifers himself, stripped to the waist and his long arm greased to the shoulder. It was a dirty, distasteful job, but one that had to be done. They managed to get three, and sometimes four, heifers impregnated per bull, twice each day. The women brought food to the barn door but were not allowed inside. Neither Fontaine nor Gonzalez were allowed to help; it was not part of the deal as understood by Mr. Anderson in his version of fairness.

During the first day, Linus stood guard at the edge of the road leading to town and Fontaine watched the Andersons. He also made an entry in his book:

Got the bulls back. It will make a great story, and get bigger with each telling. It will also help in recruiting men. . . .

The vaqueros in this area are so proud they almost bust their britches. . . . Come to think of it, that's where their pride is. . . .

It was almost dark, late in the second afternoon, and it was obvious that the bulls were spent, at least for the allotted time. Fontaine was watching from the barn door; they had used the center of the barn as the breeding arena. He was standing in the shadows from an already lighted lantern when he heard a rustling from a stall and he saw Greta staring at him, wide-eyed, with her finger to her lips. Fontaine moved deeper into the shadows and waited for her to join him. As she turned silently from the partition he saw that her dress was unbuttoned to her waist and she was breathing deeply as she moved toward him. She pulled him into the dimness of the empty stall and quickly opened her dress and held her breasts up in her hands. They were very big and very white. She rubbed against him and whispered,

"I can't hardly stand it! Don't it make you want to do it? Right in here, nobody would see us. . . . It would be real quick!"

Fontaine's eyes widened in surprise and he forced himself to keep from smiling. He didn't want to offend her, yet he didn't want to get trapped. So he carefully put his hands on her shoulders and pushed her to arm's length.

"I don't mean to be impolite, young lady," he whispered, "but I've got other plans, and I wouldn't want to fool you."

Her mouth opened in shock, she stared a moment, then bit her lip, the tears filling her eyes. She pulled her dress together and ran from the stall, biting back a sob. Fontaine shook his head and smiled, and turned to see Eric Anderson grinning at him from across the stall barrier.

"She almost gotcha," Eric whispered and smiled. "But I would be proud to have you for a brother-in-law."

"Thank you," Fontaine said politely, "but no thanks."

"Well, I don't blame ya, but I'd be grateful if ya wouldn't shame her."

"Don't worry, I won't say a word."

"Thank ya, I know I can trust your gentlemanliness."

Mr. Anderson fed them a huge meal and helped them on the road right after supper, explaining that he knew Fontaine would want to leave as soon as possible. Fontaine wasn't sure if he knew or not, but discretion percluded him from mentioning the fact. They thanked the ladies for their hospitality and headed out, accompanied by the twins who would drive and stay awake when they stopped for the night. Eric promised to trail an hour behind to make sure they weren't followed and Mr. Anderson promised to send Eric over to the telegraph the next day to wire Toby that they had the bulls and would be there in a couple of weeks.

Chapter Four

Fontaine had been gone three weeks. He was tired and dirty and thirsty. He had intended to stop at Willard's as soon as they hit town but something was changed. There were more men on the streets, and almost all of them were armed. Then he noticed that most of the horses wore the TL brand and he breathed a bit easier, though he decided that perhaps it might be better to go on to Toby's place and deliver his expensive cargo. While he couldn't decide which was more boring, riding a creaking wagon, or walking a horse alongside, it would only be a matter of a few hours and he could step down and drink all that Scotch. People stared at the bulls but no one said anything, except one TL rider who passed them on the way out of town. He nodded politely and said he'd ride ahead and tell Mr. Lane. Toby, Starrett, and six riders met them a few miles from the ranch. Toby was all smiles and pumped Fontaine's hand with glee.

"By God, Jon," he boomed, "you did it! And you made yourself a local hero to boot. . . . Old man Anderson sent me a wire that said ya killed four of the bastards by yourself. But I'll hear all that after you've cleaned up. . . . Goddam, Jon, it's a pleasure to see you."

"Thank you," Fontaine smiled, then looked past Toby and said, "Leroy?"

"Mr. Fontaine?" Starrett replied politely.

"Well!" Toby beamed. "Who's your friend?"

"Oh, I'm sorry," Fontaine turned in the wagon and motioned to Linus and the big man rode forward, his fancy vaquero outfit somewhat trail-stained. "This is your first recruit, Señor L. Gonzalez. He goes with the bulls. He's the famous professor of bull breeding from Mexico City. He was working for the major and, after his untimely demise, I prevailed on Señor Gonzalez to accept employment and see to the breeding."

"Well, good!" Toby said, extending his hand.

Linus took his cue from Fontaine and replied in a pleasant tone, "Señor?"

"And this," Lane said, nodding to Starrett, "is Leroy Starrett, my foreman."

The two men nodded and Toby looked around, then called to one of his men:

"Here, you, Billy! Bring the wagon in. And you men see that the bulls are stalled, and watered, and fed . . . uh, all right, señor?"

"Certainly," Linus said soberly while Fontaine masterfully hid a grin. "The amount of water you'd give any bull, a little more feed, perhaps, mostly grain. Then let them finish with good hay."

"You hear?" Toby yelled and the cowhands nodded, somewhat awed at Linus's great knowledge and even more so at the size of the bulls. "Goddam! They are handsome creatures. . . . And what a life they'll lead. . . . Eatin' and fuckin'! . . . But here I'm prattlin' on and you must be a might rump-sprung. Get on your horse and we'll ride up to the house and get you cleaned up, and cooled off, outside and in. . . . Uh, you do drink, don't you, señor?"

"Yes, Señor Lane," Linus said with a straight face. "In fact I was looking forward to some of your fine Scotch whiskey that Mr. Fontaine told me about."

"Well, good! We got plenty. Come on!"

Linus pulled Fontaine's horse loose from the wagon and brought it forward, and Fontaine gave the wagon reins to the cowboy and got into his saddle. As they loped forward Fontaine rode next to Toby, and Linus and Leroy followed.

"Why all the armed men?" Fontaine said. "The town was full of them. . . . Indian back?"

"No, I would've told you straight off, but, aw, I got a small problem, nothin' real big. . . . But I'll tell you after you bathe. Any trouble coming back, once you got the bulls?"

"No, the trouble was in getting the bulls. . . . And how is Miss Mary Kaye?"

"You mean that foul-talkin' bitch who mooned around here after you'd gone, and then when I said something she cussed me till my ears turned blue?"

"Sounds like the same young lady," Fontaine grinned.

"Well, I sent her back to Kansas City to visit her aunt for a spell, just in case we had a bit of trouble. . . ." Lane shot a sideways glance at his friend and grinned lasciviously. "Say!

You son of a bitch, did you knock her off the night before you left? Don't answer that, I shouldn't have asked."

"Toby," Fontaine said in mock innocence. "If I did pound her pretty little ass through your bedsprings I wouldn't tell you."

Fontaine nudged his horse into a gallop to end the conversation. As long as she was gone he would look forward to a hot bath, a good meal, lots of whiskey, and a good night's sleep.

When they were alone in the bedroom and stripping down for a bath, Linus said:

"Well, I surely do thank you. You carried it off nicely. It's certainly nicer to be accepted as a high-class Mexican than a quarter-breed anything. And, despite what Mr. Lane said, I want you to know I'm working for you, rather than him."

"Thank you," Fontaine grinned tightly. "But you've still got ten thousand dollars and own the most beautiful little valley I've ever seen. You could go back and build up one helluva ranch."

"Some men could," Linus said, his voice hardening a bit. "You could. But you were the only man I've ever met, except the major, who treated me as an equal, and didn't bother about my blood lines. . . . Mr. Fontaine, I may be a lot of things, but I know what I am out here. I'm a quarter Kiowa-Apache, a quarter white, a quarter Mexican, and a quarter just plain old nigger. . . . And a man like that might own that piece of land, but he couldn't work it for long."

"Huh!" Fontaine said. "Maybe you're right. But I can't answer the question for you. I can't even solve my own problems, let alone the world's but, in any event, I'm glad to have you. For what it's worth you're one of the few men I think I could trust."

"Thank you for that." Linus grinned. "And I won't run a sandy on you. Whatever this thing is you're in, you got one hired hand . . . and it oughta be mighty interesting."

"Good!" Fontaine smiled. "That's one."

When they came downstairs at sundown, bathed, shaved, and wearing clean clothes, they were met at the buffet by Lane and Starrett. Toby poured them both a stiff drink of Scotch whiskey and a little water and they raised their glasses.

"To a good job well done!" Toby said.

"Yes, indeed!" Leroy added. "Tell us the straight of it. The wire didn't tell it."

Fontaine downed half a glass, sighed as though a fire had just gone out in his stomach, grinned, finished the glass, and as Toby refilled it, Fontaine said:

"The first day out was all right, but . . ."

"Before you go on, Jonathan," Toby said, "let me extend my apologies for that goddam Charlie! What happened anyway?"

"Simple enough," Fontaine shrugged. "I came back from washing and I found the son of a bitch going through my saddlebags. I called him on it and he jumped to his feet and went for his gun. Fortunately for me he was off balance; his thumb got hung up on his holster and I managed to get my carbine up. I was lucky. My snap shot got him right in the chest. . . ."

Lane and Starrett exchanged involuntary glances and then Toby smiled apologetically and Starrett reverted to his poker face; Fontaine added:

"He was dead before he hit the ground. I never even had time to talk to him."

"Well, I feel terrible about it!" Lane said. "I wanted to give you my fastest rider. I didn't know the man was a common thief!"

"That's all right, Toby," Fontaine smiled, accepting another drink. "I don't blame you. I don't see how you can check on the honesty of all the men you've got working for you."

"I can't, and that's a fact. I'm just sorry it happened, that's all. . . . But tell us about the major and the bulls."

Fontaine told the rest of the story factually: about the Fords, and the major, the Andersons, and the Acostas. Then they had another round and Starrett took Linus aside to quiz him on the Herefords—whether honestly, or to see if he really knew, Fontaine couldn't tell, but he had no worries; Linus had told him that the major had sent for every publication he could get on prize Herefords and Linus had read them all. When the other two were deep into the subject of cross-breeding Toby took a bankbook from his shirt pocket and gave it to Fontaine.

"Take a look!" Toby said proudly.

"My!" Eighty-five hundred dollars were deposited to Fontaine's account at the bank. "Thank you."

"That's half your first year's salary in advance and the

bonus. I know of no other man who could've pulled it off, Jon. Now, did you incur any expenses?"

"Oh, yes," Fontaine said seriously. "I used up considerable bullets, I ate lots of jerky and beans and tortillas, I wore the ass out of a pair of levis, and two sets of long johns. . . ." They grinned at each other and Fontaine added, "But for this kind of money, pray, let us not talk of it. . . . But I would like to know about the armed men in town."

"Oh that," Lane smiled. "Well, ain't nothin' about the Indian. We've not seen hide nor hair, though those fools in town put up a fifteen-hundred-dollar reward. With that on his head we may never see the son of a bitch again! I'm sorry, Jon, they put it up while I was gone a few days and when I got back they had circulars all over the Territory. I got a feeling the town did it to put Pinyon on the map, sorta knock down Lane City, you know?"

"I should've," Fontaine sighed. Then, momentarily dismissing the Indian from his mind, "So what about all the guns?"

"Oh, that?" Lane grinned. "Well, it was a combination of the town thinkin' they could overrule me and the fact that I had to let Alfred go . . . he was my town bully, you understand?"

"No, not really."

"Well, Alfred served me a good purpose. He was a bully and a fast gun. I had him hang around town a lot to keep the local boys in line. No one dared try him, and they knew he worked for me, so I used him to sort of keep the peace in place of that half-assed marshal they got. Then, when you backed him down, he was no longer effective. Besides, after you left he threatened to get you, so I fired him and run him off the range."

"Uh huh," Fontaine said. "But that still doesn't explain why so many guns in a peaceful town, and most of 'em yours."

"Oh," Toby grinned again. "That's just a little display of force after those bastards puttin' out the poster about the Indian against my wishes. Tomorrow they'll all be back on the range workin'. My new town bully takes over. . . . I hired John Wesley Calvin."

"You what!" Fontaine exclaimed in a loud voice. "No wonder you sent Mary Kaye east! For Christ's sake, he'd shoot his own mother!"

"No . . ." Toby grinned again. "Not unless I tell him to."

Fontaine's voice had attracted Gonzalez and Starrett from across the room and they returned to the sideboard for another drink.

"Who," Linus inquired, "is John Wesley Calvin?"

"He," Starrett said in a disgusted voice, "is a no-good son of a bitch! A petty criminal who made a reputation by killin' men who aren't as good as he is with a gun. He's fresh out of Yuma, and Mr. Lane hires him just to control a bunch of shopkeepers!"

"You can see," Lane said, "that my foreman doesn't have too great a feeling for Calvin."

"Well, I don't blame him," Fontaine said. "Mr. Gonzalez, the only thing Christian about that bit of scum is his name. It seems poor Mrs. Calvin had a penchant for the religious. Fortunately for her, I understand that she has long since gone to her reward and didn't live to see the travesty she had so erroneously named. He is a bully and a murderer. If you see him, be sure not to turn your back!"

"Jonathan!" Lane said placatingly. "I know what he is, and you're right, that's exactly why I sent the girl east. But these are hard times for me. I have to start that town, and this year. I need you on the trail to bring in the good men we'll need, and I need Leroy right here to ramrod my men. . . . I had to have Calvin to keep the town under control, especially after they defied me."

"Yeah!" Starrett said in disbelief, but Fontaine wasn't exactly sure at what.

He found out shortly before midnight. They'd had many more drinks, especially Starrett, who'd seemed bent on drowning something but, to his credit, he'd managed to make it through a big dinner and cigars and brandy. Toby had been a charming host, discussing cattle and Mexico with Linus, and rehashing Fontaine's now famous exploits with the Acostas, but he had generally ignored his foreman. After a cigar Leroy had excused himself, saying he had to get up early to start picking heifers for breeding, and this broke up the dinner. Toby and Linus went to bed and Fontaine stayed up to have one more brandy and finish his cheroot. He was sitting on the steps of the front porch when a pebble landed at his feet. He looked up to see Starrett holding up a finger for silence and then motioning him to follow. When they were a hundred feet down the road Starrett took a poster from his pocket and said:

"Fontaine, I gotta tell ya something, in all honesty. I wasn't too keen on Toby bringin' ya in. I feared after your killin' that Mex that your judgment might not be too good. But ya seemed to have handled things well. . . . I want to apologize. And I thought I'd mention that if you're still here in hopes that you'll find your Injun, you're outa luck. This poster will hide him so you'll never find 'im. . . . Thought ya oughta know."

Fontaine looked at the taciturn man for a long moment, nodded, then took the poster. Something must be indeed bothering the leathery foreman for him to make the effort to see Fontaine alone and then to throw so many words together. Fontaine nodded again and decided to reserve judgment. In bold print the poster proclaimed:

WANTED DEAD MOSTLY, ALIVE IF NECESSARY. . . . FOR THE KILLING OF ONE HUMBERTO ROSALES. . . . AN INDIAN RENEGADE, NAME UNKNOWN. . . . WEARS NECKLACE OF HUMAN FINGERS, TWO EAGLE FEATHERS, ALMOST SIX FEET, BIG CHEST, AGE THIRTY TO FORTY. REWARD FIFTEEN HUNDRED DOLLARS IF APPROVED BY CITIZEN'S COMMITTEE OF PINYON AND BROUGHT BEFORE SAID COMMITTEE. INQUIRE AT PINYON, ARIZONA, BANK.

"Why, for Christ's sake!" Fontaine said. "It'll for damn sure get rid of him!"

"That's what I figgered," Starrett said. "Whoever put up that money wanted that Injun to disappear from the earth."

"Uh huh," Fontaine said cautiously. "And who is the committee?"

"That's the rub, Mr. Fontaine. Ain't no one knows who's the committee. And the banker, he ain't talkin', and he's been asked by several."

"Thank you, Mr. Starrett, I appreciate the information."

"My pleasure. One thing more, though I'm sure you know, and even though Toby told 'im to leave you alone; don't turn your back on John Wesley Calvin."

Fontaine nodded again and Starrett smiled bleakly, turned and walked toward the bunkhouse.

When Fontaine arose the next morning he found a note from Toby under the door:

JONATHAN:

I will be on the east range for a few days, rounding up selected heifers. In the meantime rest and enjoy yourself. Go to town and drink Willard's beer or stay here and drink Scotch. I think I've got a preacher lined up for you to go after (I'm waiting for a wire now) just to please Mary Kaye, and the town. Incidentally, though I failed to mention it last night, I told John Wesley to leave you alone, that you were also working for me, and your friend, Mr. Gonzalez.

TOBY

P.S. If you go to town, leave your weapon here. I'd like the town to think of you as heroic, but peaceful. . . . Ha!"

That afternoon he decided to take Toby's advice and drink some of Willard's beer. He also wanted to talk to Beesley and get his version of the reward. The liveryman acknowledged the introduction to Linus politely and in reply to the question as to who might be the committee, said laconically:

"Mr. Fontaine, you be one of the few men I'd trust in this town, and I'd give you a straight answer if I had done some investigatin' on my own, but I been busy with my string and that's a blessin', I figger, 'cause it's most likely somethin' to which I'd be better off not knowin' the answer. Besides I got a couple critters bad afflicted with the glanders and while I been treatin' them I got a half dozen more that come down with a bad case of the botts. So you can see my hands have been full; mainly with manure."

Fontaine nodded at the polite rebuke for asking dangerous questions and caught a faint nod from Linus which agreed with Beesley's approach, so he said:

"Well, all right. Then what would you say to my buying a couple of beers?"

"Ahh," Beesley grinned, "that's somethin' I can do without fear of gettin' my ass fulla buckshot some dark night."

They were about to cross the almost deserted street to Willard's when Beesley pointed to the east end of town and Fontaine got his first look at Abraham Isaacs. He was a funny little figure, pulling a small burrow with a large load. He was short and slight, and he wore a black coat and a high, somewhat dented and dusty black hat. He had a full beard which accentuated his large nose and pale, though now slightly pink skin, and his baggy pants were obviously too big for him and his miner's boots came almost to his knees. The little man stopped his burro a few feet away at the town pump and nodded politely as he let his burro drink. Fontaine shook his head and grinned at Linus; it was a hot day to be walking.

As they stepped off the boardwalk, three lathered horses galloped their way from the other end of town. The animals were pulled into a tight turn and the riders dismounted in front of Willard's and tied their horses to the rack. Then they noticed the little man with the burro and they stopped to stare.

"Calvin," Beesley whispered and Fontaine nodded.

John Wesley Calvin was well over six feet tall, but his Justin boots and tall hat made him seem even taller. He was good-looking in a weak, garish sort of way. He was wearing levis and a fancy piped gabardine shirt that had once been clean but was now stained with sweat. Everything about him was unkempt except the black pearl-handled .45 which was spotless, as was his gunbelt, which was slung well down on his thigh. With him were two hard-case gunmen, one white, one black. The white man was filthy; his clothes were dirty and sweat-stained and he hadn't shaved for a week. His hat, once tan, was now a uniform, greasy dirt color. The Negro was somewhat cleaner and bigger, almost as big as Linus. His skin was very black and when he smiled he showed two missing teeth. He wore a shirt open to the waist, with the sleeves rolled up, and he sported a slightly frayed planter's hat. Like their mentor, both wore serviceable revolvers.

The little man pulled his burro from the trough and turned to head across the street for the saloon. But he suddenly found his way blocked by a grinning John Wesley, and Fontaine cursed himself for not bringing his gun. He started to cross the street anyway but Beesley put his hand on his arm and inclined his head toward the steps of the saloon; the other two were standing easy, their hands near their guns.

"Hey! Lookit here!" John Wesley said in a loud voice. "In a silk hat even. Damned if it ain't a Jew!"

The little man backed away a few feet, his face impassive, and tried to go around Calvin.

"Hey, Jew!" Calvin shouted. "Stand still and face me when I talk. . . . You are a Jew, ain't ya?"

"Yes," Isaacs said quietly.

"What's yore name?"

"Abraham Isaacs."

"Well, now! Ain't you the funny one in that getup!"

"That was not my intention," Isaacs replied, turning slowly and continuing to the hitching rack in front of the saloon.

He was almost there when Calvin fired a shot into the dirt at his feet. The little man flinched and continued walking. Fontaine started forward again but this time Linus shook his head. Isaacs tied the burro to the rack and as he loosened the cinch on the pack another shot kicked up dirt at his feet. Then he turned, his face still impassive, but the jaw clenched, and climbed up on the boardwalk, went behind the two men and into the saloon.

Calvin put his gun away and started to follow, then turned quickly to see an unarmed Fontaine pass by him and up the steps, between the two gunmen, and into the saloon, followed by Linus and then Beesley. The little man was at the bar and Willard was already pouring him a beer. Fontaine went to the far end of the bar and was joined by his friends. As Willard was serving them, Linus said:

"That took guts."

"It surely did," Fontaine answered, taking a long drink of beer.

Then the swinging doors flew open and Calvin, flanked by his two guns, entered and went to the bar, between Fontaine and Isaacs. Calvin grabbed a whiskey bottle and started pouring three shots. "I'm John Wesley Calvin, Jew. Ever heard of me?"

"No," Isaacs replied.

"Think you're pretty goddam smart, don'tcha?"

"No," was the quiet answer. "I just try and mind my own business."

The little man finished his beer and turned toward the door.

"No you don't!" Calvin shouted. "I ain't through with you yet! I aim to find out what it takes to make you mad. You can't be a man, you don't wear a gun, and you ain't big enough to fight!"

"Calvin!" Fontaine said without moving. "That's enough. Leave the man alone."

The room was silent for a moment. Then Calvin turned to grin and Isaacs went out the door. "Just keep 'im here," Calvin said to the Negro.

The Negro stepped away from the bar, his gun trained on Fontaine's belt while Calvin followed Isaacs.

"Fontaine, ain't it?" the Negro grinned. "I heard of you. Ain't you the one that carries the little carbine around? Don'tcha wisht ya had it now?"

"I certainly do," Fontaine agreed in a matter-of-fact tone as though addressing a child. "If I had it now I would shove it up your black ass and pull the trigger."

The Negro grinned complacently and would not be goaded into anything. Through the window they saw Isaacs reach his burro and then Calvin backhanded him into the dirt and dug into a leather sack on the pack. His hand came out with a small, intricately carved wooden box with the Star of David on it. As he turned back to the saloon Isaacs leaped on his back and Calvin grinned and tossed him to the ground again. But this time he picked him up by the collar and dragged him back to the saloon.

"I finally got 'im mad," Calvin grinned, pushing Isaacs into a table.

He tried to open the box but it would not yield, so Calvin impatiently pulled his gun, reversed it, and smashed the box open on the bar. "Aw, there ain't nothin' in here but a tintype of a gal. . . . Kinda purty, though."

"Give me that, you pig!" Isaacs screamed, going for Calvin.

The little man reached for the picture with his left hand and Calvin's gun butt crashed down on the back of the hand. The crunching sound of breaking bones was loud in the silence, echoed by Isaacs's groan. As Calvin started to flip his gun over, Willard's scattergun was suddenly against his cheek.

"Put the gun away, John Wesley," Willard commanded.

Calvin's gun was holstered and he crumpled the picture and threw it in Isaacs's face. The little man, his distorted left hand immobile on the bar, reached for the picture with his right hand and tried to straighten it, but there was a permanent crease across the face.

"I'll kill you," Isaacs croaked.

"Ha!" Calvin roared. "Look at you! You couldn't kill a bedbug! Kill me? Why, if I ever see you with a gun, I'll shoot you on sight!"

"The day you die," Isaacs said between clenched teeth, "I'll be there."

"G'wan," Calvin sneered. "Just remember what I said about the gun."

"You too!" Willard said to the Negro, and his gun was put away. "A.J., take this feller to your place and see what ya can do fer his hand. You got bandages and such."

Beesley nodded and stepped forward and took Isaacs by the arm and steered him toward the door. Fontaine stared impassively at the gunmen as he passed but said nothing. Linus thought to pick up the pieces of the box from the bar on the way out. Fontaine untied the burro and dragged it after Beesley and Isaacs. He pulled it into a stall, took off the pack saddle, dropped it in an empty stall and went to the back room.

Beesley had Isaacs seated at the table, his swollen hand palm-down. Linus was studying it. "Bandages, couple of boards for splints, and something to bite on."

Beesley nodded and rummaged in a cabinet. In a moment he put a roll of ankle wraps on the table, a half-inch board, four inches square, a piece of leather chin strap, and a pint of whiskey. He pulled the cork and handed the bottle to Isaacs and said, "Here, take a big pull."

The little man nodded, took two long swallows, shivered, and returned the bottle. Linus inclined his head to Fontaine who took Isaacs's arm in one hand and with the other pinned his wrist to the table.

"This will hurt for a moment," Linus said gently, "but the bones must be put back in place. Here, bite on this."

Isaacs swallowed and nodded, and looked very pale. He bit down on the doubled-up leather strap and nodded that he was ready. Linus took the fingers in his right hand very gently and Isaacs groaned. Then Linus put his left hand on top of Fontaine's hand and suddenly jerked hard, pulling the broken metacarpals back into place. Isaacs groaned, sweat coming from every pore, and went limp.

"Good," Linus nodded, "he passed out. Now I can set them properly."

Working quickly he felt every broken bone to make sure it was back in as good alignment as he could get. When he was satisfied he eased the board under the palm and started wrapping the hand so that it would be firmly in place without cutting off the circulation.

"You've got quite a medicinal touch," Fontaine grinned.

"Practice," Linus replied. "There, that should do it. He'll be in pretty good shape in a month or so. The fingers might be a bit stiff, but it's better than no hand at all."

"A.J., can you keep him here?" Fontaine asked. "I'll pay his bed and board."

"Shore, but there'll be no charge, he's welcome."

"Good," Fontaine said, getting to his feet. "Don't let him outside. We'll be back tomorrow to look in on him. Come on, Linus, let's go."

Toby didn't return that night but he sent a rider with the message that he would be in tomorrow with some heifers, and for Fontaine to make himself at home. They did just that. They had another bath, lots of whiskey, and the cook fixed them a big dinner of roast beef. Fontaine saw Starrett ride by once, but he stayed away from the house and Fontaine concluded that Starrett thought that he had already said too much.

The next morning they rode into town again, with their rifles this time. Isaacs and Beesley met them at the stable door. The little man shook both their hands and said:

"Thank you, gentlemen, I am most grateful. Mr. Beesley told me who you are, and I appreciate your taking your time to help me. If there's some way I might repay you . . ."

"There's no payment necessary, Mr. Isaacs," Fontaine said as they went to the back room where they could talk while Beesley brought their horses in off the street. "What brings you to Pinyon? You don't look like the usual peddler, and you talk like a man of some education."

"Thank you," the little man smiled. "Education? Yes. I have that. Though I never thought anyone in this Godforsaken land would be interested in such a commodity. You see before you, gentlemen, one of the most highly educated failures west of the Atlantic Ocean. I came here as an accountant to survey the assets of a British-based concern that promptly went into receivership the moment I got to New Mexico. . . . Well, from there to now, it was just a small step, and a most appropriate one, one jackass selling scarves from the backside of another jackass."

They grinned and Fontaine said, "Well, maybe the hard times are over. As a matter of fact, I may have need for a man good with figures, though I wouldn't want it known."

"I think I'll go tend my animals," Beesley said.

"All right," Fontaine said. "We'll be out in a bit."

"Take your time," Beesley said, closing the door.

"Mr. Fontaine," Isaacs said, "if discretion is all you're worried about . . ."

"Well, a few other things too. But I admired the way you stood up to that bastard yesterday, and, if you're good with figures . . ."

"I have a degree in mathematics."

"Excellent," Fontaine smiled. "Now, here's what I propose. . . ."

Beesley opened the door and said, "There's a TL rider out here, says Mr. Lane said to tell ya that he got his wire and he wants ya to leave now so's you can ride to Holbrook and catch the night train east."

"All right," Fontaine nodded. "Tell the man to go on, I'll be there directly." When the door closed he turned to Isaacs. "Now, I will need a bookkeeper, but not for a while, maybe several months. In the meantime I will pay you eighty dollars a month. You will be working for me, but no one, except Mr. Gonzalez here, must know of it. Until I return, you peddle your scarves, all right?"

"Certainly," Isaacs beamed, extending his hand. "I'm flattered that you'd trust me on so short notice."

"Well, one thing that sold me was the fact that we agree on John W. Calvin. Here." Fontaine took a wad of bills from his shirt pocket and peeled off four twenties, "And stay away from Calvin."

"Yes, sir!" Isaacs grinned. "Besides, I can't do much until my hand heals anyway."

"Fine," Fontaine said, heading for the door.

When they were riding down the street Linus said, "That was rather sudden, wasn't it?"

"No," Fontaine smiled. "There may really be a need for a bookkeeper. Besides, though he's not very big, you can bet your ass I've hired a man who'll kill John Wesley if it ever comes down to it. . . . I'll be gone a while, Linus. You be sure you stay the big breeding expert, and Señor Gonzalez from Mexico City. And keep your eye on Isaacs, but don't let anyone except Beesley know about it."

Linus nodded, and wondered.

Chapter Five

ꘖꘖꘖꘖꘖꘖꘖꘖꘖꘖꘖꘖꘖꘖꘖꘖꘖꘖꘖꘖꘖ

It would have been an uneventful trip, except for William Lacey and his barrel. It was because of Lacey that Fontaine met fat Alfred again.

Toby had been gone again when he'd reached the ranch but there was an envelope with train fare and expense money and a note:

JONATHAN:

I'm off again, this time to Young. Seems the fight is going good and I might be able to buy a few acres cheap. I've taken Calvin with me and I expect to find some real use for him. . . . Pick up the train at Holbrook and take it to Santa Fe. Leave your horse at the livery at Holbrook, I'll have someone pick it up the next time through. Get off at Santa Fe, buy yourself a good animal and a pack mule and go to Hooray, Colorado. There you will find the preacher, the Reverend Josiah Manley. Perhaps you've heard of him. He's a real hellfire and brimstone missionary who's been doing work among the savages. I understand, through an exchange of correspondence with him, that he now has a small parsonage in Hooray. Of course, he is amenable to a further call, as the religionists say. And, because he is also a reformed gambler and one-time hired gun, he is somewhat suspicious. Thus the reason I think you should pay him a personal visit: to tell him, in person, what we have here, and that it is not blatherskite's dream, but a real opportunity to help his calling.

Incidentally, you are authorized to offer him a new church, one that will seat three hundred, and built to his specifications—out of local materials, of course.

The best of luck, Jonathan, and if I hear something of interest, I will wire at once.

TOBY

The train ride had been, as it usually was, hot, tiring, monotonous, and filled with cinders. It had been a relief to get a good horse and ride alone through the high plateau of the San Juan Basin and slowly make his way up into the eastern edge of the Rockies. During the last few days he had wondered from time to time about Iron Shirt and the damn fool reward. But he was philosophical about it; he had been looking for so long that it had become a way of life, and a thankless one. With the passage of time he'd decided it was like looking for a particular wisp of smoke in a forest fire.

Ultimately he decided that he was glad he had a job and something to keep him moving; he'd keep looking, but he wouldn't hope too much.

He had taken a cutoff and was resting his animals at the junction of the main road some four miles from Hooray when he first saw it coming up the road. He blinked his eyes in some disbelief but, sure enough, it was a barrel. But like no barrel he'd ever seen before. It was a good eight feet in diameter and fully twenty feet long. It was sitting on a giant wagon bed that had obviously been made to hold it. The big wheels were digging deeply into the road, indicating the great weight of the cask. The driver was a large, blond young man wearing overalls and a slouch hat common to the hill people. Tethered next to him was a small pig and across his lap was a double-barreled shotgun. He watched Fontaine carefully as the wagon drew close but there was a pleasant smile on his face.

"Morning," Fontaine said.

"Good morning, sir," the young man replied cheerily. "Whatsa matter, got a lame horse?"

"No, just resting a bit before going into town. How about a ride?"

"Shorely, glad to have ya. Hitch 'em in the back and climb up."

Fontaine tied his animals to a ring at the end of the giant bed and returned to the front, and the young man extended a big, rough hand and pulled him effortlessly to the plank seat. Fontaine put his carbine between his legs, smiled at the pink and black pig which grunted at having to share the seat, and said:

"Who's your friend?"

"His name's George. He don't say much, but he's company, Mr. . . . .?"

"Fontaine. Jonathan Fontaine."

"Howdy, Mr. Fontaine. Pleased to make your acquaintance. I'm William Lacey. . . . Didja see anybody on the trail, like three men, mebbe?"

"No, not a soul. Why, you expecting company?"

"Yes, sir. Figger they be along pretty quick."

William flicked the reins and the four mighty horses leaned into the traces. They rode in silence for a while, each sizing up the other. Fontaine liked what he saw, a brawny mountain lad, who, from his speech, was from the hills of Tennessee or Kentucky. William must have been equally pleased at his first impression because after a respectable silence, during which he eyed the carbine, he said:

"That's a pretty fancy weapon ya got there, Mr. Fontaine. Any good with it?"

"Passable," Fontaine replied, trying to decide what was in the barrel. It had a faintly familiar odor which escaped him for the moment in the clear mountain air.

"Well, sir, you might have to be, iffin them fellers ketch you with me 'fore we git to Hooray. You look like ya might make a livin' with it?"

"Me? No. I'm no gunman. . . . Why, these men trying to rob you?"

"Yes, sir," William said and paid attention to his horses, his brows knitted.

"I see," Fontaine said, hiding a smile because this was obviously important to the young man. "I don't know what you're hauling, but it's heavy enough. Even a city man could follow those tracks."

" 'Fraid so," William sighed. Then, "I might as well tell ya, you'll know as soon as we hit town anyway. . . . It's whiskey."

"Whiskey?" Fontaine turned to stare up at the barrel in amazement. "In there? You mean full?"

William nodded primly.

"Why, for God's sake, we're sitting on a fortune," Fontaine laughed. "That's enough to get every man within a hundred miles drunker'n a hoot owl!"

"Yes, sir. Shore would. That's my inheritance from ma pappy."

"You mean he left you all that whiskey?"

"Well, yes, sir, sort of."

"What do you mean, sort of?"

"Well . . . Pappy wuz a planner. He thought years ahead.

And old Pap, he knew that to make eny kinda money out of a corn crop in Kentuck, ya gotta turn it into white lightnin'. So he run most of our crop through the still every year, and he always saved some fer me fer when I was growed. Some of this stuff is well aged."

"No doubt," Fontaine said dryly, still shaking his head at how many gallons of whiskey there might be in the barrel. "And what brings you this far west?"

"Well, when Pap died, that jest left me. So I figgered the farther west I got the more it's worth. A feller wuz tellin' me about this here town of Hooray, says it's real woolly. So I figger I can git a good two bits a shot, right out the barrel, in a boomin' town."

"You surely can. If you can hang onto it. This is pretty rough country."

"Yes, sir, with the strike'n everything. But I figger this is where the money is."

"Why, young man," Fontaine smiled again, "do you realize that this much whiskey is worth a fortune in the East?"

"But not to me. I'd a had to sell it to a big company fer almost nothin'. No siree! Not after Pap put twenty years of his life into it. I decided to take it direct to the drinker and cut out the middle man."

"Well, I admire your enterprise. . . . Tell me, how in the world did you get the barrel this far? Didn't you ever bog down? Didn't anybody ever try to take it from you, or put a hole in it?"

"Yes, sir."

"Yes, sir, what?"

"Yes, sir," William smiled shyly. "The answers to all them questions is yes. I been on the trail a couple months now and all them things has happened to me. I got bogged down once or twice. But I always found me a dry rancher, or a cowboy. Funny how much harder a man will work fer a jug of whiskey in place of money. As to takin' it, yes, some's tried, but not too hard. I got down the big river on a flatboat, and I took the train to Santa Fe and from there I been trailin'. . . . As to shootin' a hole in it, you didn't reckon with Pappy."

"Oh? How's that?"

"Them staves is hard oak, three inches thick. And it's got double bottoms with old blankets between. A six-gun don't do nothin' but bounce off. A rifle gets in if it hits the side head on."

"Then what?"

"Oh, I got a trough on each side to catch the spills, and I got corks and bung starters up and down both sides, and I—"

A bullet ricochetted off the barrel and they flinched. The echo told them the rifleman was a good two hundred yards to the rear. William flicked the reins and took a long whip from a socket and laid it on the lead horses. Fontaine stood up on the seat with his carbine and looked down the trail.

"Nothing," he said. "Back in the bushes somewhere. . . . Take it easy, boy. You don't think you can outrun a horse, do you?"

"No, sir, but we're fairly close to town, and any distance helps."

The horses picked up some speed and were helped by the fact that the road was slightly downhill, not enough to run them off the road, but enough to make them go at a good clip. Fontaine grinned, held onto the edge of the giant barrel and watched the trail behind. They made a good quarter mile before he saw anyone. Then a pinto pony appeared and the man raised his rifle. The shot was to one side and Fontaine answered with two shots of his own, holding the carbine high. His shots dropped on the trail in front of the pony and it slowed a bit.

"Ah'm shorely glad you're here, Mr. Fontaine," William shouted.

"No doubt," Fontaine replied with a wry grin and shook his head. He'd had a notion to pull out of it when the boy first mentioned the three men, but the boy's youthful innocence had made him stay. Now he was in it, it wouldn't be considered proper to pull out.

"And ah mean it! Other fellers have tried to get my barrel, but these is the first ones tried to kill me fer it!"

"What makes you think they're trying to kill you? All they had to do was run us down. Seems to me they're just trying to get you to dump it. They could've ridden ahead and shot you right out of that seat."

"Mebbe, but a feller in that town a ways back, and ridin' a pinto, got awful mad when I wouldn't take five hunnert dollars fer it, and he said I'd never make it to Hooray!"

"Wonder why?" Fontaine said over the pounding of the

horses as they increased their speed down the gently sloping road.

"Seems to me that somebody don't want my whiskey in Hooray!"

"I can't see how the hell you got this far! Surely not many people knew it was full of whiskey!"

"Oh, that's so true, Mr. Fontaine!" William shouted. "People are shore greedy. But I always said I wuz deliverin' the barrel fer a feller and kept it fulla water so the staves wouldn't dry out. . . . See that spigot there? I got a little keg in there fulla bad water fer them that don't believe."

"And you got away with it?"

"Shore! Who'd believe this thing is fulla whiskey?"

"Ha! Nobody, I guess!" Fontaine laughed. "But then how'd they find out?"

"I sprung a little leak. I stopped to get some grain fer the stock and when I come out these fellers wuz standing there. After jawin' a while I got right out. I been on the trail all night. I stopped off a while by cuttin' off on some hardpan and got a couple hours' sleep, and rested the horses—"

A rifle slug zinged off the side of the barrel and they flinched.

". . . And I thought I lost 'em, I shoulda known better!"

"Hey! That's it!"

"That's what, Mr. Fontaine?"

"They probably could've got you right out of town, but they didn't. They let you get close! They wanted you to deliver it for them!"

"Why shore! Everybody'll buy it. But they ain't a gonna get it!"

Fontaine grinned and turned to watch the pinto. It stayed out of range as the road continued downhill, but when the road leveled and the wagon slowed it got closer. Fontaine put a slug near it and the pinto dropped off the side of the trail. When they were but a half mile from town and could see some of the clapboard buildings, the trail rose sharply and went in between two big boulders. The horses slowed to a labored pull and the pinto suddenly appeared for a moment, a bare fifty yards away. Fontaine sighed and braced his elbows on top of the barrel and got ready.

"Mr. Fontaine," William said, a worried frown on his face, "iffin you help me outa this, and we make it to town, and protect me to where I kin git set up and sell my whiskey, I'll pay you five hunnert dollars!"

"Whoa!" Fontaine grinned. "I won't leave you now. . . . And forget the money. They're shooting at me too."

"Thank ya kindly," William grinned.

They passed the boulders and there was an open space on the trail. William laid the whip to his horses and forced them into a tight turn. He made three quarters of a circle and brought the side of the wagon facing the trail, a boulder on each side. Fontaine smiled at William's driving and jumped down and ran to untie his horses, which were now exposed. As he pulled them loose, a slug thudded into the barrel near him and he ran his animals to the shelter of a boulder and tied them to a bush. He turned to see William about to raise his shotgun.

"No!" Fontaine said. "They know you got that scattergun?"

"No, sir."

"Good. Don't use it until they're right on top of us." At William's white-faced nod Fontaine added, "You scared, boy?"

"Just a mite."

"No doubt," Fontaine said dryly. "Now, sit tight. They're probably lookin' to scare us away from the barrel, then they can take it in. Hooray might not believe a stranger, and a young one, at that. Now, don't use that scattergun unless you can't miss, you hear?"

"Yes, sir."

Fontaine jumped up on the wagon bed and ran to the far end and looked down the trail. They were coming on foot, he could see the brush move on either side of the trail forty yards away. He snapped a quick shot from around the end and three quick slugs bounced off the barrel.

"You still feel like stayin', Mr. Fontaine?"

"Certainly," Fontaine replied calmly. "I'm fascinated by all that whiskey."

There were a few shots from down the trail, they didn't seem to be getting closer, but Fontaine considered the fact that they might have sent a man to approach from the town side.

"Well, iffin we make it, the offer still stands."

Fontaine looked down the length of the barrel and exchanged grins with the eager young man. Then the grins faded as they heard a horse coming from town. Fontaine turned, the carbine ready, and in a moment he saw a horse coming toward them at a dead run. He was about to raise his rifle when the wind blew the rider's coat open and he saw the badge. Fontaine breathed a big sigh of relief and lowered his weapon. The lawman was tall and wiry, and wore a black frock coat and a big hat, and he sported muttonchops that were turning gray. He ran his horse to the left front wheel, stopping at the last possible moment, and dismounted with a flourish and tied his horse to the wheel.

"What's goin' on here?" he demanded.

"We is bein' shot at, Marshal," William explained seriously, and Fontaine stifled a grin.

"Umm," the marshal nodded, he agreed with that. "Know who?"

"No, sir, but they ain't too friendly."

"Umm," the marshal agreed again.

Another shot bounced off the barrel and the marshal then showed his displeasure. He pulled a rifle from the saddle boot, jumped on the side of the wagon and levered a shell into the chamber. "You men! This is Marshal Neller! Cut that out!"

Three more shots bounced off the barrel and the marshal stood erect, laid his rifle on the top of the barrel and sprayed both sides of the trail. "God damn it! I said cut that out!"

There were no more answering shots and in a few moments they heard the sounds of three horses crashing through the brush.

"Lookit!" William pointed down the trail. "They's lightin' out!"

"That's good shooting, Marshal," Fontaine said, though he didn't mean it.

"Balls! Didn't hit nothin'." He turned to eye the two men as he reached into his coat pocket for more shells. As he reloaded he eyed the barrel and sniffed. "What you boys got in the barrel that's worth killin' over?"

"Whiskey," William replied.

"In there?" Neller pointed, with an astounded look.

Fontaine sat on the edge of the wagon and shook his head and smiled. "It affected me the same way. . . . By the way, my name's Fontaine, Marshal. The owner of this magnificent container is William Lacey."

"How'd do, Marshal?" William bobbed his head politely.

"Whatcha plannin' to do with it?"

"Set up shop and sell it in Hooray . . . iffin it's all right with you?"

"Fine. We could use another saloon. Come on, I'll ride you in."

They rode in silence for a while and then William said, "Thank you, sir. I couldn't a held 'em off without you. . . . And the offer's still good."

"You're a strange one, William. You kept your secret for all those miles and then you told me right off. Why?"

"Why, Mr. Fontaine," William smiled shyly. "I trusted you right off. . . . Besides, I wuz in a bind. I hadda trust somebody!"

"True," Fontaine allowed.

"Mr. Fontaine," William said, "if I ain't bein' too nosy. We been talkin' about me all day, can I inquire what your business might be?"

"Certainly. I'm here to get a preacher for our town."

"Aw, that's nice," William said sincerely. "And here I thought you wuz a gun."

"By the way, I'm also interested in Indians. Seen any on the way?"

"Been mighty lucky, sir. Ain't seen a one!"

Fontaine grinned and wished he hadn't.

As the wagon creaked slowly down the street it became the object of all eyes. Like most strike towns Hooray was over ninety-five percent men. What women there were confined themselves to their profession in the saloons. At one end of the town was the mine—several two-story board buildings with tin roofs. Then there were several hundred shacks, tents, lean-tos, and a couple of small, unpainted wooden houses; then the block-long business district—Mangan's saloon, a general store, a jail, many small businesses in small clapboard structures, all designed to relieve the miner of his money, and at the far end a big livery stable with several corrals to hold the mules used to haul ore. William stopped the team in front of the town pump, and the marshal stopped a moment, as a crowd began to gather, and grinned:

"Well, you're here. I suggest you put up at the livery stable till you get a spot set up."

"Thank you kindly, Marshal," William said, bobbing his head.

Fontaine stayed on the seat as William jumped down, took a canvas bucket from the wagon and began watering his team. Within two minutes there was a crowd of more than fifty men staring at the barrel and more were coming. A hairy old miner was nudged by several of his cronies and stepped forward and said in a loud voice:

"Hey, sonny! Whatcha got in the barrel?"

"Whiskey!" William said, loud enough for most to hear.

"In there?" the old man asked incredulously. "Plumb full?"

Fontaine shook his head and grinned. The barrel had the same effect on everyone.

"Whatcha gonna do with it?" another asked.

"I thought I'd sell it fer two bits a shot," William beamed.

"Whoo-ee!" someone shouted. "Hey! This here fine young public-spirited citizen is willin' to part with a whole barrel of whiskey at half price!"

As the crowd pressed forward to see the beautiful sight Fontaine thought that William might be the one who had struck it rich. Then his grin disappeared when he saw three horses, one a pinto, coming in from the other end of the street. The man on the pinto looked familiar but from the distance Fontaine couldn't be sure. They stopped their horses at a rack and two of them disappeared quickly into the crowd while the one on the pinto pulled his rifle and started toward them, down the other side of the street. Fontaine casually climbed down and stood near the pump.

"William!" he said quietly. "We've got company."

"Yes, sir, I seen 'em. I'd appreciate it if you'd back up a ways and keep any offen my back."

"Don't you think you'd stand a better—"

"No sir, I don't. Meanin' no disrespect, of course."

"All right," Fontaine said. There was no time to debate the point.

He worked his way through the crowd to the buildings, then slowly went up the boardwalk some fifty feet and waited. In a few moments he saw a man who, though dressed like a cowhand, wore a .44 tied low on his thigh. The man was coming toward him but didn't notice Fontaine as he tried to blend with the crowd. William left the pump and walked to the street side and was reaching into the wagon bed. Then Fontaine's eyes blinked in amazement. The man with the white hat and rifle was Alfred!

Then Alfred was joined by the third man and they stopped thirty feet out in the street and some twenty feet apart. A miner stepped in front of Fontaine and Alfred, and shooting from the hip, put a rifle bullet into the side of the barrel and whiskey spurted into the trough. The crowd behind the barrel broke into two segments to get out of the line of fire and Fontaine had to shift to his right to keep behind his man. William reached into the trough and came up with a bung starter and a wooden plug and quickly filled the hole.

"That's pretty good, boy!" Alfred shouted. "Let's try it agin!"

He put another shot into the barrel, near the front, and Alfred and his friend roared in laughter as William scurried forward and reached into the trough. But this time he didn't come up with a bung starter, it was a shotgun. The boy whirled and fired in one fluid motion before Alfred could lever another shell into his rifle, and suddenly Alfred was rolling in the dirt, screaming, with his hands to his face.

"No, sir," William said. "I don't think I'd care to try it agin. How about you?"

Alfred's companion made a motion to draw his gun and William turned in his direction and cocked the second hammer. The man froze.

The man in front of Fontaine decided it was time to make his move but before his hand got close Fontaine raised the barrel of his carbine between the taller man's legs and slammed it into his crotch.

"You do and I'll blow your balls off!" Fontaine whispered. The man shivered and his hands went to his shoulders. Fontaine eased the man's .44 from its holster and pushed him toward his prone companion. Alfred was now on his knees, wiping his bloody face with a bandana and groaning in agony.

"Now don't carry on so," William said. "Ain't nothin' but rocksalt. You'll be all right in a day or so."

Then the marshal pushed his way through the crowd, followed by a man dressed in gambler's black, with a fancy lace shirt and an expensive planter's hat.

"What is it this time?" the marshal said to Fontaine. "Can't I leave you two fer a minute?"

"It's all over," Fontaine grinned as William repaired the second hole. "This one put some lead in William's whiskey and William put some salt in his carcass."

"It certainly is over," the man in black said. "And I want to apologize for these ruffians. Alfred, you should know better! Now if there's any damage I'll pay for it. I certainly don't want to see good whiskey, even somebody else's, go to waste. It is good whiskey, is it not?"

"Yes sir," William smiled. "Best in Kentuck!"

"By the way," the man said, extending his hand, "my name's Mangan, co-proprietor of the saloon. And your name, sir?"

"Ah'm William Lacey," William grinned, pumping the white hand.

"And, uh, this gentleman, is he with you?"

"Yes, sir. His name's Fontaine."

Mangan arched an eyebrow and nodded curtly. Fontaine grinned widely and coldly, and didn't even bother to return the nod. Mangan turned back to William.

"Mr. Lacey, I wonder if I might sample your product?"

"Shore!"

William replaced the shotgun and returned with a jug. Mangan took a small, collapsible cup from his pocket and William poured an ounce. Mangan sniffed, took a small sip, rolled it around in his mouth, swallowed, then tossed off the rest and smiled.

"Ah, that's the way they like it. Clean and smooth, and strong as a kick in the head. Tell you what, Mr. Lacey. I've got the only saloon in town and you've got whiskey. I'll buy the whole barrel for five cents an ounce. You figure how much that is and it comes to a small fortune."

"No, sir, thank ya, but I figger on goin' into business fer myself."

"Cash, Mangan?" Fontaine said, not really knowing how much the gambler was talking about. Then, of course, Mangan didn't know either, but it must be way up in the thousands.

"If you'll pardon the poor joke," Mangan replied, "cash on the barrelhead."

"No, sir," William replied. "I aim to git two bits a shot."

"Better take it, boy," Mangan's voice now had a sneer in it, "otherwise you're in for a shock."

"Whatcha mean, Mr. Mangan?"

"I got an idea that, unless you sell to me, you may have trouble rentin' a place to sell that moonshine. You see, I doubt if anybody would want to bid against me for the rental, or sale, of a building."

"Marshal," Fontaine said, stepping forward. "Is there a law in this town against selling a commodity to anybody else?"

"Why no," the marshal grinned. "You kin open up a whore-house and run it by hand, if you're a mind to."

The miners roared with laughter at this and Mangan frowned.

"Then," Fontaine continued, "if my young friend wanted to sell this direct from the barrel it'd be all right?"

"As far as the law is concerned, it's fine."

"Thank you," Fontaine nodded, then turned to Mangan. "Then my young friend chooses to take his chances on the open market. And open it may be, at least until it rains, and that's many moons away."

The crowd roared its approval, William nodded in agree-ment, and Mangan turned on his heel and left, followed by the two gunmen, pulling a still moaning Alfred to his feet and dragging him along. The marshal watched them for a moment, then said to Fontaine:

"First round to the boy, but it ain't over yet. 'Course, now you know who tried to drygulch him."

"We certainly do," Fontaine nodded, handing the marshal the gunman's .44.

Had he known his stable was the only place in town large enough to house the barrel the liveryman would've charged more but, by the time he figured it out, the deal was made, and a week's rent paid in advance. Of course the liveryman had an added advantage: once he found out that William was going to sleep with his barrel, he could go out every night and know someone would be there in case of emergency. Fontaine wanted to get about his business, but he had taken a liking to young Lacey and decided to forgo his interview with the preacher for a few days to see if Mangan would pursue the thing. Alfred must have recognized Fontaine, though he saw him through a bloody bandana, and Fontaine knew that Al-fred's vanity would demand revenge. But that was all right, he wanted to talk to Alfred anyway.

The animals had been fed and watered and were stalled for the night. Fontaine and William had taken turns spending a dollar each for a greasy meal at the only public eating house, and when Fontaine had returned, William had piled straw under the wagon, covered it with blankets, and made a handy, if somewhat pungent bed. He was ready to sleep and Fontaine waved him to it, showing a cheroot and signifying that he would get some air. Lacey smiled and turned down the lantern, and Fontaine went out into the night air. A few crickets stopped their chirping and Fontaine pulled the rickety chair out of the dim light of the door lantern and sat down. When he was settled the crickets started again.

His cheroot had gone out, though it was only half finished when he heard the sounds of the girl's running feet. She left the boardwalk and made but a few feet in the dirt when a man caught up with her and she groaned as though her mouth was muffled. Fontaine got to his feet and silently crossed the dark street. When he was ten feet away he cocked his carbine and the man pulled away and mumbled:

"Aw, I wuz only funnin'."

He turned and disappeared into the night and Fontaine said to the young girl, "You all right, miss?"

"Yes, thank you," she sighed, pulling her cloak tightly around her. "I was visiting my uncle and had just stepped out for some air, when this ruffian accosted me, and . . . I ran. . . . I know I should've screamed, but . . . thank you."

"That's all right." She was young, and rather pretty, but he couldn't tell too much in the dim light. "Where are you staying?"

"Behind the general store."

"Uh huh," Fontaine nodded. "Come on, I'll walk you."

He took her arm and steered her back to the boardwalk. They turned the corner and started up the main street, and she breathed easier. There were a few people on the street, all men. As they passed a man idly leaning against a building, he tipped his hat and said:

"Evenin', Lucille. How come ya ain't workin' tonight?"

Fontaine stopped short and shook his head in anger. With a quick motion he turned her and pulled open the cape, confirming his suspicion; she wore a spangled low-cut dance-hall dress.

"Goddam whore!" he said through gritted teeth. "Lady, you'd better hope that boy is all right, otherwise I'll skin your ass off!"

Fontaine turned and sprinted back to the corner, mentally

kicking himself for being taken in by the oldest decoy in the world. As he got to the corner his first impulse was to fire a shot to warn William, but his natural caution stopped him. Instead he removed his hat and peered around the corner. Everything was silent at the stable and he could see no one. Then it came to him, it was silent. There were no crickets. As his eyes grew accustomed to the dark, he saw a man standing in the shadows by the corner of the stable. Fontaine pulled back, sprinted up the street a hundred feet, went between two buildings and approached the stable from the rear. He silently climbed through the corral, moving easy so as not to disturb the mules, and made his way to the open back door of the stable. From the light under the barrel he could see inside, but there was no one in sight. To his left was the tack room; that had to be checked first. He silently turned the corner, the carbine first, and saw two big feet, tied with rope. William was bound hand and foot, and gagged. Fontaine dropped to his knees and pulled the gag loose. William nodded his thanks, swallowed and inclined his head toward the barrel, and Fontaine put his ear to the boy's lips.

"They's two of them," William whispered. "One out front and the big mouth, he's doin' something to the barrel."

Fontaine nodded and pulled his knife and cut the boy free, handed him the knife and pointed to the back door. William nodded and Fontaine stepped out of the tack room and moved along the back wall. Alfred was sitting on top of the barrel, boring a hole with a brace and bit. Fontaine started to shoot, then changed his mind, not out of any feeling of fair play, or any qualms about shooting Alfred in the back, but because he wanted to talk to him. There was a hayloft ladder immediately to his left and he started climbing, carefully testing each rung. When he reached the top he took his time and made his way silently along the outer rafter of the loft until he was within four feet of the busy Alfred. Behind him was a five-gallon jug and when the bit was through the oak Alfred turned to reach for the jug and Fontaine swung his carbine, butt first, and caught the fat man on the side of the head with a dull thud, knocking him off the barrel. He hit the ground and didn't move. Fontaine flipped his weapon over and the man outside came to the doorway and said:

"You all right, Alfred?"

Fontaine cocked the hammer and the sound was loud in the silence. "Move and I'll kill you!"

The man froze, staring at the top of the barrel.

"William!" Fontaine shouted.

The boy ran from the darkness behind the man and relieved him of his weapon, then prodded him into the stable and kicked the door closed behind them. Fontaine picked up the jug and climbed down the ladder. He paused to nudge Alfred with his boot, came to the lantern light, sniffed the jug and made a wry face.

"Whew! That dirty son of a bitch!"

"What is it, Mr. Fontaine?"

"Concentrated lye, I think, maybe sulfuric acid. Anyway it smokes. Those bastards could've killed half the town. Goddam!"

"Yeah!" William said in awe of the consequences. "Should we call the marshal?"

"Uh huh," Fontaine nodded with a cold smile. "I think he'll be happy to help. Besides, keeping Alfred locked up a few days might make him more of a conversationalist."

The saloon was doing a booming business and no one paid any particular attention to Alfred's friend as he stopped at the batwings and peered inside, closely followed by Fontaine, wearing Alfred's dirty white hat. The man wore his revolver, though it was empty, and Fontaine kept Alfred's six-gun on the man's spine.

"Just like I told you," Fontaine whispered, tapping the man's spine with the end of the gun. The man swallowed hard and nodded.

In a moment the man caught Mangan's eye and called, "All set, boss. We'll see ya tomorrow afternoon."

"Fine!" Mangan grinned and nodded at the white hat. The hat nodded in return and the two men disappeared.

The next morning at eleven, as was his habit, Mangan came outside his saloon, stretched, took a couple of breaths of clean air, and went back inside for his morning drink. Fontaine, carrying a quart of William's whiskey, and William, carrying his pig, stepped up on the boardwalk and Fontaine nodded to the marshal who was standing at the corner, holding the poison jug. The marshal held up two fingers, meaning that he'd come into the saloon in two minutes.

The place was empty, except for a bartender cleaning glasses and Mangan, sitting at his table with a bottle and a glass in front of him. They sat at his table and Mangan and Fontaine exchanged barely civil nods while William smiled broadly. Mangan's ruddy face was more flushed than usual and a big vein in his temple throbbed.

"Mornin'," William said. "Ya still wanna buy my barrel?"

"Nope, not now," Mangan said with a faint smile. "You had your chance. Now I've decided to do something else with my money."

"My employer," Fontaine said carefully, "has suddenly discovered that he needs money. He is prepared to make you an exceptional offer."

"Nope," Mangan replied. "Not now, or ever."

"Well," Fontaine grinned, "let's have a drink anyway, you might not be able to pass it. . . . Bartender, two glasses."

Two shot glasses were tossed from the bar. Fontaine caught them one at a time and poured a shot from William's bottle. "Here, Mangan, have a shot of fine Kentucky lightning."

"No, thank you," was the curt reply. "I'll drink my own."

Mangan poured himself a drink and Fontaine nudged William's boot. The suddenly wiggling pig was dropped to the floor, and as Mangan turned to watch it, Fontaine deftly switched glasses with him. William beat the pig to the door and picked it up, scolding it gently.

"Here's to competition, Mangan," Fontaine said raising his glass.

Mangan grinned and tossed off his drink.

"Hey, boss," the bartender grinned, "thought you didn't like moonshine."

"What d'ya mean?"

"That feller jest switched glasses on ya!"

Mangan swallowed hard and his face grew redder. "Why . . . you . . . what the hell did you do that for? That stuff makes me sick!" His voice rose, then cracked. "You think you're pretty goddam clever. . . ."

Mangan's chair crashed to the floor as he rose and his hand went under his coat toward the shoulder holster, but suddenly the carbine appeared over the edge of the table and Fontaine said quietly:

"Patience. Now sit down and enjoy your whiskey, and if you go for that gun again I'll blow your arm off. . . . Marshal!"

The marshal entered with the jug and put it on the table. Mangan stared at it wide-eyed and shrank away as the marshal said, "It's empty, Mangan, the whole goddam thing. And them two hired idiots of yours said you put 'em up to it."

"It's a lie!"

"What's a lie?" the marshal grinned.

The room was suddenly silent, and the only sound was the buzzing of a fly. Mangan was sweating but he clenched his jaw, determined to say no more. The marshal nodded and said:

"I got 'em, Mangan. Now if you don't tell me, I'm gonna force that bottle of whiskey down your lyin' throat."

"No!" Mangan whispered, his mouth dry. "I . . . I'm sick. . . . I told them only a little, just a little!"

"You fucking animal!" Fontaine said. "You could've killed half the men in this town! You got enough, Marshal?"

"Yep. Mangan . . ."

The gambler suddenly turned and ran for the stairs, shouting, but the sounds weren't words. Neller started after him but Fontaine grabbed his coat. Mangan got to the landing and turned toward them, clawing at his collar. His eyes were glassy and he was drooling; the shouting had subsided to little cries of pain. Then his body was convulsed by a spasm and he fell on his face, the body landing on its back at the foot of the stairs. Neller got there first, followed by Fontaine and then the bartender and William. Neller knelt by the gambler a moment, then turned and said:

"He's alive, but it don't look like much. A stroke, mebbe?"

"Or a heart attack," Fontaine said.

"I think," the bartender nodded, "that's why he come here from Denver and give up runnin' the tables, he couldn't stand the strain."

Sincere as always, William said, "Gosh, that's a shame."

Fontaine and the marshal exchanged wondering looks and the marshal turned to the bartender. "Close up shop and go find the doctor. We'll git him upstairs. . . . And don't plan on opening up fer a few days."

Mangan died that night and the next day Fontaine met the preacher. The marshal had sent a rider for him and they met at the burying ground, a small hill a half mile from the north end of town; Fontaine, Neller, Lacey, two whores from the saloon, the bartender, six or eight miners who had nothing better to do, and the Reverend Josiah Manley. When the preacher arrived the box was already in the hole so the introductions were of necessity brief; the hole was shallow and it was a very hot day, and there was no shade.

The minister shook hands with William and turned to Fontaine. He was a big man, dressed in black, with a wide-brimmed black hat, as befitted his profession. He wore a full beard and his hair was almost shoulder length, making him an indeterminate age, but by the lines around the eyes Fontaine judged him to be in his fifties. His big hand was firm and strong, but unusually smooth, and Fontaine remembered that he was shaking hands with a former gambler.

"Reverend?" Fontaine said politely.

"Yes," Manley said in a booming actor's voice, "you would be Fontaine. My dear friend, Brother Lane, accurately described you in his letters. And I must say, sir, that I am indeed flattered that he would send a man of your reputation to persuade me to follow my calling in Brother Lane's bailiwick."

"My reputation?" Fontaine said with a slight frown, letting pass the remark about "dear friend." He knew Toby had never seen the man in his life.

"Oh, yes indeed, sir. Not only did Brother Lane mention your exploits with the evil Acostas and their league with the Devil, but several travelers have passed through with the same tale."

"Uh huh," Fontaine replied. "Stories like that are likely to get bigger with each telling."

"True, sir, too true, as I well know. But were there four?"

"Yes."

"Then it would be hard to change the mathematics of the thing, no matter what else was added." Then, turning to Neller he said, "I see Mangan finally got his. Well, let's get on with it. . . . Are there any relatives here?"

"No," Neller said. "He had none."

"Neither did the Devil," Manley said. "Good, then I can preach the truth."

He walked to the head of the grave, tipped his hat to the two whores who were sobbing softly, mainly because they enjoyed funerals, took his hat off and held it in his left hand, under the open Bible, and went to work.

"Brethren!" he said in his loud, deep voice. "We come here today to bury this man and consign his soul to the Lord, if He'll have 'im. As befits the circumstances I will say a brief prayer and then if you men will kindly fill in the hole?

"Lord! We are here today to bury this sinner, and ask if You'll take a look at his soul and see if maybe, after a proper stay in Purgatory, You might want to take him in. Of course if, in Your divine justice, You decide not to, well, we poor mortals will certainly understand. . . .

"Because sinner he was, as those here will testify!" (One of the whores sobbed loudly for a moment.) "Drinker, gambler, wencher! Guilty of many sins of fornication with scarlet ladies, 'scuse me, ladies, but it's true, Lord. He was guilty at one time or another of every known crime except murder and buggery. . . . He was as guilty as any of us, O Lord, and in the sure knowledge of the Resurrection and the Light, if You was to take him in, then the rest of us poor mortals would know that for sure, if we believed—and we do, O Lord! We do! But if You was to take him in then we'd know that there would be a chance for us and we would sing Thy praises until the day—and it's surely coming—when You will call up the dead and we'll all meet on that Great Judgment Day. . . . Amen!"

"Amen!" William and the miners chorused loudly. Fontaine and Neller remained silent. The two whores sobbed loudly and one crossed herself.

The miners turned to on the shovels, William politely helped the women to their buggy, and Neller and the bartender stayed to supervise. That left Fontaine and Manley to ride into town alone, which was fine as far as Fontaine was concerned; it would give him an opportunity to size up the reverend. The first thing he noticed was a Henry rifle with a fancy stock sticking out of the rifle boot.

"I see you travel with a little more than the Bible, Reverend," Fontaine said.

"Oh, you mean the Henry? Merely a memento of former times, Mr. Fontaine. And, of course, my place is farther back in the hills. One can never tell when one might run into a snake."

"Uh huh," Fontaine wasn't convinced, remembering Toby's

letter. "Surely the Indians among which you do your work would cause you no harm?"

"No," Manley said, almost wistfully. "I have no fear from them. . . . I'll tell you the truth of the matter, as long as you're here to see me anyway. Mr. Fontaine, before I saw the Light I slew thirty men. Thirty men, Mr. Fontaine! Not counting the ones who have crippled arms and hands because of me. Now some of those men had relatives, and family, and it's not unlikely that someday I might run into a poor soul who is racked with vengeance and, though I now believe in the might of the Lord, I don't think He'd take it unkindly if I protected myself. The Lord helps those who help themselves, sir."

"Amen!" Fontaine said cynically.

Manley grinned broadly at Fontaine and chuckled, "You don't believe in God?"

"Let's put it this way, I don't disbelieve."

"Then there's hope for you," Manley nodded. "Mr. Fontaine, you have a right to know, if you're to hire me. I was a killer, always fair and square, but a killer. And I did see the Light. And that's fair and square. I do believe . . . and I am reformed. Though I must admit that I do put it on a bit thick in my preaching. But that's what these simple folk must have. I can't debate theology with them! I have to give it to them in terms they can understand; the Good and the Bad, the Lord wrestlin' with the Devil. And, if it helps them live a better life, then I've done my part in this life."

Fontaine looked at the man and decided that there was no doubting his sincerity. "Well, good. I can't argue that. . . . Come on, I'm thirsty, I'll buy you a beer. Neller said he's opened the saloon, as it's the only fair way to dole out Mangan's estate."

"A most democratic solution," the preacher grinned and gigged his horse.

They had just crossed the narrow-gauge tracks leading to the mine and had turned the corner to the main street when they saw Alfred on his pinto coming toward them. His two friends were a few feet behind him.

"Goddam!" Fontaine said in a low voice, pulling the carbine. "Reverend, you'd better unlimber that Henry. Bein' a preacher's not gonna help."

Without wasting words Manley pulled the rifle, threw a shell into the chamber and laid the rifle across his saddlehorn, waiting Fontaine's pleasure.

"That's far enough, Alfred!" Fontaine shouted from eighty yards. "I don't want to have to kill you!"

"God damn you, Fontaine!" Alfred shouted. "Today it's my turn. Now, git away from that preacher! I ain't got no quarrel with him!"

"Reverend," Fontaine sighed and shook his head as he dismounted. "I'd be obliged if you'd keep those other two out of my way."

"My pleasure," Manley nodded, watching the two horsemen move their mounts to the other side of the street as Alfred dismounted and slapped his horse out of the way. "That weapon primed, boy?"

"Certainly," Fontaine said conversationally. "I could kill him from here. But I want to talk to him. He knows something of interest."

"Don't wait too long. He's got a fair chance at forty yards, certain at twenty."

Fontaine stepped forward and nodded, holding the carbine down. Alfred stopped, pulled his gun slowly, checking the loads. Then he cocked it and stepped forward, pointing it at the dirt. Fontaine stood his ground, distance being in his favor, and shouted:

"Alfred! Don't make me kill you! I just want to know how you happened to come here!"

Alfred grinned and started to run. Fontaine shook his head and gauged the distance and Alfred started shooting. The first shot kicked dirt on Fontaine's boots and he was forced to throw himself forward, snapping off a shot in mid-air. He landed on his elbows, holding the gun high, rolled over twice and came up again on his elbows, the carbine coming to bear. His first shot had caught the fat man in the thigh, throwing him off stride, and bringing him to one knee. But now Alfred had the range and was holding the .45 in both hands and Fontaine had no choice; he shot the fat man in the chest, just under the outstretched arms. The impact threw Alfred on his back, the .45 flying clear.

As Fontaine raised himself up he saw one of Alfred's friends in full flight, spurring his frightened horse madly down the street. Fontaine watched him for a moment and it almost cost him his life. The other man had chosen to fight and snapped a shot at Fontaine. The slug slammed into the boardwalk behind him and then Manley let go with the Henry, but the shot was wide by more than a foot, thudding into the wall of the store, and giving the man time to leap forward and crouch behind a low bed wagon where he could pick his moment and raise up and shoot from a mere fifty feet across the street.

"Goddam!" a thoroughly angered Fontaine muttered as he quickly pulled himself to his knees and snapped a shot into the side of the wagon. Then he was on his feet and risked a glance at the preacher. Manley was aiming at the corner of the building; somehow he had completely missed seeing the man leap behind the wagon. "Goddam!" Fontaine said again as he decided he had no choice and began walking toward the wagon. Now he could see the inside of the wagon bed and he laid a line of six shots at the base of the bed. Then he ran around the far end to see the gunman on his back, a hole in his neck which was bleeding profusely. The man made an effort to raise his revolver and Fontaine shot him in the chest from a distance of six feet. The body jerked and was still. But Fontaine was now too angered to observe any possible amenities. He put another bullet between the eyes.

Then, the corners of his mouth turned down in hate, he turned and sprinted to Alfred and knelt down. He was still alive, but the parchment color of his face under the rocksalt wounds told Fontaine that he was dying. A crowd was gathering and out of the corner of his eye he saw Neller pull his horse to a sliding halt and jump down. Fontaine ignored him and, to the gasp of the onlookers, slapped Alfred in the face.

"Goddam you, don't you die on me now!" Fontaine said between clenched teeth. "Talk first!"

Alfred's eyes were open and he smiled faintly, signifying that he understood. "All right," he said, blood trickling from his mouth. "Fuck you!"

The eyes rolled back in the head, and he was dead. Fontaine got to his feet, his face an angry mask, and the crowd drew back. He went to his horse, reached in the saddlebag, drew out a handful of shells and started reloading. Manley and Neller arrived at the same time to pat him on the back in congratulations.

"By God!" Neller said, "that wuz fancy shootin'!"

"My congratulations, sir," Manley said. "That was as calm a performance as I've ever seen!"

"Bullshit!" Fontaine said, continuing to reload his carbine.

"Whatcha mean?" Neller said.

"I mean bullshit!" Fontaine said, inserting the last shell. "You told me the third one had left the country! What the hell happened?"

"I wuz wrong. He stayed around, though God help me, I didn't think he would, and he musta busted 'em out of jail while we wuz at the buryin' ground."

"Uh huh," Fontaine said, turning to the preacher. "And we'll talk on the way to your place. I've decided to accept your invitation to see your church."

"Uh . . . oh, I'd be honored, sir," Manley said lamely.

"I . . . uh, don't suppose you'd read over 'em?" Neller said to the preacher.

"No, sir, I would not. Inasmuch as I was a participant, it would not be fitting."

Fontaine grinned cynically and said to Manley. "I've got to send a telegram. I'll meet you at the saloon in a few minutes."

No one looked directly at him as he rode slowly down the street, yet he sensed that he was being watched from every door. He nodded the telegrapher in from the street and the man was most eager to present him with pad and pencil. Fontain wrote:

THINK PREACHER IS IN THE BAG HE SHOULD BE EN ROUTE SOON STOP MET ALFRED AGAIN TODAY DOWN THE BARREL OF MY CARBINE STOP ONLY MEANT TO ASK HIM ABOUT INDIAN BUT HE GOT FOOLISH STOP PAID FOR A NICE FUNERAL AND CHARGED IT TO YOU ONLY I DID NOT ATTEND DID NOT THINK IT WAS FITTING.

FONTAINE

They rode silently north for five miles or more and climbed steadily into the high mountains. Finally Manley said:

"Ya got somethin' on your mind, Mr. Fontaine, and I think ya got a right to ask. Spit it out."

"You missed an easy shot today. A kid with a rabbit gun could've done it."

"Yes. And you've a right to ask."

"All right then, two things: Did you miss because you've run out of guts and did Toby Lane hire you more for your gun than your Bible?"

"No!" Manley fairly shouted to the echoing mountains. Then he regained his composure and added, "No, to the first question, and probably to the second."

"All right," Fontaine said, reining up his horse to face the preacher. "I'll accept the answer to the second question, because I suspected that while he wants a preacher, he also wants a gun that lots of people might not recognize. But what about the miss? You left my ass sticking out a mile! Why?"

"You don't relent, do you?" Manley asked with an air of resignation. "First, let me extend my apologies. It was certainly not my intention to risk your life, you must know that. But I have so much vanity left that I couldn't tell you when you asked me to keep them off your back, and I thought I could do it. And I, like everybody else, am guilty of sins of the flesh. I wasn't man enough to tell you the truth. . . ."

"And that is?" Fontaine persisted.

"That my eyesight is almost gone, at a distance, that is. Close up I can see fine. At over fifty yards, it becomes a blur."

"Well, for Christ's sake!" Fontaine demanded. "Why the hell didn't you speak up? We could've ridden in closer."

"Yes," Manley said sadly, "and had you known, you would've, too, I've no doubt of that. And it would've exposed you to two revolvers, and they would've been in range. I had a half a second to make a choice, and I chose that one."

"Well," Fontaine shrugged. "I can't fault you for that." After a short silence, and further consideration, Fontaine added, "And your secret is safe with me. I'd rather have a man with poor eyesight I can trust, in place of the fastest gun who ever lived."

"Glory be!" Manley said. "You know, Mr. Fontaine, there's a flaw in my religion. I find as much charity in agnostics as I do in genuine Christians. But, be that as it may, I am beholden to you and if you can indeed help me get the church in Lane City, despite the fact that my credentials are somewhat remiss, at least in certain quarters, I shall be forever grateful."

"All right," Fontaine grinned, "let it be our secret."

"Mr. Fontaine," Manley beamed, "as a practical man, I will not forget this. And rest assured, sir, that should the occasion arise, I would be only to happy to prove, in a more practical way, the truth of my words."

Fontaine nodded and said no more; Manley was still a man of the world.

They rode another five miles and came to Manley's mission, a shack with a steeple, high on a mountain, designed to succor the weary traveler and, if he happened to be a local resident, as were some of the Indians, perhaps he would come again and perhaps, just perhaps, he might get a bit of religion. Manley showed him around; it was a brief trip, and Fontaine could see the reason for Manley's acceptance of Toby's offer. The Indians were few, and didn't really comprehend, and the town of Hooray had no use for a preacher, except for an occasional chore like today, and would not have. Hooray would probably remain a woolly town until the mines played out, then the men would move on and Hooray would be nothing more than a few lines in even the biggest of history books.

"I'll make you one offer, preacher, take it or leave it," Fontaine said. "Here is three hundred dollars advance. A hundred for the trip in style, two for your Indians, and a guarantee of a church that will seat three hundred, and a parsonage; nothing like in the East, but as good as you'll see in the Territories."

"Mr. Fontaine," Manley said with a smile and a nod, "I was determined to take your offer had it been half that. And I will not forget, should the occasion arise, that you could have been far less generous. Thank you, sir."

The two men shook hands, and understood each other.

Fontaine spent five more days in Hooray waiting for word from Toby. He had asked Manley about the Indian and had received the reply he'd expected; there were no Cheyenne locally, but he would have his Indians check and get word to him in town before he left. Fontaine spent most of the time watching the erection of the Barrel House. It was a success from the day it opened. William picked a spot at the edge of town, erected a huge roof to keep the rain off his customers and the rough tables, and he was in business. The barrel was parallel to the street and painted a flaming red. On the roof was a big sign which read: 25¢ THE BARREL HOUSE . . . KENTUCKY'S BEST 25¢. A bar ran the length of the barrel and two bartenders were busy pouring from two new brass spigots.

On the fifth morning the Reverend Manley rode in with a pack mule and met Fontaine at the stable. After a handshake and an exchange of the amenities of the day Fontaine said:

"You moving out?"

"Yes, headed for Lane City, and what I hope will be my last stop. Oh, by the way, I heard from the last of my bucks last night. I trust them and they reported to me that there were no Cheyenne anywhere in the area, and have not been for several years. I'm sorry, I would liked to have told you something more encouraging."

"That's all right, Reverend," Fontaine smiled faintly. "I didn't really expect anything different, it's become the usual pattern."

"Without prying, may I ask if you intend to kill him, should you find him?"

"No . . . no, I don't plan to," Fontaine said. "At first I would have, but now, just like Alfred, I merely want to ask him some questions about . . ."

Fontaine stopped talking as a small boy ran up to him, an envelope in hand.

"Telegra . . . telegraf . . ."

"Telegrapher?" Fontaine grinned.

"Yes, sir," the boy said, extending the envelope. "He said give you this."

"Thank you, young man," Fontaine said, handing the boy a dime.

"Oo-wee!" the boy said, running off a few feet. Then he stopped and said, "Thank you, sir."

"You're welcome," Fontaine nodded and said to Manley, "Excuse me."

The telegram from Toby said:

TELL PREACHER HE IS WELCOME SOONER THE BETTER STOP GO TO HINKLEY NM THINK 250 SOUTH OF YOU STOP NEXT MAN IS DR MICA PURDY ADDRESS LOCAL JAIL STOP MEET MY MAN JOE BRITTMAN HE WILL BRING DEPUTY AND PARDON FROM GOV STOP GET PURDY OUT SEND TO LANE CITY

TOBY

"Well," Fontaine said, "looks like I'll be going too. But we can ride a ways together. It's from Lane. He says you're welcome, the sooner the better. . . . You ready to go?"

"Yes. And I'll be pleasured to have your company. Where you headed?"

"Couple hundred miles south, so I'll ride a day with you anyway."

"Good, good," the preacher nodded. "Mr. Fontaine, there's one thing I've been meanin' to ask, if it's not too personal?"

"Ask."

"Well, as a former collector of firearms, as it were, I noticed one thing of singular interest and that is the fact that neither of the dead men had your bullets in them, they went clean through. This, of course, seems somewhat strange and I am prompted to ask, do you use a particularly heavy charge or a special bullet?"

"Both," Fontaine grinned, reaching into his pocket and taking out a bullet which he handed to the preacher.

Manley examined it with interest, hefting it, and then looked at the slug. "I will assume the heavy charge, though it is obvious from the results I saw. But the slug seems steel-tipped, must have a tremendous penetrating power."

"Steel-tipped, and steel core, lead to run through the riflings. Your guess is correct, they were made specially for me in New Orleans."

Manley nodded, returned the bullet, and politely dropped the subject.

They made two stops on the way out of town; first at the general store where they purchased supplies for the trail, and then at the Barrel to say good-bye. Though it was barely eight o'clock there were six miners at the bar, quenching their thirst after a night shift. Standing in front was the proprietor, Mr. William Lacey. He was dressed like Fontaine; black pants and shirt, and black, flat-crowned Stetson hanging down his back by the leather cord.

"Mornin', Mr. Fontaine, Reverend?" William said politely. "Looks like you both is headin' out. Kin I buy you a drink fer the road?"

"No, thank you," Fontaine said, nudging his horse close to the boardwalk to shake William's hand. "Just stopped by to say good-bye."

"I hate to see ya go," William said, pumping Fontaine's hand, "without payin' the five hundred I owe ya, but I'll have it less'n a month and I'll send it to the address ya give me."

"William," Fontaine smiled, "you don't owe me a thing."

"No, sir, a promise is a promise! I will do it! It'll be along toward the end of the month. I'll send it by the Wells Fargo, or whatever they got down that way. Besides, Hooray may not last long and I'll want to set up shop in your place, and I couldn't do that without payin' ma debts."

Fontaine nodded seriously and clapped William on the shoulder. "I'm not worried, William. And we'll be glad to have you in Lane City . . . anytime."

"Thank ya kindly," William said sincerely, and nodded to the reverend.

As they rode out of town the reverend said:

"I've heard tell that imitation is the most sincere flattery."

"Uh huh," Fontaine said unconvincingly, "if he lives that long."

Chapter Six

He had figured seven or eight days to make the two hundred and fifty miles; it took him two weeks. A summer storm blocked a pass and he had to go around; that took three extra days. His horse went lame and he had to detour to a way station for a small stage line and pay an exorbitant price for an old horse, and trade his in; that took another three days. Finally the old horse gave out as he approached a small town and he paid two hundred dollars for a good horse that should have gone for no more than a hundred.

He thought he was within ten miles of Hinkley when the road started to get crowded. There were farm wagons with families, buggies, small wagons of every description, and many men on horseback, mostly cowmen by their dress. They were all headed toward town and none of the wagons carried anything but people. After a few miles he overtook a huge wagon hauling an expensive commodity, ice. The load was covered with straw, topped with heavy tarps. It had obviously been brought down from the mountains during the night.

"Morning," Fontaine said as he drew alongside.

"Morning," the man replied.

"I, uh, I've been on the trail for a while," Fontaine said. "Must have lost a day. Is this Saturday?"

"Nope. Friday."

"Then what's the big occasion? All these people going to Hinkley?"

"I reckon," the man replied, "but don't know what fer. I got a big order fer ice, direct from one of Sheriff Hinkley's men couple days ago, must be some big doin'. . . . We'll find out when we get there, I suppose."

"I suppose," Fontaine smiled and gigged his horse into a lope.

As he rode into town he concluded that it must be a fair, the town was crowded to overflowing, and everyone was in a festive mood. Concession stands had been erected along the main street selling candy, and ice cream, and lemonade made from lemons shipped in from the Rio Grande, and cake sold by the local Ladies' Aid Society. There were game booths, and a rifle shoot set up in an alley, and the town's four saloons were jammed. Fontaine let his horse slowly walk to the livery stable before he decided to ask again. As he dismounted the liveryman came forward and took his reins and said:

"Can't put 'im inside, no room. He'll have to stay in the corral, but I'll feed 'im good fer fifty cents a day. Ya can put yer saddle and gear in the tack room, it'll be all right there."

"Thank you. What's the big occasion?"

"Everybody's here fer the hangin'."

"Who's?" Fontaine said, afraid he already knew the answer.

"Doc Purdy; tomorrow afternoon. He shot his mistress. Now folks around here don't hold a fair fight between two men against the winner, but they takes a dim view of shootin' a woman."

"Is he, uh, guilty?" Fontaine asked conversationally.

"Jury thought so," the man replied. "I sorta think so, myself. His story of someone else doin' it don't hold too much water. Besides, everybody knows he was beddin' her down."

"Uh huh. What time tomorrow?"

"Two o'clock."

"That's a funny time for a hanging, isn't it?" Fontaine asked.

"No, seems it's a pretty good time, to me. All the doin's in the mornin', get the hangin' over with, celebrate tomorrow night, sober up Sunday, back to work Monday. All except Doc, that is."

"True," Fontaine said dryly. He pulled his carbine from the boot and slung his saddlebags over his shoulder and then stepped back to allow the man to unsaddle. "Where's the jail?"

"In the next block, on the right-hand side."

"Thank you."

A big, fat deputy with a big shotgun barred the door.

"I'd like to see Mica Purdy," Fontaine said.

"Cain't, without Sheriff Hinkley's word."

"Then I'd like to see the sheriff."

"Sheriff!" the man bawled, opening the door without taking his eyes from Fontaine. "Feller here wants to see Doc."

"Let 'im in!"

The deputy stepped back and Fontaine entered, and the door was slammed behind him. The sheriff was a ruddy-faced man with a trickle of tobacco juice running from the corner of his mouth. He stood as Fontaine entered, his hand hanging loosely near the big six-gun, and his eyes darted to the carbine in Fontaine's left hand for a moment, making sure the weapon was not cocked. Fontaine nodded civilly to the sheriff, and then at the three men with pale faces who were wearing suits. "I'd like to see Mica Purdy, if I may?"

"What's your business with him?" the sheriff said in a whiskey baritone.

"Our town had hired the doctor, and we sent him an advance. . . ."

"Ha!" the sheriff laughed. "Well, sir, it looks like you got took. But I guess you got a right to inquire about your money. . . . You'll have to shuck that weapon."

Fontaine nodded and placed the carbine on the desk, the barrel pointing away from the sheriff. On top of it he put his saddlebag, then reached behind him and drew his knife and put it on the bag, and the thought crossed his mind that he was glad that he carried his paper money buttoned in his right shirt pocket. The sheriff opened the desk drawer and took out a big ring of keys and unlocked the door to the three-cell block. There was only one prisoner, a handsome, somewhat disheveled man in his late fifties.

"Ten minutes," the sheriff said, returning to the office, leaving the door open.

Dr. Purdy struggled to his feet and used a makeshift cane to hobble to the bars. His left leg was badly bent and only his toe touched the ground.

"Dr. Purdy?" Fontaine said, extending his hand through the bars. "I'm Jonathan Fontaine. Toby Lane wrote you, I trust?"

"Yes," the doctor said sadly, shaking Fontaine's hand. "But it appears that you might be a bit late."

"How so, for God's sake!" Fontaine whispered. "You're supposed to have a pardon coming from Santa Fe. Lane wired me about it two weeks ago! Hasn't a man come from Santa Fe, or a man named Brittman?"

The doctor's eyes flashed and then he whispered, "Ah! That was it!"

"What was it?"

"Three, four days ago a man shows up outside, the door was closed and I never saw him. Then he's hustled outside and later that night I heard the deputy tell his friend that the 'guest' went and got himself drunk, on the sheriff. It must of been him, of course, I knew nothing of a pardon."

"Nothing?"

"No, Hinkley has kept me absolutely alone since the conviction. He said I could see my lawyer, but it seems that worthy has left town."

"Uh huh," Fontaine said, his brows knitted in thought. "Tell me, if a man is pardoned isn't the local law notified by telegram, and then a deputy brings the release?"

"Yes!" Purdy said. "Then Hinkley should know. . . . Oh, that's it. . . . You see, Mr. Fontaine, Hinkley and his family control the town, and all the saloons but one, and one of the cousins is the telegrapher. So if a wire did come, he got it. But no one would know."

"Why? The sheriff hate you?"

"Oh yes! We're old enemies. In fact, it was his shotgun that crippled my leg, the dirty son of a bitch!"

"All right, tell me quickly, I've only got a few minutes."

"He was sweet on the lady in question, the one who was allegedly my mistress? Well, when she was killed he came for me, questioned me, then said he was releasing me but for me not to leave town. The old Mexican trick, and I fell for it! As

I was walking out the door he filled my leg full of buckshot, shouted that I was trying to escape. Of course, he had that big, fat deputy as a 'witness'!"

"Uh huh, so he probably did get a telegram."

"I . . . I don't know," the doctor said, shaking his head. "True he hates me, but I don't think he'd actually stand by and see me hang if he did get word from Santa Fe. Word would get out sooner or later, besides, there's even a squad of cavalry in town to keep order . . . . And, if he did hang me, and it got out that he knew ahead of time, he'd be all through, even if he is a Hinkley."

Fontaine scratched his ear, thinking about it for a moment. Then he said, "All right, I just don't have much time but I'll nose around. You got any friends?"

"Just one. Kate, across the street. Chinese Kate's? It's a combination saloon, hotel, and whorehouse deluxe. She's the madam. And she is the only person in this town that I would trust. Maybe she can help. She's got lots of people working for her."

"I'll try her," Fontaine nodded. "Now, play along with me, let's have a fight."

"A what?"

"A fight. It'll help if Hinkley thinks you took my money and I got cheated." Fontaine raised his voice and shouted. "Now, God damn it! Where the hell's my money?"

"Ha!" Purdy shouted back and winked. "I spent it on my defense! I suggest you come back about three o'clock tomorrow and sue me for it!"

"You son of a bitch!"

"Here now!" the sheriff said from the door. He was smiling broadly. "Time's up. Can't have no fightin' in my jail."

"You bastard!" Fontaine said to the doctor, then turned and walked out.

The sheriff closed the door behind them and Fontaine gathered up his gear.

"Just a word of advice before you go, Mr. Fontaine," Hinkley said. He wasn't smiling now. "It took me a bit to place you, 'cause there ain't no wanted posters on you. But I heard about your killin' that Mexican a while back and, though I can't say as I blame you none, I also heard about you gunnin' down the whole goddam Acosta family, too. Now, maybe you hadda do it, I don't know, but it 'pears to me that you're a pretty woolly feller and I'm tellin' you right now, you un-limber that thing and you'll have an ass fulla buckshot before you get off the second round. You understand me?"

"Plain enough," Fontaine replied.

"All right. Now, you're free to stay and watch the hangin', same as any other citizen. In fact, the way you feel about the doc, you got a right to a front-row seat. But just you mind what I say. I got me a squad of Army here, and all my deputies, just to keep the peace, and by God, I'll keep it!"

"I'll be very careful," Fontaine said, a flat note in his voice.

"You do that," the sheriff nodded.

Outside Fontaine took a deep breath and watched the crowd for a moment, knowing he was being observed from the jail. He went a few feet and stopped at a lemonade stand run by a man and his small son and pointed to the sign that read: "SMALL GLASS, 2¢, LARGE GLASS, 3¢." Fontaine took a large glass, handed the boy a dime and waved that he should keep the change. The boy tipped his cap and grinned and put the money in a cigar box. Fontaine sipped his lemonade and turned his head slowly. The deputy was no longer at the door. In a moment the big man came out of the jail and hurriedly crossed the street and mingled with the crowd. To the boy's father Fontaine said:

"I'm looking for the best place in town for two things."

The man grinned and took Fontaine's elbow and they walked a few feet away from the boy. "Like what?" the man said.

"I need somebody who knows everything that goes on. I also want a decent room."

"Same place," the man said, pointing across the street to Kate's. "It'll cost you mebbe four dollars a night, even without a girl. But if you're lookin' fer somebody, she knows everything what goes on in town."

"Thank you," Fontaine said, setting the glass on the rough board counter. He put a half dollar on the counter and said to the boy, "Young man, that was the finest lemonade I've tasted in my entire life, and I've traveled the world over. Here, you may have to buy some more lemons."

"Why, thank you, sir!" the boy fairly shouted, and put the half dollar in the box.

Fontaine nodded, exchanged winks with the boy's father,

and crossed the street to the saloon. He made his way through the crowd and put a dime on the bar, ordered a beer, and when it was brought added a silver dollar to it. "That's so I can talk to the lady who runs the place."

"Why, shore!" the bartender beamed, pocketing the dollar. He disappeared across the room for a bit and Fontaine drank half his beer. In a few moments the bartender returned and started wiping the far end of the bar. Then there was a Fancy Dan gambler at Fontaine's elbow, who said:

"Pardon me, sir, but Kate would like to buy you a drink."

"My pleasure," Fontaine nodded.

He put down the glass and followed the man in the frock coat and lace shirt across the big, noisy room to a table by the front window. There sat the madam, Chinese Kate, herself. She was a buxom woman in her early forties, heavily made up, with a low-cut dress that revealed the upper half of her ample bosom. Her hair was piled high on her head in the latest fashion and, despite the makeup, Fontaine could see that she was an attractive woman. He bowed slightly and smiled.

"Sit down, sir," she smiled while the gambler, who was probably more of a bodyguard stood behind and slightly to one side, his back to the wall.

"Thank you," Fontaine replied, carefully placing the carbine on the table in a neutral position. "May he sit with us? Or must he wait for me to go for my gun? Please note, sir, it's not even cocked."

"Then why bring it to the table?" the man inquired softly.

"I would hesitate to leave it at the bar . . . it might get stolen in this crowd."

"May the house buy you a drink, Mr. eh . . .?"

"Fontaine, ma'am. Jonathan Fontaine. Yes, thank you kindly."

"What's your pleasure, sir?" she smiled.

"Well, the beer quenched my thirst, but, if I may, I'd sample your bottle," Fontaine replied, turning the wine bottle in front of his hostess. "I haven't seen a bottle of Tannier, especially 1858, in many years. My compliments, dear lady, on your wine cellar."

"See that, Rollo?" Kate said to the gambler with a wide smile. "I told you he was a gentleman."

Rollo nodded once, but said nothing.

"Look!" Fontaine said, slightly irritated, as he got to his

feet. "Search me, if it'll make you feel better. My only weapon is on the table, except for the knife in the back of my belt. Now, if you can't beat me on that, you're not much of a bodyguard anyway."

"True," Rollo admitted, with a small grin. "Then I'll sit, if it's all right."

"Sit," Kate said.

She waved her hand and in a brief moment a bartender appeared with two more wineglasses. Rollo filled all three glasses and then they were raised.

"A toast," Kate said, "to friendship."

"Fitting," Fontaine allowed and they took a sip. "Why, in particular?"

"Because," Kate said, pointing out the window, "I saw you talk to a man and then give his little boy a tip."

"The father told me you knew everything that went on in town. Dr. Purdy told me you were his friend and that you would help."

"How do I know the doctor said that?" Kate asked.

"Go ask him," Fontaine replied. "I hired him and now he's got a problem."

"I can't do that," Kate smiled. "The sheriff doesn't exactly like me."

"And why is that?" Fontaine asked conversationally.

"Because Kate won't cut 'im in!" Rollo said vehemently.

"Oh," Fontaine replied. "Purdy said the sheriff and his family run the town. I gather that you're not exactly in with him."

"Yeah," Kate replied noncommittally. "But Hinkley has a suite of rooms upstairs all the time. Just in case he might ever end up on the wrong side. . . . But tell me, why would you hire Dr. Purdy?"

"I work for a man named Lane. He's starting a new city. And it looks like to me that it might go. Anyway, he hired Purdy and sent me to get him out of jail and see that he gets to Lane City."

"What's your name again?" Rollo asked with a frown.

"Jonathan Fontaine."

"I thought that carbine jogged my memory!" Rollo said to Kate. "He's the one who shot up those Mexicans down below Lordsburg a few months ago." Rollo raised his glass to Fontaine. "My compliments, sir, on a job well done!"

"Thank you," Fontaine said. "But how did you know?"

"A rider came in about two weeks ago and spread the word. He was just passing through. . . . Of course, anyone could carry a sawed-off carbine."

"Uh huh," Fontaine agreed. "Wire Toby Lane, give him my description."

"I don't think that'll be necessary," Kate smiled. "What can we do for you?"

"I want to know if there was another Lane man here, named Brittman, and a man from Santa Fe with a pardon for the doctor."

"What do they look like?" Rollo said.

"I have no idea," Fontaine said, "but one's got a pardon. And that's what I'm after." He glanced toward the bar and saw the fat deputy watching them through the big mirror. "Hey! Is that fat deputy watching you or me?"

"I think," Kate said, "he's watching you. He just came in. If you want to, Mr. Fontaine, we can put it to the test and see just how interested in you he is. Suppose you go to the bar and order four big whiskies, but they'll be nothing but cold tea. Then the barkeep will give you a room key and you go up and wait. Then you'll find out. We will help any way we can."

Fontaine looked at his hostess and nodded slowly. He didn't particularly like the idea but it was the best chance he could see. He got to his feet and said:

"All right. Thank you for the wine."

He made his way to the bar followed by Rollo, who said to the bartender, "Give this gentleman some of Miss Kate's private stock."

The bartender nodded and took a fresh bottle from under the bar and poured a stiff shot. Fontaine nodded, sniffed the glass and, to his pleasant surprise, it was tea. He tossed it off, paid for it and loudly demanded a refill. He drank that one and demanded a room and made a fuss, but paid the four-dollar fee for the key. He drank another one, became louder and ordered a fourth. This one he tossed off, made a wry face, spilled some and dropped the glass, and then picked up his gear and staggered up the stairs. He bumped his way down to the end of the hall, singing softly to himself, found the proper room and fumbled with the key. While he was trying to insert it in the lock he heard the floor creak somewhere behind him but he gave no notice. He opened the door and went inside, slammed the door and flopped on the bed with a groan. In a few moments he let his carbine drop loudly to the floor and then he got quickly, and silently, to his feet, picked up his weapon and cocked it quietly, and took a place behind the door.

He had to wait only a minute or so and then the door opened and the fat deputy entered. He got his head inside the door and then the butt of the carbine crashed into his temple and the big man fell to the floor with a thud.

When the deputy came to, he was tied to the edge of the closet door, his hands and feet secured through the crack by a torn sheet. His face was covered with blood and he could see the horrible fact from the mirror across the room.

"Do you know who I am?" Fontaine asked, holding his knife to the man's throat.

The man nodded fearfully and swallowed hard. "Yeah. You're the man who cut up the Mexican . . . and who killed them four a couple months ago."

"The same," Fontaine nodded. "Now it's your turn. You're bleeding to death. But it will be very slow. They think I'm drunk so no one will bother us, but if you don't tell me what I want to know you'll bleed to the point where you'll lose your senses. Then you'll talk to me anyway. Now, I'll cut you until you talk. You can save us both some time if you'll talk now, and save yourself a lot of blood."

Fontaine ran the knife down the man's chin, no more than a razor cut on a hangover morning, but the blood flowed out. Then he ripped the man's shirt open to his belt, undid the belt and exposed his navel.

"Whatcha want?" the man said in wide-eyed fear.

"I thought you knew," Fontaine replied. "But, of course, you're well paid. It'll probably take all night with you."

"No! I ain't paid that much!" the man croaked.

"You mean not enough to get your whang shortened by a few inches, if you got that much," Fontaine added with a cold smile.

"No!" the deputy said. "Whatcha wanna know?"

"Well, now! A man came in from Pinyon a few days ago and met a man from Santa Fe. I want 'em."

"What for?" the deputy said in a whisper.

Fontaine's knife made a quick, sharp circle around the man's navel.

"He's in the room across the hall!" the deputy said quickly. "In the sheriff's suite! But there's only one."

"He all right?"

"Sure. We just kept 'im drunk."

"What was he carrying?"

"I don't know! Honest!"

The knife slipped under the navel and Fontaine looked like he was coring an apple.

"He's got a pardon from the governor! That's all I know!"

"He still got it?" Fontaine's cold voice persisted.

"Yes! Yes!"

"All right. How do I get in?"

"Knock twice, knock twice, then once."

"How many inside?"

"Just one man . . . and him. Honest! We give 'im more whiskey when he comes to, that's the orders until tomorrow. Then he's to be sober by two o'clock. That's all I know, honest!"

"What for?" Fontaine persisted.

"I don't know! Honest to God, mister, I don't know!"

"I think I do," Fontaine nodded. He took another length of sheet and gagged the man, checked his bonds and said, "Stay here, will you?"

Then he cocked the carbine and opened the door a crack. Kate and Rollo were coming down the hall. He motioned them in silently and when Kate got inside she glanced at the prisoner and turned away quickly. Rollo grinned and whispered so that the prisoner could not hear:

"Kate, he's not hurt bad. He's only sliced enough to talk. And again my compliments, sir."

"Thank you," Fontaine smiled, nudging them into the hall.

He closed the door and whispered to Rollo that one of his men was in the room across the hall with a Hinkley man and asked that Rollo assist. Rollo's reply was to the point:

"Cover me."

Fontaine put Kate to the right of the door, the side with the hinges. He flattened himself against the other side, cocked the carbine and laid it across his chest. Rollo stood in front of the door and nodded and Fontaine knocked the prescribed five times. In a moment the door opened a crack, then wider as the man recognized Rollo and stepped into the doorway, gun in hand. The carbine poked the man in the ribs and Fontaine's left hand pushed he six-gun toward the floor. But the man was sensible, though his eyes were wide with a mixture of fear and surprise. Rollo stepped forward and took the six-gun and the man was pushed inside while the carbine scanned the room. It was empty. Fontaine went to an inner door, and slowly turned the knob and pushed the door open while he stood to one side. Then he leaped into the doorway, fanning the room with his rifle, but there was no need. The light was on and the only person in the room was in no condition to stand. He was on the bed, dead drunk. Rollo grinned and herded his prisoner across the hall and closed the door. In a moment Fontaine heard a thunk and winced, then there was the sound of a falling body as it struck the floor. Fontaine grinned and turned to watch Kate.

She crossed the room quickly and examined the man on the bed with an experienced hand. She lifted an eyelid, listened to his breathing, and then stood up.

"Soused to the ears," she pronounced.

"Can you have someone bring some coffee?" Fontaine asked.

"No," she smiled, "raw eggs and oil. He's had way too much. We'll make 'im vomit first. Then we'll start on the coffee. Rollo!"

When Rollo returned, Kate went for the necessary ingredients while Fontaine and Rollo took the drunk and dragged him outside. The door was closed and then they carried him to the third floor where they were met by a colored maid with a towel across her arm. Rollo whispered to her and she grinned and nodded and pointed to a room. The man was dumped on the bed and then they went back for the guard and dragged him upstairs. Kate met them at the room and opened the door and stepped back. Then Fontaine learned why she was called Chinese Kate. In the room were four beautiful young Chinese girls dressed in kimonos, talented whores all. The ladies took over while Fontaine and Rollo had a drink in a fancy sitting, perhaps more properly waiting, room across the hall.

"You know what this is all about," Rollo said as more of a statement than a question.

"Yes. I think so, but I won't be able to prove it until tomorrow at the hang—Goddam! The pardon! Come on!"

Rollo followed him across the hall to where the five women were holding the man propped up with a washbasin to his face. Fontaine made a wry face and waited a moment. Then Kate held a steaming mug of coffee and the man took a sip and promptly threw it up. When his chin was wiped Fontaine raised the man to a more upright position and opened his coat and pulled out a wallet and a large paper. He opened it up so Kate and Rollo could see and grinned coldly:

"That dirty, lousy son of a bitch!"

The paper was a pardon from the territorial governor. Purdy was free; the alleged "witness" had left town, got himself into a shooting in Santa Fe and, when he lay dying, confessed that Purdy was innocent because the witness had heard a shot at the woman's house and looked in to see an unknown man leave the room, then turned toward the street to see Purdy approaching from town. The witness did not know who the murderer was and died before he could, or would, explain who got him to perjure himself. Fontaine handed the paper to Kate and turned to the man and shook him by the lapels until the eyes opened and the man nodded.

"Why the hell didn't you deliver this?" Fontaine demanded.

"I was going to," the man whined, "but him, the deputy, met me at the door and said the sheriff wasn't in, that he was at a saloon and he would take me there. He bought me a drink and that's the last thing I remember."

Fontaine let the man fall back on the bed and stepped aside while two Chinese girls moved in with their nursing instinct.

"How the hell could they get him in here?" Fontaine demanded.

"Easy," Rollo explained. "Hinkley sometimes comes in with a bunch of his cronies to play poker. He comes in the back way; be easy to bring in a drunk."

"Will this get Mica off?" Kate asked.

"Yes, but we'd better wait until the hanging. I'd hate like hell to lose that paper again, especially in view of the feelings of our esteemed sheriff."

"All right," Kate nodded. "I don't understand it all, and right now I think it's healthier if I don't. What do you suggest?"

"We wait. If he'll be safe here I suggest we keep 'im here, if nobody can get in."

"Gam Gin! Liling!" Kate said and two beautiful young girls were suddenly holding nasty-looking little two-shot derringers.

"That . . . uh, answers my question," Fontaine grinned. "All right. Get 'im sober. And don't let 'im leave. Deputy! If you go out that door you're a dead man!"

The deputy, sitting in a chair, was conscious but pasty-faced; he had sense enough to nod and hold still while one of the girls tied his hands and feet.

"Good!" Fontaine said. "Kate, Rollo and I will take turns watching. And tomorrow I would like you and Rollo to go to the hanging. Deputy! Before the hanging you will serve this paper and, if you don't, my fancy-dressed friend will put a bullet in your spine. Not enough to kill, mind you, but enough to make you a cripple begging on the streets. Do you understand me?"

The man nodded seriously and his eyes widened when Rollo showed him a beautiful .32 in his shoulder holster.

"Fine!" Fontaine smiled as though explaining something to a child. "We do understand. And if you think for one minute that we will again chance letting an innocent man hang you'd better consider how you'd like to spend the rest of your life crawling on your hands!"

The deputy nodded, thoroughly frightened. Fontaine nodded and Rollo escorted him to a room at the head of the stairs where they could watch the arrival of the paying customers while all Kate's girls but one went back to work to cash in on the overflow business. Rollo took the first shift and Fontaine napped on a couch. At two A.M. Rollo woke him with a plate of cold meat, bread, and a bottle of wine. While he ate, Fontaine laughed at the situation.

"What's so funny?" Rollo asked.

"First time I ever spent the night guarding a whorehouse."

"It's not bad," Rollo shrugged. "The pay's good."

At a quarter to two the next afternoon Fontaine made his way through the crowd behind the deputy. The man was wearing a coat, though it was a warm day. Under the coat was Fontaine's carbine, shoved up his back. Fontaine kept his finger on the trigger and the deputy moved very, very carefully. In front of them strolled Kate and Rollo and the man from Santa Fe, hungover, wiser, and more frightened than he'd ever been in his life. Several local devotees of Kate's establishment got quickly to their feet to give Kate and her escorts front-row seats on the rough benches, while Fontaine, because everyone recognized the deputy, was able to get to the foot of the steps of the scaffold.

In a few moments the crowd quieted and the sheriff, four deputies, Purdy, and the local preacher made their way through the crowd behind the armed cavalry squad. As they got to the steps the squad dispersed and took positions against various buildings on the main street, their backs to walls, Army rifles ready. The preacher had to help Purdy mount the steps because of his bad leg. The sheriff went to the noose and waited until the preacher got Purdy to the corner of the platform. As he turned to read the order of execution Fontaine nodded.

"Wait!" Kate shouted, jumping to her feet. "The doc's been pardoned!"

Her resonant voice, which Fontaine thought had been nurtured by hog-calling in her native Iowa, carried to the farthest spectator. There was a mass roaring and then the crowd grew silent. Rollo prodded the governor's emissary to his feet and the white-faced man shouted:

"It's true! I'm here from the governor! I couldn't get through before but I've got the pardon right here!"

At the fierce stabbing at his spine the man waved the paper and Rollo pushed him toward the steps. The two deputies at the foot of the steps raised their shotguns but the deputy with the carbine against his backbone said:

"Let 'em through! They're with me!"

Fontaine forced his man up the steps, closely followed by the man from Santa Fe and Rollo. Hinkley, not a stupid man, quickly guessed what had happened and his face became a mask.

"Read it!" Fontaine shouted. "Loud and clear!"

"The witness . . . the witness lied!" the governor's representative said, after his voice cleared. "This man is innocent! I came here three days ago! But I got waylaid!"

In the silence all eyes turned on Sheriff Hinkley. Dr. Purdy started forward and somehow his cane got entangled in the lever that released the trap and it was sprung and the sheriff dropped the twelve feet to the hard-packed dirt below. The crowd gasped in horror as the sheriff screamed and landed with a sickening thud. Two deputies started forward, and suddenly Fontaine's carbine and Rollo's revolver froze all those on the platform.

Then the tension was broken and the doctor was guarded by the preacher and Rollo with his beautiful revolver, and Fontaine ran down the steps to see about the sheriff as the squad of cavalry moved in to keep the scaffold clear.

Sheriff Hinkley was groaning in pain when Fontaine forced his way through the deputies. His right leg was at a funny angle, just below the knee. Fontaine yelled "Doc!" and the doctor was brought down; Fontaine pulled his knife and cut the boot and pants leg free. Both leg bones just below the knee were pushing at the skin and the foot was turned where it should not have been. Dr. Purdy, his face composed, looked at the injury and nodded to the two deputies who were holding the sheriff steady. He took the foot and pulled it back into position and felt the bones with his experienced hands. Hinkley screamed in pain and pulled away, shouting:

"No! No! Get away from my leg, you son of a bitch! I don't want you messin' with my leg! Get away!"

Purdy grinned slightly, quickly grasped the leg and flipped it back into the position he'd found it and struggled erect with the aid of his cane. "All right," he said calmly over Hinkley's screams. As he turned away, Fontaine said:

"If you don't help him he'll probably be a cripple."

"Mr. Fontaine," Purdy said with his teeth clenched, "if I understand this situation correctly that bastard lying there knew for several days that I'd been pardoned and yet he let it go on and dragged it to the limits of my endurance merely to make the town a lot of money and sell all the whiskey his saloons could serve. Is that correct?"

"Yes, Doctor," Fontaine nodded. "He did exactly that."

"Fuck 'im," the doctor said, looking up through the trap a moment, then turned away.

Fontaine shrugged; he couldn't disagree with the philosophy. Then he looked up through the trap and saw the noose gently swaying in the wind and slowly nodded and remembered something in the Bible. . . .

The crowd had dispersed, having been rewarded by an emotional cathartic, though it was not the one expected, and the spectators had taken their children and wives home. The cavalry squad had seen that the people disbanded in an orderly fashion and that Sheriff Hinkley was in jail, though the charge was rather vague because it could not be decided what he specifically had done, though it was agreed that Hinkley would never be sheriff again. Purdy was in Kate's upstairs rooms, recuperating from the rigors of jail, and the saloon was full of drinkers celebrating the triumph of right, which they knew would prevail all along. Rollo was watching the downstairs, seeing that the unwanted never made it to the third floor as the ladies were currently unavailable. Fontaine was in the room of the four Chinese girls, being attended by Kate as a reward for saving her friend, and being served wine and cold meat by the four tender, desirable young ladies.

There was a knock and Kate brought in the doctor. Fontaine got to his feet and they shook hands.

"Mr. Fontaine," Purdy said, "I owe you my life. And any career I might make in Lane City I will owe to you. If you ever need a hand, just call."

"Thank you, Doctor," Fontaine said. "All I can ask is that you take the next stage to the railroad and go to Pinyon. And don't forget what you just said."

"I will not," the doctor replied.

"The next stage is Tuesday," Kate grinned. "By that time you both might be ready to go together."

"I will," the doctor grinned. "But first I've got to close up what's left of my office, pack my medicines and the tools of my trade and, if there are any left, say good-bye to what few friends I may have."

"You'll have a number," Kate said.

"I hope so," the doctor nodded. "Mr. Fontaine, I'll see you at the stage early Tuesday morning. In the meantime . . . enjoy yourself."

Fontaine grinned widely.

Kate saw the doctor to the door, closed it and turned to her girls and said something in Chinese. The girls grinned, one giggled, and they pushed Fontaine back on the white chaise lounge and began to take his clothes off.

"Hey!" Fontaine protested, but only verbally, and still grinning.

"My dear sir," Kate smiled. "Most men in this town would

sell their souls for what you're going to get in the next couple of days. Relax and enjoy it. One of my lovely ladies will be with you at all times. The door will be closed and locked. Your weapon is by the door, should you feel the need of it. And, for this evening, you will be entertained by all of them."

"On a Saturday night?" Fontaine said. "One, or maybe two, should do me."

"It's on the house," Kate explained, leaning over to pour more wine. "My way of thanking you for saving one of my very true friends."

"Won't, uh, you join us?" Fontaine said, staring into her ample cleavage.

"Why, thank you, Mr. Fontaine," Kate smiled. "But I've given it up and . . . well, you're a man of the world, I can tell you. Once in a while I enjoy one of my girls. In fact, I've got a sixteen-year-old white girl now that's new and . . . Never mind, enjoy yourself."

"Thank you, ma'am," Fontaine said as two girls slipped off his boots. "Pardon me if I don't get up."

"Take your time," Kate said and slipped out the door.

While two finished undressing him the other two slipped off their kimonos and advanced on their knees. It took less than a minute and then he was taken to the next room and put in a large tub and bathed, then fed and wined and pampered until he was in a state of euphoria such as he had never been in his life. Then they pulled him out of the tub, dried him with soft towels and put him on a large bed and covered him with four soft young bodies instead of a blanket.

He awoke early during the evening and was quickly smothered in soft young breasts and vaginas and was made love to without moving a muscle, save one.

He awoke sometime Sunday morning, not caring about the exact hour, and there were two in attendance, waiting for him to awaken. He was allowed to go to the fancy bathroom alone, but that was all. He could not light a cheroot, pour a glass of wine, or even eat the steaming plate of eggs and ham by himself. When he had finished eating and was about to doze off again he was brought to wakefulness by one putting her pointed young breast in his mouth.

In the early afternoon Kate looked in on him and he asked her to send a wire. It was to Toby:

DOCTOR EN ROUTE STOP CONDITIONS NOT TOO BAD HERE
STAGE LEAVES TUESDAY.

FONTAINE

On Monday afternoon, after a partially restful night, he
began to think again of the events surrounding the good
doctor. The first thoughts that actually penetrated his, for
once in years, sexually sated consciousness were: What happened to Toby's man? Neither the deputy nor anyone else
admitted to seeing a man from Pinyon, or having heard of
anyone named Brittman. And then the fact that several people
knew of Fontaine and his carbine became a subject of wonder.

Then three of the Chinese girls came at him again on his
chaise lounge. They pulled off his kimono, and then theirs,
and he promptly forgot about any questions he might have
had and filed them away in favor of man's oldest, most basic—
and certainly Fontaine's most basic—drives, pure carnal enjoy-
ment.

Just before he boarded the stage with the doctor for Santa
Fe, Rollo appeared with a wire from Toby:

SEE THAT DOCTOR GETS EVERY CONVENIENCE TO PINYON
STOP HAVEN'T HEARD FROM BRITTMAN HAVE YOU STOP
GO TO JOSHUA WELLS SW OF PRESCOTT AND ENLIST
MARSHAL P.J. ROBERTS STOP HAVE WRITTEN HIM HE
IS INTERESTED AND HONEST AND WILL WORK FOR 100
MONTH BUT WILL HAVE TO HAVE CUT OF SALOON AND
GUARANTEE OF PENSION STOP GIVE IT AS 200 ACRES
PRIME LAND HOUSE STOCK PLENTY WATER FOR FIVE
YEARS SERVICE LAND AND STOCK TO START AT ONCE STOP
AND ANYTHING ELSE YOU DEEM NECESSARY THEN RETURN
FOR REST

TOBY

Fontaine kissed Kate's hand and whispered "Thank you,"
shook hands with Rollo and boarded the stage. As the stage
was pulling out he wrote these cryptic lines in his journal
(though he later explained them to several close friends):

SPENT TWO DAYS AT CHINESE KATE'S RESTING AND FORNI-
CATING WITH FOUR LOVELY ORIENTAL LADIES. . . . MOST
REFRESHING.

Chapter Seven

When he got to Ash Fork the train was met by three immobile Indians leaning against the depot wall and a stationmaster who reluctantly helped him pull his saddle and camping gear off the baggage car. He asked the man to watch his things and set about buying a horse and mule. Unfortunately for Toby's money there were no mules for sale at the local livery so he bought two horses, and to make sure, he bought two good ones. They cost Toby a hundred and fifty dollars each and Fontaine thought that he might go into horse raising. He returned to the depot, got the stationmaster to reluctantly show him a map and figured that it would take him two days to Prescott and another day, at least, to skirt the mountains and get to Joshua Wells. He bought four days' supplies and left town as soon as he was loaded. He preferred to sleep on the trail, or, more precisely, to sleep off the trail in a draw somewhere, rather than spend the night in a dirty hotel.

He guessed he was but a few miles out of town when he came to a fairly wide stream with what looked like a decent ford, and he stopped. But it was not the water that stopped him, though he let his animals drink, it was the funny-looking wagon stuck in the middle. It was long, but narrow, and had a canvas cover like a Conestoga. The wagon was drawn by something less than a healthy horse and, though he could only see into the rear of it, the sight of another animal inside the wagon made him raise an eyebrow.

"Hello!" he shouted. A man's arm waved from the front of the wagon and Fontaine started through the shallow water, skirting the deeper part where the wagon was stuck. As he was halfway to it a man appeared from the far bank on horseback and started toward him. Fontaine leaned forward to draw the carbine but stopped when he saw the sun glint from the marshal's star. It was probably just as well that he stopped, the marshal held a shotgun across his saddlehorn.

Fontaine patted his horse on the neck and then raised his hand in a wave to the peace officer. The man nodded and both horses started forward. They met in the middle of the ford, a few feet from the wagon.

"Afternoon," Fontaine said.

"Howdy," the marshal replied with a friendly grin. "Name's Roberts, marshal of Joshua Wells. . . . That a carbine you got in the boot?"

"Yes," Fontaine replied.

"Then your name'd be Fontaine, I reckon."

"My name is Fontaine," he nodded slowly. "How'd you know? Did Toby Lane describe me that well?"

"Didn't describe ya at all, just said you wuz comin'. 'Nother feller, a drifter, looked like, come through here a few days back, fulla tales 'bout you killing all the Acostas in Sonora. Said what ya looked like and said ya used a sawed-off carbine. Well now, that's sorta an unusual weapon. It ain't a handgun a man could draw, and it ain't a long rifle he could shoot two, three hunnert yards with, sorta in between. . . . Interestin'. . . . When I seen it I figured it wuz you."

"It's me, all right," Fontaine grinned as they leaned across their horses to shake hands. Despite his colloquial speech, the marshal looked thoroughly efficient. He was burly, quick-moving, and had a rugged face with numerous battle scars and squint lines around the eyes that showed little if any trust for his fellowman; the look of an ideal lawman. "But I'd like to know a little—"

"Hey now!" a loud voice with a broad Irish accent said from the front of the wagon, "what about me?"

"Who's he?" Roberts asked.

"I have no idea," Fontaine grinned. "I just got here."

The two men walked their horses through the knee-deep water to the front of the wagon. There they saw a small man with a freckled face and blond hair sticking out from under his tall silk hat. He was standing, holding the reins of the ancient horse. He tugged at his ascot tie and grinned broadly.

"Gentlemen?" the little man said, "may I introduce myself? I am Sean O'Rooney. Late of St. Louis, come west to make my fortune."

"Roberts."

"Fontaine. Can we help you out of the water?"

"Oh no, thank you kindly, gentlemen," O'Rooney answered. "But I must decline your generous offer. You see, I am carrying a valuable cargo, a genuine, thoroughbred Kentucky racing horse, and I mustn't chance gettin' it wet. It's a sprinter, you know, sometimes asthmatic, but generally sound. My man is cutting a pole. . . . Abe!"

A huge Negro, somewhat ludicrously dressed in a dirty shirt and pants far too small for him, came out of the rushes carrying a long sapling. He nodded and smiled at the two horsemen and went to the back off wheel, inserted the pole, got a good grip and nodded to O'Rooney. The little man lightly touched the old horse with his whip and it leaned into the traces. With a mighty heave the Negro lifted the mired wheel, then dropped the pole and leaned on the back of the wagon and pushed it clear.

Fontaine and Roberts exchanged nods of appreciation at this feat of strength and Roberts guided the old horse to dry ground. O'Rooney tipped his hat, Abe climbed aboard and O'Rooney said:

"Should I see you at the local watering spot in town, gentlemen, it will be my pleasure to buy you a drink."

"Why, thank you," Roberts smiled. "Can we ride with you a ways?"

"Thank you, sir," O'Rooney replied grandly, "but it's not necessary. My man will want to change his clothes and, poor as we are, we will want to make as presentable an appearance as possible under our somewhat strained circumstances."

The two men nodded and let their animals move forward into an easy lope. After they'd ridden in silence for a bit Fontaine said:

"I'm curious, Marshal, about the man who rode in and told you about me."

"Nothin' special, just a saddle tramp relayin' the latest news about a shootin' or a range war, or an Indian killin', just current event stuff. . . . Why?"

"It seems a bit curious. . . . As well as possibly dangerous. I'm not a gunfighter, Marshal. And stories like that could lead the town bully, or some kid trying to make a name for himself, to try and choose you off, and I don't like to fight. . . . Anyway, you say the man is gone?"

"Yeah. Left a couple days ago fer Tucson."

"Uh huh. . . . Well, let's get down to business. What prompted you to take Toby's offer?"

"Ain't taken it yet," was the short reply. Then, "I ain't agin the hunnert a month, mind you, but lookit me, I ain't gettin' any younger and I got to think of the day when I cain't go agin every young buck who wants to put a hole in this here star. I got to think of what then."

"How about this for what then," Fontaine said. "Two hundred acres of prime land, plenty of water, a house and barn stocked with the beginning of a good herd of Herefords. And started now. The deed to the land and cattle is yours after five years' service as marshal. . . . By the way, how old are you?"

"Forty-five," Roberts replied. "And I figger I'm good fer at least five years. Five years like any lawman, iffin I don't git drygulched first. See, Mr. Fontaine, I'm sorta like you. I don't cotton to the revolver. They's always some kid whose eyes and hands is far faster than mine ever wuz. But I prefer the twelve-gauge. If I hit anything it's down fer good, and I can turn away and pay attention to what else might be comin' at me. 'Course I got but two chances, then I have to reload, but the shotgun gits such respect from everybody that I've always had enough time. Besides that, it's the best thing fer drunks on a Saturday night. No foolin' around with a draw, I jest walks up to the loudest one, or biggest one, and clouts him a fair one on the head. He drops and the rest don't aim to try buckshot. . . . I'm honest, I take only a fair cut of whatever I'm allowed from the saloon business. I don't take a cut from the girls, and I don't allow any crooked gamblin'. . . . In fact, Mr. Fontaine, I'm a rare bird among Arizona lawmen. I do my duty, and I'm honest."

"That sounds like what I'm looking for," Fontaine nodded. "I've got a couple men in mind, but you're the best of the lot. Give me a couple days to see how you run your town and I'll let you know."

"Fair enough," Roberts nodded. "Thank you kindly."

Fontaine checked in at the local livery, then the local hotel, then the town's main saloon downstairs. He ordered a beer from a table against the wall and reflected on his conversation with Roberts. He'd lied about having anyone else in mind, mainly because he wanted Roberts to think he had to work for the job and perhaps be a bit grateful. Roberts was obviously a good man with guns and fights and Fontaine didn't want him to think he was to be hired with no effort. Fontaine was on his second beer when Roberts entered, acknowledged the nods of the two silk-hatted gamblers and the barkeep and joined Fontaine. The bartender had a beer on the table before Roberts had moved his chair to a point where his back was not to the patrons.

"Drink only beer," Roberts said, raising his glass. "I can drink lots of it and never get drunk. Makes men relax to see the lawman having a beer and they're not so edgy. Never drink whiskey unless I'm home and got a deputy on all night. . . ."

Sean O'Rooney walked in, high silk hat and all. He nodded pleasantly around the room, ordered a beer and began to watch the play at the tables. Though it was early evening there was a goodly crowd. Joshua Wells enjoyed a varied commerce. There were several large cattle outfits nearby, numerous small ranches, and sevaral silver mines which were producing—nothing near a strike, but paying a day's wages for a man who would dig. One of the gamblers walked by Fontaine's table and said to the marshal in a low voice:

"What is that?"

"That's what you money-grubbin' bastards live on," Roberts replied jovially, "a greenhorn. A real, genuine greenhorn. He's out here with a broke-down racehorse to, as he says, make his fortune. Now, wouldn't you like to help 'im?"

"I certainly would, Marshal," the man grinned widely. "Thank you for the tip."

"Hey now!" Fontaine chided mildly. "Little O'Rooney will have enough trouble. No point in hurrying it."

"I don't think so," Roberts said seriously. "Consider this, Mr. Fontaine. That funny-lookin' little feller and his big nigger ain't made it this far west of St. Louis on nothin' but luck. He's got somethin' goin' in the back of that crafty little Irish mind, and if I kin help him, legal like, mind you, I will. Besides, that's the best thing I coulda done. If a gambler thinks a mark is real green he's apt to get a mite careless. It should help the little feller."

Fontaine's eyebrows went up at this bit of basic philosophy and the marshal's stock went up.

"Lookit!" Roberts whispered. "This oughta be good. And

if O'Rooney is about to be took, best he be took here. At least the tables are honest."

"Hello there, sir!" the gambler said, his oily professional smile in place. "May I buy you a drink? My name's Williams and I run this sporting establishment. Our neighbor, the hostler, tells me you are a racehorse owner of some renown, come west looking for matches after having run out of competition in the East."

"Thank you, kindly," O'Rooney beamed, extending his hand. "Sean O'Rooney, at your service. And yes, thank you, I will have a small drop. . . . But, as to my being a big racehorse owner, no, sir, I am afraid the man has misled you. I do have a horse, but I brought him west to recover from a breathing ailment he contracted along the big river."

"That son of a bitch!" Roberts said, shaking his head in admiration.

"Which?" Fontaine asked with an amused grin.

"Both! Especially Williams. That bastard knows every stranger what comes to town. He musta checked the horse and seen that it had fine lines. But he didn't do it right. I looked at the horse as soon as the little feller left fer the hotel, and I'd stake a lot on my knowledge of horses, Mr. Fontaine. That animal ain't got a natural winding problem."

"How do you know?"

"Well, fer one thing, we can figger O'Rooney rode him here in that wagon, so the animal ain't suffered on the trip. Fer another it's been dry fer more than a thousand miles so the animal should've cleared up. But it wheezes. I figger the little bastard give it some snuff jest before we hit town. . . . This oughta be good. Any bets, Mr. Fontaine?"

"None at all, sir," Fontaine grinned. "Now I don't know who's working on who."

With an open mind, Fontaine sat back to watch the shearing, not knowing who was the sheep, but silently betting on O'Rooney. The little man was either the perfect mark or he was a great actor. After his free drink he bought the gambler one, and Fontaine was willing to bet on O'Rooney's Irish heritage backing up his drinking. Then the gambler bought one and O'Rooney professed an interest in roulette. Roberts nudged Fontaine, waved for another round of beer and whispered:

"This is like watching one of them morality plays the travelin' preachers bring through, everything happens according to plan. Tonight the little man will win; couple a hunnert, maybe, then maybe tomorrow, then they move in to take all he's got. . . . 'Course, if the little guy ain't a mark, on the third night he'll outsmart 'em, or turn crooked. If he does that, I gotta warn the gambler, of course."

Fontaine took a large drink of beer and grinned, "Oh, of course!"

But it didn't quite work the way the two observers thought. True enough, the first night O'Rooney won two hundred dollars at roulette and promised to come back the next night to "take the house." Enjoying the rest, and the protection of Roberts' shotgun, Fontaine decided to stay a few days and drink, and sleep, and see how the charming little Irishman made out. So he wrote a telegram and Roberts sent it to Prescott by the next rider. It said:

ROBERTS PROBABLY STOP WILL BE HERE A WEEK STOP
ANY INDIAN SIGN

FONTAINE

The next night they "taught" O'Rooney to play poker while Fontaine and Roberts watched from the next table. "Morality play" was an apt description, Fontaine thought. The conversation was so broad, with such exaggerated gestures of surprise and joy, that it was a wonder that it didn't upset the participants themselves, but, true to form, they followed the precise pattern. O'Rooney won a fifty-dollar pot on two pair while the gambler folded with three tens and a protestation that O'Rooney learned quickly. . . .

"Any Indians around here, Marshal?" Fontaine asked, lighting a cheroot.

"None any self-respecting cavalryman would saddle his horse for. Why?"

Fontaine repeated his desire to find a certain Cheyenne and at the mention of the tribe Roberts nodded.

"Oh, that one. . . . Now don't look so surprised, Mr. Fontaine. Yes, I checked with the marshal at Pinyon on you, right after I got Mr. Lane's letter. I wouldn't be much of a lawman if I didn't do a little nosin' around."

"I suppose," Fontaine nodded, and his appreciation of Roberts went up a bit more.

O'Rooney, when it was his turn to bet, asked if a spade flush was better than a heart flush, won a twenty-dollar pot when the gambler and his friends folded. . . .

"You got a whorehouse in town, Marshal?" Fontaine said to change the subject.

"Why, you feel the need?"

"No, not particularly, just wondering how you kept order."

"I got a rulin' posted. Works pretty well. To answer your question, yes, we got one, such as it is; two forty-year-old biddies and their half-wit niece. I should check it anyway; come on, I'll show ya, it's just next door in the back."

Over the door was a dim lantern with the panes painted red. One knock and it was opened by a dumpy woman wearing a grease-stained shift. At the sight of the marshal she grinned and stepped back. They entered a dingy sitting room with a battered table and chairs and two often missed cuspidors.

"Evenin', Marshal," the woman said in a raspy voice.

"Evenin', Priscilla, Any customers?" When the woman shook her head Roberts said, "All right, line 'em. Might as well check ya now."

The woman nodded and disappeared through a back door and Roberts pointed to a big printed sign on the wall which said:

NO FIGHTING, NO SHOUTING OR DRINKING, NO WELCHING. VIOLATORS GET 20 DAYS OR $20.

In a moment the woman reappeared with two others. One was about her age, the other was maybe twenty, but it was hard to tell. At a nod from the marshal they stood in a line and dropped their robes. Their feet were dirty and their pale bodies reeked of sweat, cheap perfume, and rotgut whiskey. The two older women had big, baggy breasts, flabby stomachs and their bulging legs were marked with blue varicose veins. The young one was skinny, had a wall eye, and very small breasts. At a nod from Roberts they held up their breasts so he could look under them, though there was no need on the little one. Then they held their arms up, then sat on chairs and spread their legs and parted themselves. Finally they stood up, turned around, and bent over. Fontaine swallowed and tried to keep a blank face.

When he was satisfied the marshal nodded and they left quickly. Outside Fontaine took a couple of deep breaths and said:

"Whew! You mean men pay for that around here?"

"Yes, sir. Dollar apiece."

"Christ! That's enough to make you give it up!"

"Mebbe. But the local miners and cowhands think it beats playin' with themselves."

"I suppose. . . . What about you? Married, or got a gal?"

"No. I'm widowed some years. After that I sorta give it up, 'cept for an occasional clean Injun gal. By the way, what you just seen in there I done 'cause we ain't got no doctor and I run a clean town. A woman gets the pox and I put her outa business."

"Very commendable," Fontaine said dryly.

When the bartender served them a beer he informed the marshal that the little man had not only lost back the two hundred he'd won the night before but was now almost two hundred in the hole. O'Rooney was sweating, his coat was on the back of his chair and his face was contorted with agony. They were playing five-card stud, O'Rooney to the left of the dealer. His first card was a king, high card.

"What is it when you don't bet, but stay in?" he inquired, fingering the dwindling supply of money.

"Check," the gambler said.

"O'Rooney nodded and the gambler bet ten dollars. The next two men stayed and O'Rooney stayed. On the next card the king was still high and O'Rooney checked again and the gambler bet twenty. The other two folded and O'Rooney reluctantly stayed. The process was repeated on the third card; king high, check, the gambler with no pairs showing bet fifty dollars. O'Rooney, sweated some more, agonized some more, finally called. The last card gave O'Rooney a king high, no possible straights or flushes, the gambler had a jack high, no possibles. The gambler grinned and O'Rooney sighed and said:

"Well, sir, I know you'll bet, and all I have, no doubt. But I cannot let you bluff me out, so I will, what do you call it, go in the pot for my last two hundred dollars. Is that correct?"

"Yes, sir, it is," the gambler beamed. "We run a fair and square house here. A man is not run out of a pot because his opponent crowds him out with a bigger bankroll. No matter what I may bet, you are in for the amount now, plus my two hundred dollars."

O'Rooney nodded, and almost reluctantly pushed his two hundred to the center of the table. The gambler beamed, added his two hundred, then counted out two hundred more and set it to one side.

"Now, sir," he grinned widely. "I plan to raise another two hundred, if you care to cover it."

"But I have no more funds, sir!" O'Rooney protested.

"Ah, but I would allow you two hundred for that fine racehorse, and these gentlemen will witness the fact."

"Oh no, sir!" O'Rooney protested. "That animal may not be the best in the world but he has a sentimental value far exceeding a thousand dollars. I could not!"

"How about four hundred?" More bills were added.

The little Irishman, his face contorted, bit his lip. "Except for the fact that I would not have you bluff me out, I would not do it. But I'm sure my king is the better hand. . . . Very well. Marshal? Is he correct?"

"Yes, sir," Roberts said as he and Fontaine got to their feet to watch the final scene. "You win and you get the money on the table. Lose and he gets the horse."

O'Rooney nodded once more. "Very well, sir. You are, what is it? Called."

The gambler beamed and turned his hole card; a pair of jacks.

"Two kings, I believe, wins," O'Rooney grinned, turning over the hidden king and started raking in the money.

"Why goddam!" the gambler said, his mouth open in the realization that he'd been had. "You checked a cinch! You had the high hand every single turn!"

Fontaine and Roberts grinned and the bartender laughed, then quickly shut up, realizing that his job might suddenly be exposed. O'Rooney pulled in the money, a broad Irish grin on his face, and stacked the bills and put them in his coat pocket. As he got to his feet he said:

"Yes, sir! I did indeed do all those things. But remember, sir, you spent the evening in a voluntary effort to teach me this fine game. You volunteered everything and never once asked me if I had ever played before. . . . Abe!"

The big Negro stuck his head over the swinging door.

"We go. Good night, gentlemen, and thank you."

O'Rooney started for the door while the gambler sat there, his beady little eyes narrowed to slits, his mind working.

"Wait!" the gambler said, getting quickly to his feet. "Surely you would be gentleman enough to allow me a sporting chance to regain my money?"

"Certainly, sir," O'Rooney said grandly, "but not tonight. Tomorrow, perhaps."

"I had, sir," the gambler said, his oily smile back in place, "another thought. Perhaps you'd care to put the five hundred you won on your horse in a match race?"

"Well," O'Rooney said, returning to the table, "I hadn't thought of racing him for a while. He's well out of shape, he'd need a few days workout. . . ."

And so the wager was made. Once they agreed on terms they went to the marshal as final arbitrator. He agreed that the race should be held in five days; time enough for O'Rooney to work out his animal and for any other entrants to get ready. The fact that it would be on a Sunday was not overlooked by the gambler, the town would be crowded. Over O'Rooney's objection the marshal agreed that local custom dictated the race would be run in three, two-mile heats. The little Irishman worried the thought for a moment, then asked:

"And what if there is no winner of two?"

"Then the winner is judged on points, five for first, three for second, two for third. Me and the mayor is the judges."

"Then, sir," O'Rooney said with a nod of finality, "I will accept. My champion is a good distance horse and if the atmosphere gets to him I yet feel sure he will last over the locals on the point system."

Thereupon O'Rooney took five hundred dollars from his pocket and gave it to the marshal and the gambler added his five hundred.

On Thursday afternoon, feeling the need of a bit of practice, Fontaine bought a hundred rounds of carbine shells from the general store, not wanting to use his good ones, and rode a few miles out of town toward the edge of the desert where he picked off a tarantula, three running lizards, and shot the branches off numerous mesquite bushes. His timing was good, his accuracy was undiminished and feeling satisfied he sat under the shade of a large palo verde to clean his weapon. He had just put his own shells back in the piece when he heard a horse galloping down the trail. He quickly mounted but there was no need; it was O'Rooney and his racehorse. Abe was far behind on a rented animal. Fontaine waved and the little man pulled his horse to a controlled canter with a tight rein, the animal still wanted to run. Fontaine studied the racehorse for a moment and decided that O'Rooney was a lying Irishman. O'Rooney turned the horse toward town and Fontaine rode along.

"Are you ready, Mr. O'Rooney?" Fontaine asked with a smile.

"That I am, sir, that I am," the little man grinned.

They rode a ways and talked about the heat and the race-course, which was laid out in a circle, starting and ending in front of the saloon. Finally O'Rooney, who had started to say something several times, got it out.

"Mr. Fontaine, I would be imposin' on ya to ask a kindness."

"Ask anyway," Fontaine grinned. "I might."

"Well, the marshal assures me that you're an honest fellow and you're the only one in this God-forsaken town who has been nice to me, and the first time we ever met, too, ya offered to pull me wagon outa the mud. . . . Anyway, would ya place a small wager fer me?"

"Not if you're going to bet on the other horse and throw the race."

"Mr. Fontaine!" came the remonstration in a broad accent. "I'm an honest fellow! I wouldn't do such a dastardly thing!"

"Oh no! Like you didn't take that gambler playing poker!"

"Oh, that was different!" the little man grinned. "He wuz askin' fer it. Besides, a gambler's fair game at his own table."

"All right!" Fontaine laughed. "So what do you want?"

"I want ya to bet five hundred dollars for me to win the first heat."

"Why you little crook!" Fontaine grinned. "I shoulda known. . . ."

"Whoa!" O'Rooney said, holding up his hand. "It's a fair wager. All the entries will be tryin' like holy hell to win the first one. The man with the first leg has the best chance, everybody knows that!"

"Well by God that's true," Fontaine agreed. "All right, I'll do it."

The little man nodded and stopped his horse, made sure there was no one but Abe around, opened his vest to a money belt and pulled out five one-hundred-dollar bills and gave them to Fontaine.

"Perhaps we shouldn't be seen together until after the race," he said, and when Fontaine nodded the little man gigged his horse and rode away.

"Trusting little bastard," Fontaine observed. Then added, "My honest face."

By Saturday night the town was jammed with people coming to see the big race and the marshal was busy watching the drunks. A crude tote board had been set up behind the bar in the saloon which was presided over by the mayor. There were four entries; O'Rooney, two horses put up by two rival ranches, and the gambler had brought in a part Morgan, part Arab from Prescott and had hired a sharp-faced little man of no more than a hundred and twenty pounds to be the jockey. Betting was heavy on the final winner at two and a half to one, take your choice, and there were all kinds of bets on individual heats and between individual horses in given heats. Fontaine watched the board during the evening and about midnight decided that it was time to bet. When he offered a thousand dollars on O'Rooney to win the first heat the mayor hesitated at the going rate of two and a half to one, but a quick nod from the gambler and the bet was confirmed. Fontaine paid his money, got a receipt, and headed for the marshal's office with a frown; the gambler was too quick to take the bet.

He found the marshal putting away his fourth drunk and letting the first one, who was now sober, free. He told him the story and Roberts nodded seriously.

"I figger you're right, he knows somethin' we don't. And, uh, by the way, O'Rooney got to me too, and the hostler, and one of them old whores, she said he reminded her of her baby brother."

"What, uh," Fontaine said suspiciously, "does that mean?"

"It means what you think it does," Roberts nodded. "He

got us all to bet five hundred on him too, with his money. That means he bet two thousand dollars. He wins and he wins five thousand dollars! The little son of a bitch must be mighty sure he'll win. 'Course he told me to mention it to you so we'd be sure to get together. . . . How much of your own did you bet?"

Fontaine grinned almost sheepishly. "Five hundred."

"I bet two hundred. That's a month's take. . . . 'Course you figger like I do? The gambler is gonna fix the first heat so's his horse wins?"

"Uh huh," Fontaine agreed. "Now, how many ways to fix a horse race? If the animal doesn't start it's no bet, so we're all right there. Now, they can't very well shoot the rider or the horse, that's too obvious. What about the other two entries?"

"No indeed! Perfectly honest, both of them."

"All right. . . . Think I'll take a run around the track just before daylight."

"Good idea. Why don'tcha sleep in my office. I'll wake ya, you take a look-see, then I'll sleep in the mornin'."

Fontaine nodded. "He's a shrewd little bastard! Getting us to place his bets he figured we'd put down some of our own money and at least insure him an honest run. Goddam, he's got guts!"

At four o'clock in the morning Fontaine rode around the staked-out racecourse at an easy lope. Through town it looked all right, and into the first and second turns the land was wide and clear, except for a bit of sagebrush for hundreds of yards on either side. The last turn (the course wasn't a perfect oval) passed among some trees near the creekbed, then into the last long straightway, all clearly visible from the main street. If there was to be any chicanery, it would be on the last turn. Fontaine turned around and rode through the turn again, this time at a walk, watching the outside of the track. There were trees and bushes enough for a man to hide, it might be there. When the land opened up he turned around and walked his horse back through the turn, only cutting it short by five yards. The brush was five feet high and anything could be hidden. . . .

"Mistah Fontaine! It's me, Abe!" the big Negro whispered.

Fontaine raised the carbine at the first sound but then lowered it as the big man appeared from the shadows.

"Abe!" Fontaine whispered. "What the hell are you doing out here?"

"Same thing you is, suh. And I found it! Looky here."

Fontaine dismounted and followed Abe to the middle of the turn and some fifteen feet from the inner edge of the marked course. The end of a coil of rope was buried in the sand. Fontaine nodded and they followed it across the course to where it was securely tied to the trunk of a palo verde. Buried across the course by a foot of sand it made a perfect trip wire.

"You had the same idea I did," Fontaine nodded.

"Yes, suh!" the big Negro grinned. "Mistah O'Rooney, he's a smaat fellah."

"Yes, he certainly is," Fontaine grinned. "In more ways than one. I take it you'll be here tomorrow?"

"Ah plans to go back, tell Mistah O'Rooney, git me some food and watah and be back 'fore dawn and waits till the race."

"Good!" Fontaine said, clapping Abe on the back. "I'll see that things go properly in town."

They exchanged grins and Fontaine remounted and headed for the marshal's office.

The pre-race festivities made the town coffers several thousand dollars. Most of the miners and cowmen from miles around drank huge quantities of beer and whiskey, lost most of their money at the tables, and were ready for the big race. The contestants lined up their animals for last-minute instructions, dressed in diverse ways. The two cowboys rode light western saddles, the gambler's jockey had an English saddle, and O'Rooney showed up wearing riding pants, no boots, stripped to the waist (showing big arms and chest for so little a man) and his animal was bareback. The mayor went over the instructions again, the marshal raised a kerchief and the horses lined up ten feet behind the overhead rope that was the finish line. The kerchief dropped and the race was on.

They got off to a good start and went the length of town by twos, the cow ponies with their lightning start getting a twenty-foot jump. They turned the corner to the right and the spectators ran between buildings to see them run down the backstretch. Then the Arab and O'Rooney's horse took over and began to make it a two-horse race. Fontaine saw the gambler nudge a big, pale-faced man wearing a low six-gun and the man nodded and ran back toward the street and Fontaine followed. The man quickly pulled a horse from the front of the saloon and ran toward the last turn. Fontaine sprinted for his horse, got mounted, waited until the man was out of sight, then pounded down the street after him, dismounted at the last building and ran into the brush with his carbine.

He advanced, mostly on his hands and knees, and got there in time to see big Abe creep up on a man holding the rope, grab him by the throat with his two big hands and raise to his feet, the muscles of his bare arms contracted. The man didn't have time to scream, he let go of the rope and tried to save his life. Abe shook him and held him off the ground until the man grew limp, then he flung him ten feet away in an inert heap. Fontaine kept looking for the other man while he was watching Abe, hoping the man wouldn't shoot before he could spot him.

But the man didn't want to shoot, it would draw attention to the turn and now they could hear the sound of advancing hooves as they pounded toward the end of the backstretch. The man stood up, holding his gun by the barrel, and advanced on Abe, intending to brain him.

"Good!" Fontaine said to Fontaine, and advanced silently across the sand. Abe was watching for the horses and as the man raised his gun Fontaine closed the gap, released the hammer on his carbine, and brought the butt flashing around in an arc, catching the man on the side of the head, mashing his ear to a pulp. He dropped with no sound other than the rifle butt hitting his head, and Abe turned and stared wide-eyed, then grinned broadly.

Then the two leaders were within sight and the Arab was giving O'Rooney a real run for his money, they were head and head, driving hard. As they got close to the place where the rope was the rider pulled hard on the Arab to let O'Rooney get himself tripped and that was the horse race. O'Rooney flashed by the spot and shot them a quick grin, the soul of confidence from the fact that he ran his horse to the spot as hard as it would go, relying on his friend, pulled into a long lead coming out of the turn, and the Arab didn't have a chance.

Fontaine and Abe heard a great cheer go up from the finish line; Fontaine motioned to Abe and the big black man dragged the two bodies to the gunman's horse and Fontaine helped tie them by one ankle each to a stirrup. Then he mounted his own horse and pulled the other horse behind him, dragging an unconscious body on each side.

He approached the laughing, shouting crowd silently as the winner and second-place horses returned to the starting line for a breather. The marshal spotted him and pointed toward the jail. Half the crowd saw him and they grew silent. Fontaine left the horse in front of the jail and the marshal and a part-time deputy ran to pull the two inert bodies into the building. Fontaine rode to the crowd, which parted for him, and stopped his horse in front of the saloon. He dismounted, smiled at O'Rooney and said:

"Run the second two heats just like the first. In fact, I think you'll have less traffic this time. Your gambler friend and I will stand here and watch from the porch."

O'Rooney nodded and saw to his horse and Fontaine crossed quickly to the gambler, his carbine nudging the man in the thigh.

"I don't suppose you know anything about those two brigands?"

"Absolutely not," the man protested in strained innocence.

"Of course not," Fontaine replied dryly. "Now, just stand here and watch."

O'Rooney was badly beaten in the second heat, the Arab winning by twenty lengths. O'Rooney was second, making it a tie. In the third heat his horse broke down just as they reached the last turn and he walked his limping horse to the finish line. The Arab won by thirty lengths this time. There was lots of cheering and congratulating the winner and then they turned to laugh at the little Irishman who was walking a lame horse to the saloon. But the funny thing was, the little Irishman was smiling. The gambler, still held by Fontaine, had a sickly look on his face and Fontaine grinned; the gambler had finally done his mathematics. O'Rooney turned his lame racer over to Abe and walked up to the winning jockey and stuck out his hand in a sportsmanlike gesture. The other little man took it and they shook hands and everyone cheered. Then O'Rooney smashed the jockey full in the face with his left fist, knocking him to the ground.

"You dirty little cheatin' bastard!" O'Rooney roared.

"That'll teach ya! Now git up again and I'll change yer face
for ya!"

But the little jockey had no desire. His nose was broken and
he didn't feel like fighting. But a burly six-footer did. He
stepped forward, dropped his gun belt and shouted:

"Why, you little son of a bitch! Hit me little cousin, will
ya? I seen ya! You professional bare-knuckle fighters think
ya can hit a little man and git away with it. Why, them fists
of your'n is like pistols!"

"I'm not a fighter!" O'Rooney said in some amazement.
Then he smiled, realizing that the bigger man had said it to
make him look like he wasn't a bully. "But maybe you're
right."

The little Irishman spit in the big man's eye, ducked the
anticipated roundhouse right, and darted in and reached up
and popped his opponent on the right eye. The man roared
and swung a backhand, which was ducked easily, and as the
man came around he was jabbed in the left eye by three
stiffly extended fingers. The crowd roared at this extra added
attraction and moved back to give them room. The big man
charged again, with no purpose or direction, only intending to
get a grip on his elusive opponent. O'Rooney, smiling and
dancing about like an Irish clog dancer, moved lightly out of
the way, waiting to blind the other eye. On the third charge
he got it, the man hesitated, and O'Rooney's extended fingers
closed the right eye. The man roared in pain, his hands to his
eyes and staggered in a circle. O'Rooney, grinning like an
ancestral banshee, danced in and out, pounding the man's
face at will. O'Rooney broke his nose, knocked out a couple
of teeth, and was about to permanently blind him as evi-
denced by the fact that he had given up using his fists and now
kept his fingers stiffly extended.

"Abe!" Fontaine roared and the big man rushed in and
pulled his angry employer away. Then the marshal joined
them and the fight was over and the winners began to line
up to collect their bets.

Under the stern eye of the marshal the mayor and the
gambler paid off each and every bet. Though he'd won the
race and made fifteen hundred dollars there, the gambler
had lost five thousand to O'Rooney, five thousand to
O'Rooney's friends and backers, and while he'd made some
four thousand off the cowboys he still showed a net loss of

forty-five hundred dollars, precisely the amount O'Rooney had won, which would make the gambler a pauper for some time to come.

The racehorse was in the wagon, Abe was ready, and O'Rooney was washed and dressed and ready to go. He had collected all the bets made for him by his friends and grandly given back ten percent as a gratuity. As Fontaine was seeing him to the wagon the little man turned and said:

"Mr. Roberts wuz tellin' me of the grand and glorious opportunity you had offered him in Lane City. Do ya suppose there would be a place fer the likes of me?"

"Well, now, I don't know," Fontaine grinned. "What can you do?"

"I can be damn tired of runnin', fer one thing. And fer another I can run an honest saloon with honest tables and I can spot a crook a mile off."

"I've no doubt of that," Fontaine laughed. "Tell you what, I'm sure there's a place for a brave man who is smart and quick. Show up in Lane City and I'll see there's a place for you. It might not be the saloon but you can make money at it. And Abe will be welcome, also."

"Thank you kindly," the little man said, "especially fer Abe. I appreciate that. And it's time we settled down to something a little less, shall we say, sporting like? It's like the name of me horse. Did you know what it is, Mr. Fontaine?"

"No. What?"

"Tempus Fugit."

"Time flies," Fontaine said.

"The same sir!' O'Rooney said, laying the whip to two newly acquired wagon horses. "And me congratulations on your knowledge of the Latin language! See you in Lane City!"

As the wagon hurried out of town the marshal came out onto the boardwalk and a man stepped down from the just arrived stage, obviously a drummer by his clothes and the sample case he carried. He saw the marshal's star and grinned and said, as he pointed to the departing wagon:

"Is the race over, Marshal?"

"How'd ya know?" Roberts asked in some wonder.

"That's Sean O'Rooney," the man smiled, pointing at the wagon. "He's the biggest gambler I ever seen. And I seen him in Santa Fe, Tucson, Tombstone!"

"Yeah, we know," the marshal said as the drummer hurried into the saloon.

Fontaine broke into gales of laughter and punched the marshal in the chest with a finger. "Sure! Now we know!"

"Yeah," Roberts grinned. "Say. I must know now. Do I have the job?"

"You got it, Roberts," Fontaine grinned, "you got it. But why now?"

"Two things. I ain't too popular with the mayor right now and, if I got the job I thought it only kindly, seein' as I made all that money, to make sure the Honorable Mr. O'Rooney gets to Lane City without a slug in his Irish ass."

"Good idea," Fontaine nodded. "You'll get there first. Go to Toby Lane and tell him I sent you. Tell him I'll be along in a week or so. I'm going back by way of Flagstaff and check out the Indians."

Roberts nodded and they shook hands, and the lawman added:

"Mr. Fontaine, I know it's Lane's money, and he's the biggest man in the Territory, or will be if he lives that long, but I jest want ya to know that I never yet picked up my bread butter side down."

"Good boy!" Fontaine grinned tightly. "That's the right answer."

In recording the events of the horse race in Joshua Wells and the story of Sean O'Rooney, Fontaine concluded with this observation:

O'Rooney, typical of his race, is either full of bullshit or rotgut, but he's got a way about him that will make him a pile of money, if he doesn't get killed first. Big men don't like being taken by little men, but O'Rooney knows that.

Chapter Eight

Fontaine took two weeks longer than Roberts and O'Rooney. They went east and along the Mongollon Rim to Pinyon while Fontaine went north to Flagstaff. There he made the rounds of the saloons and the outlying ranches, even stopped by the sheriff's office inquiring about a stray Cheyenne. People thought he was either crazy or a dumb greenhorn, everybody knew there were no Cheyenne in Arizona, only a few on reservations in Colorado and mostly they were up north in Wyoming and maybe a few farther east on the plains, but anybody who was looking for a Cheyenne in Arizona must be a little strange. When Fontaine began to agree with them he headed for Pinyon. He had been gone seven weeks.

When he arrived at Lane's ranch no one was there except the Indian woman and a few hands whose duty it was to take care of the local stock and the ranch itself. The Indian woman, never one to volunteer anything, confined herself to answering his questions. No, Mr. Lane did not say when he would return. Yes, she knew he was past the new town, up on the Rim somewhere with a bunch of hands to bring in some cattle. From that answer Fontaine knew he wasn't bringing in cattle; there weren't enough up there to make it pay, he was probably closer to Young, and with an armed party, gobbling up some more land. No, Mr. Starrett wasn't with them. Where, then? With the rest of the men on the range some fifty miles east, expected back in a week or so. No, Miss Mary Kaye was still gone, return not known. Yes, the Señor Gonzalez was still here. Where? In town, picking up supplies for the bulls. Fontaine thanked her for this fountain of information, prevailed on her to fix him a bath; shaved, changed clothes and headed for town.

As he rode into town he saw Linus loading grain on the back of a wagon. Fontaine gigged his horse and rode close, leaned down and put out his hand.

"Linus!"

153

The big man turned quickly, his face split into a broad grin, and he gripped Fontaine's hand. "Am I glad to see you! I was about to chuck this play-acting and come look for you when that marshal and the funny-looking little Irisher rode in and said you'd only be a week or so. . . . Did you find what you were looking for?"

"Naw, hell no! It got to the point where I was making an idiot out of myself by asking. If the Indian isn't dead he's long gone; north, probably. . . . What's new around here? How's little Isaacs? Is Calvin in town?"

"Whoa!" the big man said, wiping the sweat from his brow. "Let's get a beer and I'll bring you up to date."

Fontaine dismounted, hitched his horse to the back of the wagon, pulled the carbine, and they crossed the street to the saloon. Willard nodded like Fontaine had been in just the day before and brought them two beers to a table against the wall. Linus drank over half a schooner before he put the glass down. Fontaine took a sip of his and waited for Linus to catch his breath.

"Well, let's see," Linus said. "Where's the best place to start? I guess with Mr., oops, sorry . . . Señor Lane. He's very proud of the bulls, and they've been doing their duty. He's given me a long rein with 'em, and left me pretty much to myself. 'Course, he comes and goes a lot. Right now he's over near Young somewhere again. This time he took John Wesley Calvin and his two killers with him, and ten of his fastest men. From what I gather, picking up bits and snatches, he bought a lot of land over there and he went over with enough guns to make sure he got what he thinks he bought. Anyway, they've been gone several days now.

"The preacher and the doctor got here all right, and they're up at Lane City with Roberts and the Irishman. Señor Lane left word with Starrett that if anyone you sent came in while he was gone they were to put them up at Lane City and set them up however you'd agreed. So far, they all seem satisfied.

"The young lady, Lane's niece, is scheduled back later this month."

Fontaine grinned into his beer. "What about Isaacs, he all right?"

"Oh, he's fine. But that's a good long story, and I got involved in that one. I'd have to have another beer to be sure I got through it."

"No doubt," Fontaine grinned.

He held up three fingers to Willard, pulled out a cheroot and match, put his feet in the empty chair next to him, and sipped his beer. The three schooners were delivered, Fontaine paid Willard and pulled his hat to his eyebrows and waited. Linus finished the beer and half the third one, then said:

"Well, after you left, the town buzzed for a while at the little feller standing up to the great John Wesley but in a few days the novelty wore off and they forgot about it, but not that little Jew. He moved into Beesley's stable, they arrived at a fee of two bits a day for him and the burro, and Isaacs helps around the stable. John Wesley uses the saloon, here, as his headquarters and he spends most of his time tellin' anybody who'll listen what a fast gun he is. Well, I've got plenty of time of late. . . ."

"I'll see to that," Fontaine remarked with a straight face.

"No doubt," Linus grinned. "Anyway, I've gotten real friendly with the little man. Me, being one fourth of every second-class type we got out here, I found a lot in common with the Jew. He taught me about his religion, and it's not too far from what the Kiowa-Apaches believe, and, for my part, I taught him to use a six-gun."

"You what!" Fontaine exploded, almost spilling his beer. "Now what the hell didja want to do that for? He's a book-keeper, not a gun sharp!"

"Anybody can use a gun," Linus replied seriously. "Isaacs was determined to learn, so I thought, if that's the case, I might as well teach him the right way."

"All right," Fontaine said with a note of resignation. "You got me there."

"Anyway, he insisted on paying all the cost himself, even my ammunition. . . . Oh, that's something else you didn't hear about. The little bastard unloaded all those cheap scarves of his on the storekeeper for seventy-five cents apiece."

"How in hell did he do that?" Fontaine grinned.

"I watched 'im. You never saw a feller so reluctant to sell anything in his life. Finally it got to the point where the storekeeper just had to have them. But no matter, he'll sell them at the Apache reservation for at least a dollar apiece. He may not get silver for them but he'll get horses, and anything else the Apaches can steal to make money. . . . It was a great

American deal, everybody made money, even the Indians.
They'll steal enough to make it up."

"Probably," Fontaine laughed. "Okay, so what about the
gun?"

"It was a strange thing," Gonzalez said, reflecting on what
had happened. "The little feller is as nice a man as I've ever
met, except you and me, of course. But you and me, and
everybody else who lives the hard life out here and doesn't
knuckle down, or run, has some natural asset. Take me, I'm
big, and fairly strong, and I've got four different kinds of
blood runnin' in me, and I'm willin' to fight, 'cause maybe I've
got no better sense, despite what education I've got.

"And you, you're highly intelligent, educated, but you
were wronged and it made you mean, on top of being brave.
And you learned to use that carbine . . . and it's made you one
of the coldest men I've ever known. . . . No offense, mind
you. . . ."

"None taken," Fontaine said, raising his glass.

"But the little Jew, he's kindly, and honest, sort of, and
he means no harm to anyone. But he got a notion to take up
the gun to, as he said, protect himself. So I figured to help
him where I can. Now, of course, he intends to get even with
Calvin, and I can't blame him. And, you know, it took me a
bit to figure it out, but it's not because John Wesley broke his
hand, it's because Calvin, uh, defiled, that's the word, his little
wooden box and the tintype of that girl."

"Ever find out who she is?"

"No. And it wasn't my place to ask."

Fontaine nodded in agreement, that was proper.

"So, I taught him to shoot a six-gun. I didn't try to make a
fast gun out of him, he's probably too old. But I did teach
him to hit what he's aiming at, and that's half the battle, if
you can make your feet stand still!"

Fontaine nodded and raised his glass to that.

"Then I found something that will make an equalizer between little Isaacs and the great John Wesley Calvin. You ever
heard of the Rocks?"

"Sure. Old Apache sacred ground, five miles or so from
town."

"Right. Well, I got talkin' Apache one day to some Indians
who came to town and through them I found out about the
Rocks, and I got one of 'em to take me out there. Well, I was

mighty impressed; those sandstone spires rising eighty, hundred feet right out of the desert floor. Pretty spooky . . . not the size, I mean, but what the Indian showed me. There are places in there where a man's voice echoes out a hundred feet ahead of him. There's another spot where you talk into the wall and the sound of your voice seems to come right out of the desert floor fifty feet away. There are hiding places that even I missed the first time around. Some of those spires are in so many pieces that a man can step into one and not even be seen!"

"So?" Fontaine inquired suspiciously.

Linus grinned. "Isaacs and I both saw it as an equalizer."

"Are you out of your mind!" Fontaine demanded. "That little guy choosing off John Wesley Calvin?"

"I know," Linus nodded. "I felt the same way at first. But the little man is determined to go against him; I had to help him."

Fontaine nodded and finished his beer. "All right. I'll see what I can do, especially as the world would be better off without Calvin. Where is Isaacs?"

"Down at the livery, probably."

They found Isaacs and Beesley repairing the stable corral. They had a hand-pumping reunion and Fontaine was amazed at the change in Isaacs. He now wore western clothes, his face was brown, his arms were bigger, and he seemed much more confident than the pathetic little figure who had wandered into Pinyon in a dirty silk hat. Fontaine told him that Linus had brought him up to date and that he would help, but it must be done with caution, and Fontaine would be in on everything. Isaacs readily agreed; to have Fontaine on his side, in his mind, assured his success. Fontaine wasn't so sure.

Toby returned three days later with Calvin and his two killers. Toby and his men dismountd but Calvin and his two flunkies wanted to go into Pinyon as Calvin preferred to stay at Mrs. O'Bannion's boardinghouse; there were whores and the saloon was just across the street. Fontaine met them on the ranch house steps and he and Toby shook hands warmly. Then Fontaine shook hands with Leroy Starrett, nodded to the men, and ignored Calvin.

"Jonathan," Toby said, pounding Fontaine on the back, "how are you? It's a pleasure to see a friendly face."

"I'm fine," Fontaine nodded, noticing the lines in Lane's face. "What's that mean, about the friendly face?"

"Jonathan, you don't know what I've been through in Young. The hardest thing in the world for a man of influence to do is to get people to help themselves."

"Yes, I can understand that."

"Well, let me get a bath and a shave and I'll tell you all about it."

Toby waved at his men and turned to go into the house. As he was about to follow, Fontaine saw Starrett nod at him, so he waited. When Toby was upstairs Starrett climbed the front steps and said:

"He's got an awful burden, tryin' to run all this, and he's sore put upon. Go easy."

"All right," Fontaine nodded. "I'll let him do the talking."

But when he came down he was distant and preoccupied. They had several drinks of good Scotch and they talked of the bulls, and they toasted Fontaine's success in getting the key men Toby wanted but Fontaine never had an opportunity to ask about Joe Brittman and they didn't talk about Young, or Lane City, or Toby's problems. Fontaine knew when to shut up, and he had feeling enough to know that Toby Lane had problems that went past men and money, and into some secret mental world that Jonathan Fontaine knew nothing about. So, after a quiet dinner, Fontaine went to bed and decided to spend the next two weeks resting and drinking beer in town, and helping Isaacs. Two weeks, because Toby had imparted one bit of good news during dinner; Mary Kaye would return then.

It started with minor things at first. Like the night someone poured molasses on his saddle, and the next night somebody cut Calvin's cinch strap in front of the saloon. He put his foot in the stirrup and the next thing he knew he was flat on his back in the dust. Even his two flunkies laughed, but only for a moment. Calvin stormed back into the saloon, looking for the culprit. His eyes landed on Isaacs, having a beer at the bar with Fontaine and Linus.

"You little bastard!" Calvin roared, heading for Isaacs. "Ya cut my cinch!"

But Fontaine was suddenly in the way, the ever present carbine hanging from his left hand. "I don't really think he did,"

Fontaine grinned. "If you can remember that far back, like fifteen minutes ago, you will recall that Mr. Isaacs was here before you rode up, and he is still here, and has not left the room."

Several men grunted their assent and Fontaine, of course, didn't admit that he was the one who'd waited across the street, cut the cinch, then come back into the saloon from the back way like he'd just been to the privy, to a half-filled beer glass purchased by Linus. Willard knew, and Fontaine saw his eyes narrow for a moment, but true to his neutrality, he said nothing. Calvin, his face red with anger, searched the room with his eyes for a moment, then stormed out as angrily as he had entered.

And it would have continued that way, Fontaine and Isaacs perpetrating little practical jokes on the great John Wesley Calvin, except the next night they tortured Leroy Starrett.

Fontaine was sitting on Toby's front porch in a straight chair, tipped back against the wall, his feet on the banister and his hat over his eyes. His carbine was next to the chair, also leaning against the wall. He was waiting complacently for Linus to saddle two horses so they could go to town and think of another trick to play on Calvin, and drink lots of beer while they conspired, when A. J. Beesley pounded up the road on a lathered horse. At the sight of Fontaine he started shouting.

"Mr. Fontaine! Fontaine! Come quick! They's got Starrett!"

Fontaine jumped to his feet and ran down the steps. The Indian woman came and stood in the doorway. Fontaine grabbed the bridle of the winded horse and said:

"Whoa! Who's got Starrett?"

"Calvin! They backed him down on the street and then they brung him to the stable and kicked me out! I borrowed the first horse I could and beat it out here!"

"Easy now!" Fontaine said quickly, helping the old man down. "Why didn't you get the marshal?"

"That son of a bitch is out fishin' as usual!"

"Don't shout. What do you mean, backed down?"

"The big nigger of Calvin's, he called 'im out, Leroy! And Leroy wouldn't draw. The whole town seen it! Then Calvin and the other one come outa the barber shop, without eny guns, and they took Leroy and walked 'im down to my place. The nigger, he waved 'is gun at me and I lit out!"

Fontaine nodded, ran for his carbine, turned and started running toward the side of the house. To the woman he shouted, *"Mujer!* Shotgun! Out back!"

He sprinted around the back of the house and to the front of the stable where one of the Indian grooms had just thrown the reins over the backs of both horses and Linus was going for a saddle.

"Linus!" he shouted. "No saddle! Calvin's rousted Starrett in town!"

The Indian pulled one horse away from the other and held it while Fontaine threw himself across its back and grabbed the reins with his right hand as the animal bolted. As he reached the end of the house he saw Linus on the back of the other animal reach out and grab the barrel of the extended shotgun held by the Indian woman, then Fontaine was out of sight and running the horse flat out.

As he pounded down the main street he saw that the stable door was closed and he ran his horse another hundred feet and jerked it to a halt in front of the building next to the empty lot. There was a group of men there, taking turns peering around the corner, but making no other effort. One grabbed his horse and from several he learned that they were probably out back, from the several screams and groans they'd heard. Linus was fifty yards behind him. He waved to him and Linus ran his exhausted horse out of sight, next to the other one. As Linus dismounted, Fontaine nodded and ran between the buildings. They reached the alley, worked their way at a crouch behind some boxes to the end of the building where they could see the back of the stable.

From the light of the blacksmith fire they could see that Leroy was hanging by his wrists from the hayloft pulley, his ankles lashed together. His shirt was torn open and his pants and long johns were pulled to his boots. The big Negro had a pair of long tongs in his hand and he was touching Starrett on the thigh. Starrett groaned and kicked away and the three danced out of the way and watched him swing and laughed at the funny sight. They were too close to Starrett for Fontaine to risk a shot and while he decided what to do, the Negro put the tongs back into the fire for a moment, then brought them out, a glowing red in the night air, and Fontaine could wait no longer. He put a shot into the base of the anvil and they scattered as he and Linus ran forward. The three shadowy forms hesitated a minute, then ran around the other side of the barn and out onto the street. As Linus made sure they were gone, Fontaine cut Starrett down and leaned him against the barn while he cut the ropes around his feet. Then some of the group of men appeared, one with a lantern. Fontaine cut Starrett's hands loose and Linus half carried him into the tack room. Then Beesley appeared and began to chase the men out of his stable, shouting:

"All right! It's all over! Now git, before you scare the stock eny more!"

Linus held the front door of the stable and closed it behind the last man. Then Isaacs appeared through the back door, leading a horse.

"Where the hell you been?" Fontaine demanded as he helped Starrett sit on a bale of hay.

"Out to see the Rocks at night."

"Good timing," Linus said as he appeared from the front.

"Sorry," Isaacs said, lighting another lantern.

As he turned to Starrett with the light Beesley gasped and the others stared in shock. Starrett's thighs were fried in several places, there were four long, raw burns on his lower stomach and his penis was beginning to swell from being seared by the tongs.

"Oh, my God!" Beesley whispered and hurried to get some salve.

"All right, Leroy," Fontaine said gently to the sweating man. "What did they want?"

"I . . . I don't know," Starrett said, taking deep breaths to keep from fainting.

"Leroy," Fontaine continued in the same gentle tone, "I think you're lying."

"I don't know," Starrett said through his pain.

"Leroy," Fontaine persisted, "Beesley said the big black backed you down. That's not like you. Now, what is it? Tell me!"

"No, Fontaine!" Starrett said, his voice cracking a bit in momentary desperation. "Stay out of it! It don't concern you!"

"Calvin is an animal," Fontaine said. "You know it. And you know somebody's gonna kill 'im, sooner or later, so . . ."

Beesley shouldered his way in with a tin of branding salve and started to administer it. Then he paused in embarrassment and held out the tin. "Here, put it on your ownself."

Starrett nodded through gritted teeth and dipped his fingers and started applying the greasy cream. He sweated some more, and tears came to his eyes, but he got the job done, then leaned against the wall, took a deep breath and closed his eyes.

"Get a wagon," Fontaine ordered. "Linus, take a look around."

When Starrett was stretched out in the bed of the wagon on a pile of blankets with one over him, Fontaine called the others to one side.

"Beesley, Linus and I will go outside and make sure it's clear. When I wave, you come out, Linus will ride with you. Get him up to Lane City, we've got a new doctor there. . . . Linus, if anybody gets close to the wagon, shoot once, high. If they keep coming, kill them."

Linus nodded and Fontaine turned to Isaacs. "You still want to try Calvin?"

"Absolutely."

"You think you can do it?"

"Give me a fair chance at him."

"I'll do more than that. For once I'll see that you have the edge. I'd just as soon kill 'im myself but I don't want to cross Toby. . . . You sure?"

"I'm sure," the little man said quietly.

"All right," Fontaine nodded. "I'll give you one chance, fair and square, sort of. You stay with me, we're going to the saloon. And leave your gun here. All right, Linus, move out."

Starrett raised up and whispered, "Fontaine, come close."

Fontaine left the others and leaned close to Starrett.

"Fontaine," Starrett said, his lips barely moving, "I should tell ya. It ain't got nothin' to do with Toby, just me. Calvin found out somehow. I got night blindness. I can see well enough to git about but I couldn't see that big nigger . . . I can see fine in the daytime, mind ya, but I couldn't place 'im, and there wuz people on the street. . . . Fontaine, I hesitated a bit; he seen it, and he knew he had me. By the time I had 'im placed they wuz on me. . . . It wasn't that I wuz scairt to draw down on 'im, mind ya, it was jest . . ."

"Never mind," Fontaine nodded and patted Starrett's shoulder. "It's all right. You did the right thing. . . . And I won't say anything, your secret's safe."

"Thank ya kindly," the foreman nodded weakly.

Fontaine stepped back; Isaacs opened the stable door and

they were met by a crowd of silent men, waiting to see what would happen. When the wagon pulled out they turned silently away, somehow embarrassed for the foreman of the mighty TL outfit, and Fontaine knew Leroy lied, not about his eyes, but about the reason. Calvin had thought about the railroad.

Ten minutes later Fontaine and Isaacs entered Willard's saloon. Calvin and his two gun hands were at the bar, a large empty space on either side of them. Fontaine and Isaacs took a table nearby and Willard brought two beers. Fontaine carefully placed the carbine on the table near his left hand, cocked. He raised his glass and said in a louder voice than usual, "Mr. Isaacs, what shall we drink to?"

Isaacs raised his glass and looked around the smoky room. Then the little man seemingly saw Calvin for the first time and he grinned and said in the same tone:

"Well, sir, what say we drink to the noble and brave John Wesley Calvin, renown backshooter, and his two hired bushwhackers."

The room was absolutely silent for a moment. Then Calvin turned slowly and said:

"You little Jew bastard! I oughta kill you now!"

"No, no . . . I don't think you will," Fontaine said calmly. "And I'll tell you why. Your hand is six inches from your gun, and so's mine. And I'll bet your life on the fact that if you move I'll blow a hole in your belly. . . . Black man! Don't you try it!"

The Negro froze and Isaacs calmly took a sip of beer.

"And I don't think he'll try it," Isaacs said. "I never heard of him fighting a man on even terms. He always has to have the advantage."

"Why you buffalo chip!" Calvin said, his face growing red. "I'll fight you on any terms you kin think of!"

"Really?" Isaacs replied calmly as though he didn't believe it. "I don't believe it. How about tomorrow night, just as soon as the moon comes up; one six-gun each and a belt of ammunition; in the Indian Rocks, just out of town?"

"Why, you little Jew son of a bitch!" Calvin grinned. "You think you got an edge in there? Why I can git off five shots to yer one, runnin', hidin', or standin' on my head!"

"I hope so," Isaacs smiled and raised his glass, and Fontaine grinned.

The crowd buzzed with excitement at the prospect of a duel and Calvin turned to the bar with a grin, tossed off his drink, and said, "Come on, I gotta go practice shootin' fer tomorrow night!"

His two flunkies laughed at the big joke and they marched toward the swinging doors but halted when Willard said:

"John Wesley, me'n some others will inspect the Rocks for extra weapons before sundown."

Calvin doffed his hat, bowed grandly and said, "Any terms you want."

The town buzzed with the news; the little Jew was going to take on John Wesley. Bets were made and Willard booked most of them. By the next day every man within twenty miles knew of the duel and most of them planned to attend. By the next night—and Fontaine had stayed in town, just in case— there were several hundred men present. The east side of the Rocks, next to the road, was a series of succeedingly higher sandstone spires, with an open amphitheater, strewn with boulders and smaller spires, backed on the west side by a sloping cliff rising almost ninety feet in the air.

To this natural arena the two combatants were escorted by nearly every male in town over the age of fifteen. By the time they arrived, the odds had gone up to ten to one, favoring Calvin. The great John Wesley had spent the day in the saloon, though he drank sparingly, betting everything he owned on himself. As he correctly explained it, if he lost he wouldn't need the money anyway, and it was a considerable sum, considering the man had just been out of Yuma Prison a few months; something over three thousand dollars. Isaacs slept most of the day, ate an early supper, and drank lots of water.

Willard, the self-appointed master-at-arms, duly checked the gladiators for extra weapons and directed the searching of the arena. Then he told the rules as he returned each man his loaded gun, and a full belt of ammunition, fifty bullets. At the signal each man would run into the rocks, one on the north side, the other on the south, and take up any position he chose. When they were out of sight of the entrance, Willard would fire one shot and they might begin. The fight would be over if one cried for mercy (Calvin sneered, Isaacs grinned faintly). They were not to shoot at the north, south, or east rim as there would be spectators there. They might shoot at the west rim, no one would be allowed at that one. Both men nodded and Willard held up his hand and his watch, signifying that he would wait five minutes, time to let the spectators climb the three sides of the arena.

Calvin, who had worn a new red shirt for the occasion and a new white hat, and had stated that he wouldn't even get them dusty, stood aside to talk to his two friends. Isaacs, in a tan shirt and moccasins, wore no hat. The little man was getting last-minute instructions from Fontaine, while Linus and Beesley saw to it that they weren't disturbed.

"Now," Fontaine whispered, "you know this place, and where to hide. That won't give you an edge, it might just come close to breaking you even with Calvin's reflexes. Remember this, your life depends on it. That bastard has been used to shooting to kill and thinking about it afterward. If you stop to think about it, or waver for a second, you're dead. If you get a chance, kill him. Do not do anything fancy, do you understand?"

"Yes," Isaacs smiled, completely relaxed. "And I thank you for the . . . "

He stopped talking and turned as eleven horses galloped up in a group; Toby Lane and ten TL riders, all carrying rifles. While his men dismounted, Toby sat his horse and Fontaine's eyes narrowed a moment as he got the feeling that here was not the wealthy Mr. Lane but a feudal lord with his palace guard. Toby nodded to several men, then to Willard; then he saw Fontaine and dismounted as one of his men quickly took his reins.

"Jonathan?" Toby said, his voice properly polite, rather than friendly.

"Toby?" Fontaine responded in the same tone, a slight shiver going up his spine.

"You did this, Jonathan? You set it up?"

"Yes, sort of," Fontaine admitted.

"Why?"

"Toby," Fontaine said in a flat, measured voice, "Calvin is an animal."

"Why did you let Isaacs try Calvin first if you feel that way?"

"The little man should have his chance."

"Uh huh," Toby nodded curtly. "What if Calvin wins?"

"I'll find an excuse to kill him by Saturday," said the flat voice.

"Even against my wishes? He works for me, you know."

"I know," Fontaine replied, "so does Leroy. How is he?"

"Be all right. Won't ride for a spell."

"No doubt," Fontaine replied dryly. "Toby, tell me this; why did Calvin torture him?"

"Leroy wouldn't say," Toby lied, and Fontaine knew it. "By Saturday, you say?"

"Yes, if not tonight or tomorrow."

"Umm." Toby considered this for a moment, then said, "All right, you're more valuable to me than Calvin; I'll root for the Jew." Then, added almost as an afterthought, "Mary Kaye returns Friday morning. The invites are already out for the big party Saturday night. You and Señor Gonzalez must come, of course, as several of the guests of honor; and the little Jew, if he makes it."

Fontaine grinned at the news and said, "Thank you, we'd be honored, of course."

"Of course," Toby nodded and Fontaine wasn't sure what he meant.

Willard waved at the two principals and they ran into the Rocks. Toby turned on his heel and, followed by his men, climbed the nearest slope to watch the fight. Linus nudged Fontaine and pointed to the big Negro, who went to the left with the other man, and Fontaine and Linus followed by forty feet and climbed to where they could look down into the arena. Then Willard fired a shot.

The participants, while they rarely saw each other, were usually in sight of someone at the rim. After a few minutes of darting from spire to spire Fontaine decided that he could see each man about half the time, more than he expected.

Suddenly Isaacs took a big chance; he darted across the center opening and dived into the darkness at the north side, followed by two wide shots from the startled Calvin. Then Fontaine saw Isaacs appear to the left of a sandstone boulder and he had Calvin in his sights. The first move and the little man had outflanked his enemy. Fontaine grinned, but only for a moment. Isaacs, with an easy shot, put a slug a foot from Calvin's head and Calvin dived headlong out of sight. Fontaine said "Damn!" under his breath; Isaacs was playing games.

"I could have killed you then!" Isaacs shouted into a wall and Calvin fired four times at the echo.

Isaacs spotted the fire and put another slug perilously close to Calvin's head.

"See?" Isaacs shouted. "I could have killed you again. . . . Getting scared, big brave bully? You will be!"

"Will be! Will be! Will be!" Isaacs' voice echoed throughout the rocks.

Calvin started working his way to his left, directly below Fontaine, reloading as he went, headed toward a cleft in the rear wall. Isaacs darted through the moonlight and got there first and disappeared into the shadows. As Calvin went by, the little man stepped out and put one shot between Calvin's legs and stepped back into the dark. Calvin turned and sprayed all six shots quickly, then turned again, running blindly. The watchers saw Isaacs follow, silently and easily, and step into an alcove where his voice echoed throughout the rocks.

"You're frightened now, aren't you, Calvin?" Isaacs' voice said. "You just might die of fright yet. If I don't maim you first!"

"You little son of a bitch!" Calvin shouted at a boulder. "Come out and let me see you! Fight like a man!"

"Why should I? You never did! Name one good gun hand you killed! Just one!"

Calvin fired a couple of wild shots, cursing, then realized that he should be quiet. When it was silent again, Isaacs' taunting voice came out of the night:

"How about this, Calvin? How about if I let you live, but maybe shatter your hands so you can't use a gun?"

"Fuck you!" Calvin shouted, his voice cracking a bit, then echoing.

"He's playing with him," Linus whispered.

"Dumb bastard!" Fontaine replied. "But he's a gutsy little bastard."

The duel went on for five minutes, Calvin firing three and four times, Isaacs replying with but one well-placed shot close to his enemy. Then Linus touched Fontaine's arm and pointed. The Negro was nodding to the other man who dropped down the hill and ran toward the road.

"Get him!" Fontaine whispered to Linus. "If he pulls his gun, kill 'im!"

Linus returned the nod and slipped down the hill. Fontaine

watched him for a moment and then turned his head the other way; the big Negro was gone. "Bastard!" Fontaine whispered. He slid down into the darkness, cocking the carbine.

At the base of the sandstone he began working his way to the west, glancing up at the rim every few feet. He was almost to the west wall when he saw the outline of the Negro's floppy hat. He grinned tightly, went a few more feet, and began climbing the slope. He moved carefully and kept the carbine pointed at the broad back. During the last ten feet he tested every foothold, breathed slowly and moved slowly. Finally, after what seemed ten minutes but Fontaine knew was less than one, he was within reach. He got a grip on the sandstone wall with his left hand, then shoved the sight of the carbine up into the Negro's crotch.

"Freeze, you bastard!" Fontaine said.

The Negro jerked involuntarily but held his position, the carbine between his buttocks. He also held his pistol steady, pointed down into the arena.

"You white whang!" the Negro whispered. "I've got your little Jew friend in my sights right now. Back off or I kill him!"

"Oh?" Fontaine replied, almost conversationally. "That makes it easy. I told you what would happen."

And he squeezed the trigger. The bullet coursed upward through the Negro's rectum, body, throat, and skull and blew the hat off the already dead man. The sound was muffled and the body dropped with a small shower of pebbles and stopped on its back twenty feet down. Fontaine stared at it coldly, then whispered:

"You son of a bitch, I told you."

Then he turned and dropped down the bank in great strides until he was on the sand; he sprinted back and climbed slowly to his spot on the rim. The men to his right gave no sign, they were engrossed in watching the duel. In a few moments Fontaine heard a muffled shot from the other side, but when the men looked at him he kept his eyes on the arena. Isaacs' shots were increasing in speed, while Calvin was trying desperately to conserve what little ammunition he had left. Isaacs was relentless, pressing his advantage, whispering at the echo spots and keeping the frightened Calvin on the run. Calvin had his hat shot off, one boot heel was gone, and his voice now mumbled in fright. Then there was a slight sound and Fontaine turned his head to see a sweating Linus join him, grinning.

"Kill 'im?" Fontaine asked.

"Had to, right in the face and out the back."

"Good!" Fontaine nodded. "Me too. Up the ass and out the hat!"

"Ooh!" Linus grinned. "But you told 'im."

"That's what I said to him again, but he wouldn't listen," Fontaine complained.

"Jew bastard! Jew bastard!" Calvin shouted.

This time Isaacs didn't reply, vocally. He put a bullet in Calvin's left hand. The gunman cried in pain and retreated toward the west wall. The next shot was between his feet and Calvin screamed as his courage broke; then he turned and ran across the open arena and tried to climb the wall. The spectators gasped. Calvin was completely vulnerable; only a man out of his mind would do such a thing. Isaacs stepped into the open, aimed carefully, holding the .45 in both hands, and shattered Calvin's extended right hand as it clawed the cliff. Calvin's gun flew into the night and the gunman screamed again, stopped and turned, facing Isaacs, but not really seeing him. Then he began to whimper. Isaacs' eyes were wide now, and his face was completely twisted with unleashed rage. Calvin made a motion as if to run toward Isaacs and the next shot tore off his right kneecap and threw him against the cliff. Isaacs fired one more shot, into Calvin's left leg, and the gunman sank to the ground, an insane, whimpering, bloody mass, but alive.

Isaacs took a deep breath, got himself under control, and turned slowly, looking up at the rim. "Well?" he shouted. "Did you get your money's worth?"

The crowd slowly broke up, generally embarrassed by Isaacs' remark. Most decided to ride back to the saloon and recount the night's events, many stopped to congratulate the little man, most just nodded, not knowing if he wanted to be congratulated or not. The barber, who also acted as undertaker, enlisted the aid of two men and tied Calvin's wounds as best they could, and promised to take him to the doctor at Lane City. Fontaine and Linus settled for an exchange of nods and brief smiles with Isaacs and walked him to his horse. When someone remarked that it seemed Calvin had lost his mind, Fontaine turned to watch and saw Toby on his horse pause at the animal to which they were tying Calvin upright and stare a moment, shrug, and ride off, followed by his ten riflemen. Fontaine involuntarily shivered, though it was a warm night. Then the crowd broke up without anyone noticing that Calvin's two men hadn't returned to their horses. Fontaine shrugged at Linus and they mounted their horses.

They rode back to town with Isaacs, bought him a beer at Willard's, then Willard magnanimously bought the second round and Isaacs, who had been almost completely silent, excused himself, saying that he was very tired, and left to go to bed. In a few minutes the barber entered and announced that the great John Wesley Calvin was dead, the last shot had severed an artery in his leg and they were unable to stop the bleeding. Then the man grinned, indicating that he had not tried too hard. Fontaine shook his head and he and Linus left the saloon and headed for Toby's ranch. Linus had one comment:

"At least the little man saved you a nasty chore."

Toby kept himself busy and Fontaine didn't see him until Mary Kaye returned. Toby had ridden to Holbrook to meet her train and Fontaine thought it strange that Toby didn't invite him but, of course, it was really none of his business. He and Linus were sitting on the porch with their feet propped up when the buggy, containing Toby and Mary Kaye and her luggage, came up the drive, escorted by the ten riflemen. Fontaine grinned, pushed his hat off his head and went down the steps to greet her.

She fairly leaped out of the buggy and into his arms, smothering him with kisses. When he put her down she kissed him once more, hard, and with her mouth open, then whispered, "I'll go for a ride after lunch toward the new town. Follow me!"

Fontaine pulled away to look at Lane who was watching them, his eyes narrowed but with a deceptively disarming smile on his face.

"Jonathan?"

"Toby?"

"Ready for the big party?"

"Oh, I wouldn't miss it."

"Good."

Fontaine had saddled his horse before lunch and tied him behind the stables; he sat through a strained lunch with Toby, Mary Kaye, Starrett, who was hobbling about and told Mary Kaye that he had been thrown, and Linus Gonzalez. Mary Kaye chatted gaily about Kansas City and how the town had grown, and about the horsecars on rails and the street lights, and the theater, and the gay restaurants, and the men covered the somehow strained atmosphere by encouraging her. As soon as he had eaten, Fontaine excused himself, saying he had some business in town.

He got his horse, headed for town for a half mile, then circled around and headed for Lane City. He cut her trail a mile short of the town, spotted her a quarter of a mile in front of him and followed slowly. She went past Lane City and on up into the canyon past the place where the dam was to be built and stopped her horse at the base of a cliff. Fontaine tied his horse next to hers and began to climb to a ledge where she stood smiling down at him.

When he got there she threw herself against him and kissed him until he had to pull away to get a breath. She grinned and took the carbine from him and propped it against the wall of the overhanging cliff next to the blanket she had spread in a secluded corner.

"What's that?" he said with a knowing grin.

"That's the blanket on which you're going to make love to me in the full light of day. I want to watch you do it."

"Uh huh. And what if you get pregnant?"

"I'll chance it. I want to see if I'm in love with you."

"Yeah," he said noncommittally. "And I promise I won't marry you!"

"That's all right," she smiled. "I wouldn't mind having your child. Try me."

She pulled away from him with a smile, pushed him against a boulder and turned quickly to the blanket. While he watched she pulled off her boots, her levis, and her shirt and put them in a neat pile. Then she slowly pulled down the straps of her short chemise and stood nude in the sunlight. Undulating slowly she spread her legs slightly, put her hands above her head and began to move faster, until her big breasts were swaying from side to side. Throwing his hat next to his rifle he advanced to the blanket and she knelt quickly in front of him and began tearing at the buttons on his pants.

He had his boots on and was just buttoning his levis when one of their horses whinnied, but more in recognition than fright. He jumped up quickly and grabbed his rifle while she hurriedly dressed. He peered down through the bushes at the horses but could see nothing. Then he heard the slight sound of a horse's shoe click on a stone as it was being led quickly down the narrow canyon. He listened for almost a minute, but heard nothing more, and their horses stood silent again. He turned and put a finger to his lips and she nodded and gathered up the blanket while he put on his shirt and hat.

They made their way very carefully down to the horses and led them out of the canyon and back to the trail alongside the stream, but Fontaine saw no one, nor could he see any tracks, the trail was too rocky.

Toby kept her up late that night, talking in the study, and Fontaine had no chance at her. But then there would be the party the next night.

There was no doubt about it; it was the biggest soirée ever seen in that part of the Territory. Toby had spared no expense, and made sure his guests knew it. Twenty cases of French champagne had been imported from New Orleans, along with four cases of old brandy. For those with more plebian tastes Willard had contracted to supply five barrels of beer and enough whiskey to make every man on the ranch drunk.

Early that morning Toby had six Indians up on the Rim fishing and six more roasting sides of beef in freshly dug pits behind the house. He had his Indian woman and four helpers cooking enough food for a hundred people. The early guests would eat in the afternoon, all would be there for dinner, and most would want breakfast before they started out again in the morning. The brick ovens of the Mexican women were used for baking hams, and lamb saddles, and four kinds of bread, and potatoes and yams. Several vaqueros were busy during the morning setting up tents. Some thirty-five, maybe forty, couples were expected as well as some twenty men. The vaquero bunkhouse was cleaned out, aired of the onion and sweat smell, and curtains were put up for the ladies. When these preparations were finished the vaqueros set up three freshly whitewashed outhouses over newly dug pits and the TL ranch was ready.

By ten in the morning Toby's ten riflemen were also ready, under the direction of a hobbling Leroy Starrett. Two waited at the gate and politely rode in with the arriving guests. One was stationed at the front door of the main house, and the rest roamed the ranch area, seemingly engrossed in ranch business, but all ready to move at a signal from Lane or Starrett. Fontaine had been sitting on the front porch, idly wondering why so much precaution was necessary, when he was joined by Señor Linus Gonzalez, dressed in his Sonora best. As he handed Fontaine a cheroot and held a match he said in a low voice:

"One wonders why so many guns are necessary on such a festive occasion?"

"One may wonder," Fontaine grinned, "when one is a peasant. But when one becomes a monarch one must have enemies and therefore one must be ready."

"Uneasy lies the head . . . ?"

"Something like that," Fontaine replied, his brows creased, wondering at Toby's recently distant, almost baronial attitude.

Though the invitation was for dinner it was the accepted custom for guests to arrive early in the day if circumstances permitted. Fully three quarters of them were there by the noon meal, as Toby had expected. Only those living close would arrive after sundown. They were fed at an outdoor buffet and beer was served all afternoon, punch for the ladies. At five P.M. they retired to clean up, rest, and be ready for the evening's festivities.

The guest list was the upper echelon of eastern Arizona. They were mostly cattlemen and their ladies, a few mining men, a few investors in opportunities, a few bankers and men known to have money, but they were all men of influence from both sides of the Rim. The only guests of no major importance were Fontaine, Gonzalez, Isaacs, and the local banker and several others from Pinyon, and, of course, Leroy Starrett. Dr. Purdy, the only resident of Lane City who was invited, had to decline, his leg injury was acting up.

Fontaine, dressed in his black suit and string tie and clean shirt, courtesy of the Indian woman, came down the stairs at seven thirty accompanied by Linus, dressed to the teeth as a *haciendado*. Most of the men, of course, were dressed in their black suits. The ladies, for the most part, wore high-necked black or navy blue dresses, except for some of the younger ones who wore ball dresses cut low off the shoulder and in various lighter shades. Toby greeted Fontaine with proper cordiality, nothing more, and offered glasses of champagne from a passing tray.

"Toby?" Fontaine said, raising his glass.

"Jonathan?" Lane replied. "Enjoy the party, señor."

"Señor?" Linus replied, raising his glass in salute.

Lane, the host, grinned coldly and went to join his guests.

"You, uh, seem to have a coldness between you and your employer," Linus observed.

"You Mexican, Indian, Negro, white renegades seem to have a faculty for understatement," Fontaine replied.

"Huh!" Linus grinned and sipped his wine. Then he pointed at the stairway.

Mary Kaye, making the grand entrance, appeared in the most spectacular dress of the evening, a maroon, watermarked taffeta dress cut very low, accented with a white sash and white gloves. The women all gasped in envy, the men gasped in pure admiration, slightly laced with lust. Fontaine grinned, for once he agreed with the consensus. Toby came forward, took her arm, and made the rounds, introducing her to the ladies she had not met, renewing acquaintances with those she had, and then to the stag line where she was quickly engulfed. Fontaine had the distinct impression that Toby looked across the room at him and grinned derisively.

"Ever have the feeling you were a hired hand?" Fontaine asked Linus.

"Most of my life, if it's any consolation," came the dry reply.

Starrett joined them and they exchanged grins and then Isaacs came in and was immediately lionized by Toby. He was taken around and introduced to all the out-of-town guests as the brave man who had been forced into a duel with the infamous John Wesley Calvin and had triumphed. Then it was added that Mr. Isaacs was scheduled to be one of the permanent residents of Lane City. Fontaine raised an eyebrow at that one; he hadn't said a word, and he was sure Isaacs had remained silent. Toby must have just decided, not knowing that Isaacs was a bookkeeper.

"That, gentlemen," Leroy said with an admiring sigh, "is what you call turning a bad card into the winning hand. Toby loses the finest hired killer he had and turns it, and the winner, into a matter of civic pride."

"Yes indeed," Fontaine replied, raising his glass to Toby's back. "Whatever one might think of Toby Lane, you must credit him for being the sharpest manipulator of men I've ever known."

"Amen!" Leroy replied, and three glasses were raised.

After everyone had been introduced and all were chatting gaily, thanks largely to the champagne, Toby gave a signal and the woman he'd hired from town began to play waltzes on the pianoforte, accompanied by two freshly scrubbed and shaved cowboys on the violin and guitar. Mary Kaye was instantly beset by the stag line, and those men who brought their own women stiffly did their duty. But Mary Kaye was the standout of the unbranded ladies, though there were several local belles running a close second. Toby stood against the wall with some of the older and more influential guests and beamed; once he beamed Fontaine's way and it turned into a nasty smile. Fontaine returned the same cold smile and tossed off his champagne.

Just before they went in to dinner Toby passed him and said, "I should have some good news for you tonight or tomorrow." Before Fontaine could reply he was gone.

During the lavish meal Toby Lane was king, entertaining the many visiting princes, and the epitome of charm to the ladies. He sat at one end of the long table and Mary Kaye at the other. After dinner the men retired to the living room for brandy and cigars while Mary Kaye took the ladies upstairs. When all his guests were served Toby raised his glass and said in his most charming voice:

"Gentlemen, I give you a toast to a most pleasant evening, and my thanks for your kind acceptance of my invitation."

The brandy was tasted and the cigars were lighted and then Toby added:

"I would not spoil such an evening with business talk but I will get around to seeing all of you within a few days on a subject we have talked of before; a combine. . . . These are not the best of times for some of us. The cattle market is down; the last two winters, particularly those of us with high ranges were hit pretty hard. I am informed that several of the larger British interests in Wyoming and Montana have folded completely. With a European management they are too far away to make decisions with the speed that is necessary for survival. I predict that the British will be largely out of the American cattle market by the end of this winter. . . . Well, I don't need to tell you that this leaves an opening that strong men can control."

He paused to sip his brandy and let them think about it a bit. There was a mumble of assent, but no one would go farther. Fontaine stared at his employer over the rim of his brandy glass and the words "king and empire," flashed through his mind and he nodded to himself; a man with plans like that would, of course, become more distant and arbitrary as he progressed.

"The men in this room," Lane continued, "properly joined together, could control the commerce of eastern Arizona." He paused again for a good five seconds, then said, "We either prosper together . . . or we go down one at a time, the weakest first. . . ."

There was a knock at the door and Lane nodded to his guests and opened the door to the Indian woman and a TL rider. They had a few words and Toby took an envelope from the man, opened it, grinned, thanked the man and closed the door. He crossed the room to Fontaine and handed him the envelope and said in a low voice:

"Here's what you've been waiting for. . . . The party will break up real soon now, they'll want to talk individually and see what the other feller thinks. Wait around and we'll drink up the rest of the champagne in celebration."

Then, doing a complete aboutface, Toby clapped Fontaine on the shoulder and grinned at his friend as he used to. Fontaine raised an eyebrow but he couldn't help returning the grin, at the same time realizing that Toby Lane could charm a bird out of a tree, unless he decided to shoot it.

Lane moved away to chat with a group across the room and Fontaine opened the envelope. The only thing in it was a tintype. It was a posed group of six Indian warriors with lances and rifles; some wore buckskins and some a mixture of castoff Army uniforms. The third one from the left wore a necklace of human fingers. Fontaine kept his face composed, but took a deep breath. He nudged Gonzalez and showed him the picture, and pointed to Iron Shirt. Linus studied the braves closely, then whispered:

"These three are Kiowa, this one might be Cheyenne. I don't know about the end one, could be anything."

"Kiowa?" Fontaine whispered. "Christ! This was taken up north somewhere!"

"Probably. Colorado maybe. You can bet there are no Kiowa close by."

Fontaine forced himself to contain his impatience stoically while the men had another brandy and finished their cigars. Though it seemed hours it was only another ten minutes and then the ladies returned like a group of well-dresssed hens and the entire group chatted some more and then the guests began to say their good nights. When he'd done his duty as a host Toby took a fresh bottle of champagne and two glasses, nodded to Fontaine and they left Gonzalez, Starrett and Isaacs to have another brandy and went into Toby's office. Lane popped the cork, poured the drinks, and picked up the tintype and his glass and said:

"Well, Jonathan, here's to the end of the chase."

Fontaine nodded and they emptied their glasses and Toby refilled them.

"I should drink to your patience, too," Lane said. "Perhaps I should've waited until now to bring out the picture but I knew it was coming tonight, or tomorrow, and I knew you'd want to see it at once. . . . It is Iron Shirt, isn't it?"

"No doubt about that," Fontaine nodded. "But those other bucks look to be Kiowa."

"They are. . . . For some time I've been corresponding with an attorney for a British cattle firm in eastern Colorado trying to get him to come with us. The man writes a beautiful letter and seems to be knowledgeable about buying and selling cattle and the leasing of land and water rights, something I'm not an expert on."

"Oh sure!" Fontaine said with a grin. "You don't know the cattle business!"

"It's not that, Jonathan. It's just that I always bought my land, that way I was sure. But now I've gotten so big I can't afford to buy every piece of land I need, I'll have to buy grazing rights, and water rights, and rights of ingress, and this means corporate law. That's why I need Mr. Estes."

"All right, so what about the tintype?"

"Well, during our correspondence I inquired about the Indian and sure enough he found him . . . took 'im a bit of doing, he had to check with a local chief on one of the nearby reservations but the necklace was quite distinctive, there aren't too many of those."

The little spark of vengeance flared a bit brighter and Fontaine said: "When can I leave?"

"Whoa!" Toby laughed, pouring more champagne. "Don't you wanna know where it is first?"

"Yes," Fontaine said, leaning back in the big leather chair, "I guess I'd better."

"I guess," Toby agreed. "And while you're there, hire Estes. His name's Louis Estes, he's an attorney and he's in Jason, Colorado. Tell him I agree to his terms and give him a thousand dollars as a retainer. Seems he has some debts to pay before he leaves. The firm he was working for went bust, they couldn't survive last winter's storm. . . . Here, I'll get you some money."

Toby drained his glass and went to the safe and started twirling the dial. As he was taking out a metal box there was a brief knock and Mary Kaye entered.

"Excuse me," she smiled, "but Addie Richter is going to spend the night with me, Toby. I haven't seen her in ages and it'll give us a chance to talk. I'm going down to help her with her things."

"All right," Toby said, turning back to the safe, "but don't be long. And don't go near those tents!"

While her uncle's back was turned she raised her shoulders in an apologetic gesture to Fontaine and mouthed the word, "Tomorrow." Aloud she said, "After you poured all that champagne in half the men in the Territory, not on your life!"

She blew a kiss to Fontaine and went out the door and closed it quietly. Toby turned from locking the safe and counted out a stack of bills.

"Here's two thousand dollars. That'll pay Estes and your trip, and anything you need to spend while you're there. If you need more, wire me."

"All right," Fontaine nodded, angered that he'd been cheated out of a night with Mary Kaye. "Now where the hell is Jason, Colorado?"

Toby went to the paneled wall behind his desk and pulled

down a big rolled map of the western United States and
pointed to eastern Colorado.

"Let's see, it's in the east part of the state . . . yeah, here
it is. Jason. Right on the Big Sandy."

"That's a ways," Fontaine said. "I guess I could take the
train to New Mexico and go north from there."

"My dear boy," Toby grinned. "You'll get the train ride
of your life. From there you go north through the Raton Pass
and up through the Royal Gorge. I took it last summer, going
to Denver. It's a spectacular trip, even considering how sore
your ass gets on a train."

"Good," Fontaine raised his glass again. "I get to Jason
and look up this lawyer, and he can point me to the Indian?"

"Right. Get off at Colorado Springs. Buy a horse and go
due east. You can't miss it. . . . Here, the glasses are empty.
. . . *Mujer!*"

Toby emptied the bottle and the Indian woman appeared
with another one in response to his shout. Toby's face was a
bit flushed and he was well on his way to being drunk, something Fontaine hadn't seen. Fontaine was feeling the effects
of the wine but he'd been drinking champagne when he was
eighteen so he decided to match his host drink for drink
and see what would happen. Fontaine told himself he had a
slight edge; while he and Toby had consumed about the same
amount that night, Fontaine had a peculiar faculty of being
able to keep his senses, if not his equilibrium, and be able
to hold his tongue until he passed out. When they were alone
again Toby took a long drink and said:

"Well, Jonathan, assuming the Injun's hidin' out in the best
place in the world for him, with a bunch of Indians, and you
can find him, what'll you do, kill the bastard?"

"Oh," Fontaine replied, "no doubt about that. It's the way
I'll do it."

"Will you cut him up?" Toby asked conversationally.

"Oh no," Fontaine lied, guarding his tongue. "There's nothing I want to ask him, it's just a question of revenge."

"Good, good!" Toby replied, though Fontaine didn't think
he sounded convinced. He finished another glass and fumbled
with the fresh bottle. "I thought you might get some fool
notion to bring him back here to stand trial or something."

"Hell no!" Fontaine said, and shivered slightly. "He's too
tricky. Besides, I figure I can sell you that coat of chain mail

for a thousand dollars. It'd look mighty good over your mantelpiece."

"You son of a bitch!" Toby laughed. "Always out to make a dollar! All right, you bring me the Iron Shirt and I'll pay you . . . plus his scalp."

Toby's last word left no doubt, he wanted the Indian dead.

"And ya know why?" Toby continued, his voice getting a bit thicker. " 'Cause that red-assed son of a bitch killed one of my men and slaughtered my beef, and nobody does that to Tobias Lane, nobody!"

Fontaine nodded, a little more soberly than he was and then he refilled the glasses and decided to change the subject; they'd lied to each other enough about Iron Shirt; power was always a good subject to a man obsessed with it.

"Here's to you, Toby," Fontaine raised his glass. "To a cattleman of the old tradition! A man who knows what he wants! And is willing to . . . work for it!"

"An excellent subject to drink to!" Toby said, showing his inebriation.

They drank another and Fontaine added, "And to a man who worked and sweated for years to build his own city!"

Another toast, some spilled, but glasses were quickly refilled.

"Toby, I gotta give ya credit!" Fontaine said, leaning back in the chair again. "Ya put up a town, ya make all kinds of promises to get people from all over to come to it. . . . Then you start to run outa money and talk to all the cattlemen for miles around about a combine, which they sure as hell don't need this far south, and the beauty of it is, once you get 'em into it, then they'll bring their cattle from over the Rim, and from the east, clear over from New Mexico, to the railhead at guess where? Lane City, that's where! Ha! Goddam, and who owns Lane City? Toby Lane, that's who! Goddam!"

They drank another toast, this one interspersed with drunken laughter, and Toby finally said, "And I'll drink to you, Jonathan! Goddam, I'm glad you're on my side. You know how many men I've had to ruin, and kill, to get where I am? No! Of course not. . . . Jonathan, it's a lonely spot to be sittin' here."

"Shouldn't be," Fontaine said, thickening his voice to match Toby's. "You've got the game won now. The railroad comes in and you've got all the chips. It's . . . it, it is comin' in, isn't it?"

"Whee!" Toby roared in drunken laughter. "Dear old friend, it's comin' in all right, right straight in from Holbrook on the straightest line they could draw, and not straight north, or from Flagstaff, like I put out the rumors. . . . Whee! The shortest place between two lines is a straight point!"

"Wonerful! Wonerful!" Fontaine shouted and joined Toby in laughter. "That'll make you a millionaire and it'll make me a . . . a thousand-aire! . . . And I'm drunk! And I've gotta git up in the mornin' and go chase Indians. Can you imagine a full-grown man in 1888 chasin' Indians?"

Fontaine finished his glass, Toby finished his, then they finished the bottle in one last drink and Fontaine leaned over the desk and stared at Toby with bleary eyes for a moment, waved the empty glass to his drunkenly smiling host, carefully put it on the desk, struggled to his feet and staggered to the door and weaved toward the stairs. As he started up them Toby shouted from the doorway:

"Lookit you, you son of a bitch! You're drunk!"

Then, roaring with laughter he staggered back into the study and slammed the door. Fontaine grinned a little and continued pulling himself up the stairs. When he reached the dark of the landing he suddenly stood erect, stopped weaving and walked steadily and coldly to his room. What Toby had just said answered all his questions, now he had to prove it; if he could get to Iron Shirt.

"Linus?" he said softly as he entered the darkened room.

"I'm awake. Who could sleep with the two loudest drunks in Arizona under his bed?"

"Could you hear it all?"

"Not the words, just the shouting. . . . Hey, you're not as drunk as you sounded."

"No, and if Lane finds out I'm dead, so if anyone asks you I came in drunk."

"Lane?" Linus said in disbelief. "I thought he was your friend."

"Lane has no friends. Just his money and lots of people trying to get at it. . . . Listen, I'm leaving in the morning for Colorado."

"He did find the Indian?"

"Yes," Fontaine said slowly. "Toby said he was found by an attorney I'm to hire for him. Seems he's holed up near a reservation, probably going to spend the winter."

"Uh huh," Linus replied. "You think it's too big a coincidence?"

"Yes. . . . Listen, I'm going anyway. I'll be gone three, maybe four weeks, maybe longer. Knowing where the son of a bitch is is only half of it, trackin' him's like trailin' a ghost."

"I'm as good as any, I'll go with you."

"No," Fontaine said quickly. "You stay here. If I need you I'll send a wire . . . to Beesley. Tell him tomorrow, and keep checking with him. What about the telegrapher in Pinyon? Toby own him?"

"No. He's one who won't leave, so there's no love lost."

"Good. If I wire you to meet me . . . let's see, yeah, meet me at my old place. You know where it is?"

"Yes, four or five miles northeast of here."

"That's right. If I say to meet me, bring plenty of extra horses, four anyway. May not need 'em, but just in case."

"All right. You want me to see you off in the morning?"

"No, you'd better sleep late, or at least stay up here. If I need you I'll yell."

"Good luck," Linus said, rolling over.

"Thank you; I figure I'll need it."

The champagne began to catch up with him and he barely got his clothes off before he fell asleep. He had the dream again, for the first time in months. Only it went rapidly, and in quick flashes of still images, and he wished again for the thousandth time that he'd had sense enough to check the side of his house before he'd stormed in the front door.

There was a slight tap on his door and the Indian woman's voice said:

"Mr. Fontaine? Breakfast."

"Thank you, I'll be right there."

He swallowed hard a couple of times, went to the wash stand and splashed his face, and found his toothbrush and jar of salt and soda. He dressed quickly, checked his carbine, packed only his saddlebags, and went to the privvy. When he came out Linus had his pants on. He was sitting by the window with his rifle. They exchanged silent smiles, shook hands, and Fontaine picked up his gear and went downstairs.

The woman fixed him a quick plate of grits and eggs and several cuts of slab bacon and a big mug of coffee. He ate quickly and asked, "Mr. Lane?"

"Already at the stable."

Fontaine nodded his thanks, finished his coffee, picked up his things and went outside. Toby was nowhere in sight but he saw Leroy Starrett coming out of the stables leading two horses, his own and one for Fontaine. Starrett nodded and tied the two animals to the rail.

"Morning," Fontaine grinned. "Where's Toby?"

"Over to the tents, talkin' to some of the early risers," Starrett answered in a louder voice than usual. Then, lowering his voice to a whisper, he said, "Fiddle with your stirrups. I got a thing to say."

Fontaine nodded and began tying on his saddlebags.

"Listen close," Starrett whispered. "First off, I'm beholden to ya fer what ya done fer me, or I wouldn't be botherin' to tell ya this. And because the girl's got a feelin' fer ya, and she's the only one 'round here ain't spoilt one way or 'tother, either by money or onriness, that I'm goin' agin my boss fer the first time ever to tell ya that yer bein' sent to a killin'; your own."

"What makes you think that?" Fontaine inquired calmly.

"Listen!" Starrett hissed. "Don't go horsin' me around, there ain't time! I wuz sittin' outside on the porch last night and I heerd Lane git drunk enough to tell ya what you're better off not knowin'! Top of that Toby found out about you and the girl. The Injun woman tolt him yesterday afternoon that the two of you come back together and he said don't worry, he knowed all about it and she weren't gonna marry no broke homesteader, even if he did use all them fancy French words!"

"Stirrups are too long," Fontaine said loudly and grinned and started adjusting them. Then he whispered, "Go on, Leroy, there's more."

"That tintype's been here since the day after I got my balls burned. Toby he got two letters that day, both from Colorado. And he got drunk and made the mistake of leavin' 'em lay around and I got a look at 'em. Now I ain't much on letters but I kin read slow and this here second letter wuz from a feller who didn't sign it but he said somethin' like don't worry, the one you spoke about may git to the Injun but ain't neither one of 'em'll ever leave, and that's a promise. . . . Now, ain't that enough?"

"That," Fontaine said, nodding his head once, "should be enough. . . . Thank you, Leroy; you have my word that I'll never repeat what I just heard."

"That goes without sayin'," Starrett grinned. "If I'd a thought otherwise I wouldn't a said a word. Way I figger it, that Injun knows somethin' you wanna know real bad. Enyway, I figger you're all right till you git there, and I figger you're jest oniry enough to go enyway, but I tolt ya."

"You did that," Fontaine grinned. Then the grin faded. "He's sick in the head, Leroy, you know that, don't you? Maybe completely mad."

"Yes," Starrett nodded soberly. "I know. Knowed it fer a long time. Didn't do nothin' about it, hopin' he'd git over it. I even passed killin' that big nigger and Calvin when they wanted to know about the railroad. . . . If he weren't that way, he wouldn't be gittin' rid of ya. You two wuz always friends."

"Yeah," Fontaine said curtly. Then, changing the subject, "Hey! You're not going to ride that thing are you?"

"Christ no!" Starrett grinned. "I'm still so swole up it's awful. I got me padded with an old blanket; jest gonna walk 'im around the stables a bit. Gotta keep loose at my age."

Fontaine nodded, mounted his horse and turned it as Toby rode up and stopped his buckskin with a flourish.

"Well, Jonathan," he grinned, putting out his hand. "All ready?"

"Ready," Fontaine answered, shaking Lane's hand.

"Good luck!" Lane boomed and grinned again.

"Thank you," Fontaine replied with a grin of his own and Leroy Starrett shook his head, wondering if any other two men could be such liars.

As Fontaine got to the end of the stables he turned and waved and the two men waved back; and Linus, holding his rifle, waved from the bedroom window.

Chapter Nine

The main street of Jason, Colorado, was a typical cowtown main street, with two exceptions; it was extremely quiet and it was the cleanest town Fontaine had ever seen. The buildings were all neatly painted, mostly whitewash or red-lead, and the street was smooth and relatively dust-free; there was no trash, and no manure piles. Though it was late afternoon it was very quiet and while there were a few people on the street they hurried about their business with a minimum of noise. Fontaine rode his horse slowly down the street, the carbine hanging casually from his left hand, his eyes roving from side to side.

A man with tattered clothes and chains on his ankles shuffled toward him and Fontaine stared in some wonder; the man was pulling an upright barrel on wheels and in his right hand was a small spade with a four-foot handle. On the other end of the shaft was a sturdy ten-inch spike. But it wasn't the fact that the man was a prisoner doing the town's clean-up duty that made Fontaine stare; it was the fact that the man's face was beaten to a lumpy purple. Both eyes were black and his mouth was so swollen it was doubtful if it would ever be the same. He paused briefly and looked up; his mouth moved but Fontaine couldn't tell if it was a smile or not. Fontaine nodded, the man nodded, and each moved on.

On his left was the blacksmith and livery stable. The smith was in front of his establishment sweating an iron rim onto a buggy wheel. He paused as Fontaine stopped, looked up and smiled. Fontaine returned the smile and said, "Can you put 'im up?"

"Yes sir."

"Good. I'll be back."

Fontaine rode on to the general store in the middle of town, which was across the street from the saloon, and turned into the hitching rack and tied his horse next to a heavily loaded pack mule. He untied his saddlebags and looked at the storekeeper and a little Mexican standing in the doorway. The merchant smiled and said, "How'd do?"

As Fontaine went around behind the mule he almost tripped on a small, shaggy dog. Fontaine grinned and leaned over to pet the animal and the old Mexican scurried down the steps and quickly scooped the dog into his arms and pulled his hat from his head.

"Your pardon, señor, the dog did not see you."

"That's all right," Fontaine grinned, "I didn't see him, either. What's his name?"

"Don Benito Juarez."

"Well, Señor Juarez," Fontaine said, taking the dog's paw, "happy to make your acquaintance. My name's Fontaine."

"And we are happy to know you, señor. I am Adolpho Gomez."

"You're a little far from home, aren't you?" Fontaine inquired.

"Sì, señor," Gomez smiled. "We are returning to Sonora from Montana. Don Benito, as you can see, is very old and we would spend our last winters at home."

"Well, have a good trip."

They exchanged nods and Fontaine entered the store and took a deep breath of all the pungent odors that made up a general store; flour and leather goods, sugar and coffee, gunpowder, tea, and the musty, damp smell of the freshly mopped wooden floor.

"Afternoon," the storekeeper said.

"I need some cigars. . . . Yes, those cheroots there. How much for the box?"

"They're ten cents but, by the box, four dollars."

"Good. I'll take the box." Fontaine fished in his shirt pocket and brought out a sheaf of bills. "By the way, I'm looking for a lawyer man, named Estes. You happen to know him?"

"Oh yes sir!" the man grinned. "You must be the man he's expecting!"

"Great!" Fontaine said under his breath. Aloud he said, "Yes, I'm the one."

"Well, sir, he should be at his house this time of day, other end of town, but he always comes up for a drink."

"Good. I'll go have a beer and wait a bit."

"I'm sure he'll be along. If he doesn't come in a few minutes I'll have my boy get 'im."

"Thank you kindly," Fontaine replied.

He went outside, smiled at the old Mexican who was shifting

the load on the mule after purchasing his supplies and stopped to put the cheroots in his bag, put four in his pocket, and headed for the saloon. Except for the bartender the saloon was empty. Like the rest of the town, the place was spotless, right down to the shiny brass gaboons. Fontaine stepped to the bar, put down the carbine and the saddlebags and nodded to the fat, jolly man.

"Yes, sir!" the bartender beamed. "What's your pleasure?"

"Beer."

Fontaine put down a dime and took a long drink from the big schooner. "Sure is quiet," he said.

"Sure is," came the noncommittal answer.

"Uh huh," Fontaine agreed. "Say, your town's right on the edge of the reservation yet I never saw a single Indian. How come?"

"New law. Mayor's orders."

"Oh? I thought you did a lot of trading with the Indians."

"Used to. No more. . . . We got taxes now, and no Injuns. Mayor's out to make Jason the cleanest town in the state."

"Quietest, too."

"Yeah, if it gets any worse . . ."

The man's voice trailed off as a burly man in an eastern suit and a derby walked in. On his chest was a star and he wore a revolver tied very low. He smiled affably and stopped at the bar. The bartender put a bottle and a shot glass in front of the man and poured a quick drink. The man tossed it off, put down the glass and came to Fontaine, his hand outstretched.

"Hello, my name's Bryan. I'm the tax collector, also deputy mayor."

"Fontaine. And the town marshal?"

"In a way," Bryan chuckled. "But we hardly need a full-time marshal in Jason. You see, we've got a clean, peaceful town. Long as it stays that way, no need. . . . By the way, Mr., er, Fontaine. We've got a two-dollar firearm tax."

"I see," Fontaine said, reaching into his shirt pocket.

"Or you can check it at the jail and pick it up on the way out, that way there's no charge."

"Uhh, I'd just as soon pay," Fontaine said.

"As you wish," Bryan nodded. He took a small receipt book from his pocket, scribbled on it, tore the bottom half off and gave it to Fontaine and pocketed the two dollars. "Thank you.

A good city treasury is the key to a good city. Well, enjoy your stay."

"Thank you."

Bryan nodded again and strolled out the door. Just as Fontaine was finishing his beer the swinging doors opened again and a tall, paunchy man in his mid-fifties entered quickly. He had a red face and his hands shook badly. His once handsome alpaca suit was now worn and shiny and the man needed a shave. The bartender quickly put a bottle and glass in front of him and poured a shot and waited. The man tossed it off quickly, put the glass down and the bartender refilled it. The man drank this one in two sips, licked his lips and put down the glass and sighed.

"Ahh! Nothing like the hair of the dog." He paid for his two shots, put some more money down and indicated another one, and inclined his head toward Fontaine's beer. Picking up his glass he came, hand outstretched. "And you, if I'm not mistaken, must be Mr. Fontaine? Louis Estes, sir, at your service."

Fontaine shook the man's hand and, though he smiled, he thought to himself that Toby didn't know what he was buying this time. "Mr. Estes?"

"I've already taken the liberty of buying you a beer, Mr. Fontaine. Shall we take a table?"

Estes picked up Fontaine's refilled glass and they sat in the corner. Estes raised his glass and said, "Your health, sir!" and tossed off his third shot. "Well now!" he said with a friendly smile. "Now that I've recovered from my bout with John Barleycorn, shall we get down to business? That is, if you still want to do business, now that you've seen me."

"And why shouldn't I?" Fontaine inquired.

"Well sir, because, admittedly, I do not look like the paragon of the corporate lawyer, and I'll be the first to admit it. I've been drinking too much of late, now that I've sunk from being the attorney to a cattle empire that has gone out of business to practicing law in a town that needs no lawyer. But I am not yet a drunk, sir, nor is my mind so befuddled with drink that I cannot yet read the most involved document."

"Whoa!" Fontaine grinned, holding up his hand. "I am sure that Mr. Lane checked your background before he made you an offer. Assuming you're ready to leave, my job is a simple one; I pay you the thousand-dollar-advance agreed upon, get a receipt and put you on the stage."

"And then see to your Indian, I suppose? As you no doubt know, Mr. Lane mentioned in one of his letters your interest in the Indian with the necklace of . . . uh, human fingers, and to help my cause with your employer, I got one of the tintypes your Indian posed for."

"Do you, uh, happen to know where he is now?" Fontaine asked casually.

"Yes, generally speaking, that is. And my compliments sir, you posed the question casually, and without a show of eagerness . . . and after coming all this way."

Fontaine chuckled and took out a cheroot, offered one to Estes which was declined with a wave of the hand, and took out a match as he bit the end off.

"I've learned to be patient, Mr. Estes. What does generally speaking mean?"

"It means that he's at the far end of the reservation which is some fifty odd miles on a side. You've narrowed it down, Mr. Fontaine, to some twenty-five hundred square miles. . . . Now, I don't mean that as a cause for dismay, I merely meant to show you that your bird has not yet come to ground. However—and that brings me to several points—I may be in a position to help you and at the same time I owe you an apology."

"Oh oh!" Fontaine smiled. "I think I've got a problem."

"Not at all, sir," Estes said with a smile of his own. "I think we can be of mutual assistance. Hear me out."

"All right, speak."

"Thank you. First, as to the apology. I must confess that I have talked you up to my friends and local citizens as a marshal for hire. . . . Wait, sir, let me finish, please. Thank you. Well, I did, and I promised them to try and enlist your aid in helping us clean up the town. . . ."

"Hey now! This is the cleanest cowtown I've ever been in!"

"Physically yes; morally, sir, it's rotten to the core. . . . Say, I'm going to talk quite a bit and it's dry work. Let me buy you another."

"My turn," Fontaine said, holding up his hand to the barkeep and putting some coins on the table. "And you're going to have to talk a lot to keep me from my two chores; get you hired and chase that Indian."

"Let me, uh, put this delicately, Mr. Fontaine. Help us with the town and I can help you find the Indian. I know the local chief of the Cheyenne, Broken Hand, quite well, and he can locate your redskin in less than a day."

"Uh huh," Fontaine grinned. "This smacks of blackmail. And from an attorney."

"Heavens no, sir!" Estes protested. "It's more of a barter. Help me and I can help you."

"All right," Fontaine nodded, picking up his fresh glass and nodding to the bartender who scooped up some change and returned to his bar. "I'll listen. Talk."

"A practical approach, sir," Estes nodded, sipping his whiskey this time. "All right, you've noticed how quiet our town is? Well, quiet is not the word, no sir. Frightened is the word. We have an ambitious mayor who is taxing us out of existence. As a result, there is no new business. Our trade with the Indians has been stopped and there has been talk of an uprising or, at least, raids. And this is 1888, sir! In any event, some people have already left town. . . . Our esteemed mayor, and his noble assistant, whom I presume you just met, are looting the town."

"Don't you have a town council? Can't they do something?"

"Yes, we have one. No, we can't do a thing! Six months ago Jason was a sight. Dirty, lawless, a woman wasn't safe on the streets and we had no money in the treasury to hire a marshal. . . . Alas, we were ripe for most anything when 'His Honor' came to town and said if we'd back him for mayor he'd clean up the town."

"It's clean, isn't it?"

"Certainly! He cleaned it right into his pocket. He smooth-talked us into it and then he got us to sign a bunch of laws and the first thing we knew he brought Bryan in and the town council was powerless."

"Is it legal?"

"Absolutely. He's too good a politician for that."

"Was, uh, part of your problem the fact that the council didn't pay attention to business, and let the mayor have his way?"

"Ah ha!" Estes smiled and banged the table. "I see you're a student of history, sir. And, of course, Bryan is the weapon."

"Seems nice enough," Fontaine observed, but not believing it.

"Oh, he is! Right up to the time he kills someone. Four men in the last five months. It's called resisting arrest. Two were pistol-whipped to death."

"My!" Fontaine exclaimed mildly. "But it doesn't make too much sense. If they run the town into the ground that's sorta like killing the golden goose, isn't it?"

"In a way, yes," Estes admitted. "But there are bigger things at stake. If the mayor looks good here, he's a cinch to be appointed to the governor's staff, and that's where the real money is. . . . And that's the reason for the cleanup; no dogs allowed, no Indians, and the governor comes here Saturday and His Honor wants us to look our best."

"Well, if he gets appointed and leaves, that's what you want, isn't it?"

"Unfortunately, the appointment wouldn't be effective until the first of the year. By that time we'd all be broke. . . . Mr. Fontaine, that's why we need help. Most of these good people don't want to leave their homes . . . that's why we need you."

"I think you've got me confused with someone else, Mr. Estes. I've never sold my gun and I don't intend to start now. Sorry."

"You don't understand, sir," Estes protested. "We only need to get Bryan out of town through Saturday, then we can talk to the governor ourselves. We mean no violence."

"No," Fontaine said caustically, getting to his feet. "Just abduction with force, that's all. You'd be breaking the law yourselves, Mr. Estes. No, thank you. Besides, the mayor would just get himself another tax collector in a hurry, that's all. . . . Mr. Estes, I'm going to see to my horse, get myself a room and something to eat, and spend the night. If you still want Lane's offer tomorrow I'll be happy to talk to you. If not, I'm going to that reservation and look up the chief myself. . . . I thank you for the beer."

Fontaine put his saddlebag over his shoulder, picked up his carbine, nodded politely, and went through the swinging doors. He crossed the street to his horse, the lawyer hobbling along a few feet behind, and was reaching for the reins when he heard Bryan shout:

"Hey you!"

Fontaine turned to see Bryan come up to the old Mexican and his little dog as they were approaching the mule.

"Dogs are not allowed in the city limits!" Bryan said.

"I did not know, señor," Gomez replied, pulling off his hat. "We will leave."

"Not before you pay the fine."

"Fine, señor?"

"Five dollars and you can leave. In fact, I'll see you out myself."

"But, señor, I do not have five dollars."

Fontaine slipped his carbine into the boot and turned from his horse and stepped around the mule and said to Bryan, "I'll pay his fine."

"No, you won't," Bryan said, his voice now nasty as he poked the old man in the chest with his finger. "It's his dog. He'll pay the fine."

"Come on," Fontaine said, reaching for his shirt pocket, "he's an old man."

"How about you?" Bryan said, turning to face Fontaine, his coat pulled clear from his gun. "You're more my age."

"Please, señor," Gomez said, "I will get the money."

He put his hand on Bryan's gun arm and the collector flung him away and stepped to his left. As he did so he stepped on the little dog and it yiped once, then growled and nipped at Bryan's boot. With the smooth motion of long practice Bryan's gun flashed out of its holster and he shot the little dog in the chest. The impact flung it on its back a few feet away, dead. Keeping the gun pointed at the ground Bryan turned to face Fontaine who was very careful to stay very still. Not so little Gomez; he ran to his dog with a cry, the tears streaming down his cheeks, and picked up the little animal and rocked it in his arms.

"Well?" Bryan said to Fontaine.

Keeping his eyes on Bryan, Fontaine called over his shoulder, "Was that legal, Mr. Estes?"

"Unfortunately, yes."

"Well," Fontaine shrugged, his face calm, "can't argue with the law."

"Very sensible," Bryan grinned, putting his gun away. To Gomez he said, "We got a vagrancy law, too, so if you ain't employed by tomorrow, or outa town, you'll do thirty days, makin' little ones outa big ones. . . . You seem to be a man of property, Mr. Fontaine, so that, of course, doesn't apply to you."

Fontaine nodded and Bryan spun on his heel and strolled

up the street and Gomez stood up and said through his tears:

"I saw a little hill at the edge of town. Would it be permitted to bury him there?"

"Of course," Estes said gently.

As Gomez pulled a spade from his mule pack Fontaine turned to Estes, his eyes narrowed and said, "Is the smith in with your group?"

"He is."

"Señor Gomez," Fontaine said. "I'll take your mule to the livery. When you're through, come there."

The little man nodded his thanks and turned away. Fontaine rubbed the back of his hand across his nose, sniffed, and grabbed Estes by the arm. "Come on, lawyer, I don't think we finished our talk!"

Sometime after midnight two horsemen rode out of the back of the livery stable, around the corral to the west, swung a wide loop around the town and headed north. Once Fontaine thought that they were being followed and put a finger to his lips and they paused to listen. Then Estes pointed ahead and whispered, "Hardpan," and they took their horses across it at a canter. The hooves made a sound like running across a wooden bridge. They ran another forty yards and pulled up to listen. Nothing but the labored breathing of the horses. Once Fontaine thought he heard something but the animals gave no indication, so they rode on although they changed their route several times during the night.

As they came over a hill and started to drop down toward the river the sun came over the horizon somewhere in eastern Kansas and they paused a moment to let the horses rest, but the animals, snorting at the smell of water, wanted to continue. Fontaine held his animal a moment and said, "We got company."

"Where?"

"There's a buck behind those bushes, over there," Fontaine said, pointing.

The brave rode out in front of them, blocking the trail, a rifle across his thighs.

"Well!" Estes sighed in relief. "No warpaint."

"So?" Fontaine said dryly. "Paint's for war. They can kill without it."

Fontaine held up his right hand and the brave put up his and rode closer.

"You speak English?" Fontaine asked.

The brave grunted and shook his head.

"Español?"

"Poco," the brave replied.

"Bueno! El jefe?"

This drew a blank stare. Fontaine held out his left hand and hit it with the heel of his right hand and said, *"La mano."*

The brave grunted and pointed to a bend in the river several miles away, turned and disappeared.

"Come on," Fontaine said to Estes. "We're invited in to set a spell."

"I'm still not sure," Estes said, nudging his horse to catch up with Fontaine's. "I think maybe you're more interested in your Indian than our problem."

"Why you legal fraud!" Fontaine laughed. "Of course I am. Just as you're more interested in your town than me! It was you who stated the proposition that we can help each other. Now, counselor, use your logic. . . . I can't do what I propose alone. Then it follows that I need help. Are you any good with a gun? Would you use one if you had to? By your own admission, probably not. Your blacksmith, a physical giant, but a gentle man, he wouldn't want to hurt anyone. Bly, the storekeeper; the other merchants? No. . . . So, obviously I need help. And it seems your Indian friend can help both of us."

"All right!" Estes laughingly agreed. "You sure you're not an attorney?"

"Nope, I'm not devious enough."

Several bucks appeared at the edge of camp and rode with them along the river as an escort. They rode the length of the village, their horses skittish at being nipped by the many varieties of Indian dogs.

"See?" Fontaine grinned, indicating the dogs.

"I certainly do. Say, there's something I should've told you about Broken Hand."

Estes stopped talking as they reined up in front of a large teepee and a handsome Indian in levis, a buckskin jacket, and a black stetson like Fontaine's came through the flap and stared at the two white men. Fontaine held up his right hand and said, "How, chief?"

Broken Hand stared at them impassively for a moment, then his face split into a grin and he laughed and came to Fontaine and put out his hand. Fontaine took it in a firm grip, his brows creased at the chief's sudden humor.

"Pardon me for laughing," Hand said in perfect English, "but it's always a source of some amusement that the white man never seems to think that an Indian might speak English. . . . Lou Estes, it's nice to see you. How've you been?"

"Fine, John, fine," Estes said, dismounting and coming forward to shake hands. "John, this is my friend, Jonathan Fontaine."

"Mr. Fontaine," Hand said, "step down and enjoy our hospitality. If you're Estes's friend and he thought enough of you to bring you all the way out here, you are indeed welcome."

"Thank you," Fontaine said as he dismounted and handed the reins to a waiting boy. "As to the English, yes; I've come across many Indians who could speak it, but never like a college professor! You know, there was something Estes was going to tell me about you. Now I know what it was."

"I went to a Methodist missionary school, Mr. Fontaine. My father was chief before me, and a very astute man. He told me that if we were to survive we would have to learn the white man's ways. He sold almost everything he owned to send me to the East to school. . . . I returned almost too late, there aren't many left."

"You don't seem particularly bitter about it," Fontaine observed.

"No, things happen," Hand said quietly. Then he smiled and changed the subject. "Well, you must be hungry after your long ride. Eat, rest, then we will talk."

"Mr. Fontaine?"

Fontaine opened his eyes, pushed his hat back from the bridge of his nose, and raised up from his saddle, which he had been using as a pillow, and smiled at his host.

"Hi!" Fontaine grinned at Hand. "Sorry, I must have dozed off."

"Umm," Hand agreed. "Like three hours. But I take that as

a compliment. Most white men wouldn't dare close their eyes in an Indian camp."

"I learned a long time ago, Mr. Hand," Fontaine said, getting to his feet, "that a Cheyenne might kill you, but he won't lie to you. And we were welcomed as guests. . . . And that puts you one up on the white man."

"Yes, I think so," Hand nodded, indicating that they should stroll through the village. "And we thank you, though most of my people wouldn't understand you, but if they see you with me they won't be so inclined to be wary. . . . Estes has told me both reasons for your coming to see me. As to your wanting to talk to Iron Shirt—and I mean talk—if I arrange for you to see him you must be unarmed . . . yes, I will do that. I know Iron Shirt is a renegade and has thrown what you call a wide loop, still he is, or was, a war chief of the Cheyenne and as such he has the respect of some of my men, so I cannot chance your killing him."

"I agree," Fontaine grinned, "if you think it's safe. As to my killing him, I'm flattered that you might think I could, but I only want to talk to him. He has some information I must know."

"Good. I have already sent one of my young men to locate him. Whether he will tell you what you want to know, I cannot say. As to your questioning Iron Shirt, I, uh, presume it's about the incident of two years ago?"

"Huh?" Fontaine looked startled. "You know?"

"Not all of it," Hand replied. "But when Estes made inquiries on behalf of a man in Arizona I made it my business to see Iron Shirt. As chief it's my duty; we have enough problems without Indians adding to them. . . . Iron Shirt told me, and I believe him, that he had no part of the rape or murder, he insists that he was hired to run off a rustler."

"And why do you believe him?"

"Because he is a Cheyenne war chief."

"Uh huh," Fontaine nodded, not completely convinced.

"As to helping you with Bryan, Mr. Fontaine, that's out of the question."

"Well," Fontaine smiled, "frankly I don't care. I want to see Iron Shirt. But I promised Estes I would do what I could to get your help. Estes told you the idea?"

"Yes," Hand's face broke into a rare smile. "And I think

it's excellent. But it's out of the question, I can't risk it. Should I, or any of my braves, be killed or put in jail by Bryan the rest would put on paint."

"Uh huh," Fontaine said. "Consider this. You're facing a revolt of your people anyway, as I see it. Your people survive by doing business in town, plus what the government gives you. Now Bryan has cut you off. Soon your braves will run wild. Then the government will cut you off. Then what?"

"You do, indeed, have a point, Mr. Fontaine," Hand nodded.

"Add this to the proposition," Fontaine said. "If we do it with you and me and two or three others, Bryan just might shoot, but if fifty braves show up, or sixty, or eighty, and just before the governor is due to arrive, Bryan will not be so stupid as to shoot. . . . And, I'll add this as a promise: if Bryan shoots one of your men I will see to it that he stands trial. And I would almost like him to try me! Did Estes tell you what that son of a bitch did to that poor old Mexican's dog? The dirty bastard shot 'im down, and he enjoyed it!"

"Easy, Mr. Fontaine!" Hand said. "I appreciate your feelings for the old man, it shows you have some compassion. As to your feeling for the dog . . . well, Indians are different, we eat them."

"I know," Fontaine nodded. "But you don't shoot 'em down for sport."

Hand nodded and considered Fontaine's words. Fontaine, knowing the dangers of overselling, remained quiet. They strolled the length of the village and down to the river in silence. Finally Hand smiled, just a little. Fontaine kept his face impassive. Hand chuckled, then started laughing loudly.

"It would, indeed, be a pleasure, Mr. Fontaine, to see the look on that white bastard's face, no offense, mind you. . . . All right, we'll do it. It's a damn sight better than starving this winter!"

"Good!" Fontaine grinned as they shook hands. "Let's get Estes back to town, it'll be a long trip back with three wagons."

As they returned to Hand's teepee a brave rode up with a message. Hand nodded and turned to Fontaine. "Iron Shirt will meet us at the big tree. That's ten miles or so up the river."

"When?"

"Whenever we get there," Hand shrugged.

"He's trailing us," Hand said as they got within sight of the tree.

"How do you know?"

"I know."

In a few moments Fontaine heard a horse and turned to see Iron Shirt walking his pinto fifty feet behind them, holding a rifle.

"He's just escorting us," Hand said.

"Sure," Fontaine replied and shivered.

They dismounted at the tree and Hand spread a blanket in the shade, opened a saddlebag and took out some dried meat and corn and cigars.

"Jerked horse," Hand said with a slight grin. "You'll like it."

"Uh huh. Better'n dog, I guess."

Iron Shirt came forward and sat on the blanket, the rifle next to him, and they ate in silence. Then Hand passed cigars and matches. When they had smoked in silence for several minutes Hand said to Fontaine, "Now."

Instead of talking at once Fontaine studied the end of his cigar for a bit, recrossed his legs, slowly scratched his arm, finally looked at Iron Shirt and said:

"Do you know why I am here?"

"Maybe to kill?" Iron Shirt answered in English before Hand could translate.

"No," Fontaine replied. "Though I would have killed you once."

"You killed the Mexican."

"Yes," Fontaine admitted.

"It is said you killed him like an Indian. It is said you skinned him."

"Is that right?" Hand asked in spite of himself.

"Yes."

"Well now," Hand said with a bit of sarcasm, "which one of you is the savage?"

"Bullshit!" Fontaine said. "That Mexican was raping my daughter. After the fire I found her with her throat cut."

"I'm sorry," Hand said. "I would have done the same."

"I came," Fontaine said to Iron Shirt, "to learn the name of the other man."

"You saw only me and the Mexican," Iron Shirt said, avoiding the question. "I did not know he would do that thing. Cheyenne warriors do not rape children."

"I am told that Cheyenne warriors do not lie," Fontaine said carefully. "Tell me the name of the other man, the one who hit me on the head."

Iron Shirt did not answer, but puffed his cigar. Fontaine leaned forward and stared intently at the Indian.

"Was it Tobias Lane?" he said in very carefully spaced words.

The Indian played with his cigar some more, his face impassive, while Fontaine studied his chances of rushing the rifle and beating it out of him. Finally Iron Shirt looked at Fontaine and nodded and said:

"Yes, it was Tobias Lane . . . but you knew. Why did you come this many days to ask me to tell you what you knew?"

"Because in the white man's way we have to prove it. Now, you have admitted it and there was a witness, you also told Broken Hand."

Fontaine took a long breath and leaned back. Though protocol wouldn't allow him to smile he squinted his eyes at the pleasurable thought of telling Toby and then cutting his throat. To Iron Shirt he said:

"Because you spoke the truth I will tell you a thing. Lane has sent you here, you may not know it, but he did; this was the only place you could hide for long. If you leave he will have you killed."

"He will not," Iron Shirt said in disbelief.

Fontaine reached into his shirt and pulled out the folded copy of the wanted poster and gave it to Hand.

"Do you believe Broken Hand speaks the truth?" Fontaine said.

"He does," Iron Shirt allowed.

"Then he will tell you that this paper offers fifteen hundred dollars gold for your death!"

Hand read it, nodded and said, "It does."

"Why do you tell me this?" Iron Shirt asked.

"So you will know that if you leave this place you will be killed. Lane used you like he used me. He wanted me burned out so he could get my land. It was on the railroad right of way. He had to have it for his town. . . . You, he dishonored. You are a killer among your own people and a dead man among the whites. Your friend Lane did this to you!"

There was a long silence, then Iron Shirt nodded and said:

"Yes, you speak truly. He told me that you were one who stole his cattle. I took his money, I needed a new rifle and a horse, I did not want to steal, the white man has laws about stealing I do not understand. . . ."

"Now you know he used you," Fontaine said carefully, making his points one at a time to be sure the Indian got his message. "And should you return to Arizona he will pay for your body. Now, make sure you know my words; after I got the Mexican you were only kept alive to get me back, for Lane knew that as soon as the railroad went through my property I would know what he had done and I would come back to kill him, if I lived that long. Instead he used you to get me back from the East to get some bulls for him. He used you as bait, like in fishing?"

Iron Shirt nodded that he understood and Fontaine nodded and continued.

"All right. Then he sent me to many places, because I thought he was my friend, and every place I went men had heard of the Mexican and how I killed him. . . . You are the same now. Wherever you go, Lane will have someone waiting to kill you. Lane has ordered your death!"

The Indian thought about this for a while, then turned to Hand.

"Do you believe this white man?"

"Yes. He speaks truly."

"Why did you not try to kill me?" Iron Shirt asked Fontaine. "You are a brave man. No one would deny your right to my scalp. Then take it to Lane for the money?"

"I don't want you. I want Lane. And it's not your scalp. It is the iron shirt he wants, to hang on his lodgepole."

"No! I have taken a sacred oath. The shirt only comes off when I die. . . . If Lane dies first will the money be paid?"

"No," Fontaine replied, forcing himself to keep a straight face. "The offer, the bargain, dies with him."

"That is good," Iron Shirt said, getting to his feet. "Do not try to follow me, white man, or I will kill you."

"Where do you go?" Fontaine asked hopefully.

"To kill Lane. Unless you give your word not to follow I will take horses."

"Tell you what," Fontaine said, getting to his feet. "I have business in Jason that will take until tomorrow. How's that?"

"Your word, Broken Hand?" Iron Shirt asked.

"My word," Hand nodded.

"Good, it is time enough. With even your iron horse you cannot stop me."

With that, Iron Shirt turned, vaulted on his pony and disappeared in the brush. Hand got to his feet and started folding the blanket.

"You know," Hand said, "I think he's right. He's probably got a good six ponies nearby. He'll run each one to death in turn, eat a haunch, and keep going. You can't possibly catch him, even if you got a through train from Colorado Springs and went nonstop."

"Yeah, guess you're right," Fontaine grinned.

They had ridden but a quarter mile back toward the village when Hand stopped his horse and looked at the trail. "We've had company."

"What's that mean?"

"You white men," Hand grinned, shaking his head. "You can't read the simplest trail. Look. Tracks over ours, both ways, and the same horse. He must have been good to get that close to Iron Shirt."

"Indian?"

"Hardly. The horse was shod."

"My!" Fontaine said, raising an eyebrow. "Make some inquiries, will you?"

"You think he might have been on you, instead of Iron Shirt?"

"Oh, absolutely. I didn't tell you, somebody in town works for Lane. That's why I gave the Indian a start, no point trailin' with somebody on my ass!"

"Who is it?"

"Don't know. I'd like to think it's Bryan."

"I will inquire."

It was five o'clock Saturday morning. Fontaine, Estes, and Bly were waiting in his store for Hand. It had been arranged that Hand would come in early, make sure nothing had changed, then ride back for his men who would be on the way with the wagons. It was still dark and Bly had the two lanterns burning. Bly was at the front door, watching the street, Estes was in the storeroom, waiting at the back door. Fontaine

was standing behind the counter passing the time by trying on
Bly's supply of hats. His own was hanging down his back
while he selected from a big pile in front of him. From time to
time Bly would turn nervously from the door and Fontaine
would smile reassuringly. After ten long minutes there was a
sound in the back room and Fontaine turned to look, but
stayed by the hats. In a moment Hand entered, followed by
Estes, and shook hands with Bly, and grinned at Fontaine:

"I saw Bryan on the street so I took the long way around.
Everything set?"

"Ready to go," Fontaine nodded. "How's your end?"

"They're on the way. Should be here by eight."

"Good," Fontaine nodded. "Governor's still due at nine,
and—"

There was a pounding on the door and Bryan's bull-like
voice shouted: "Bly! Open up! The mayor's with me, open
up or I'll kick it in!"

Fontaine nodded his head toward the back room and Hand
and Estes disappeared, closing the door behind them. "Open
up, Mr. Bly."

"But . . ."

"Open it," Fontaine said quietly. "It's all right."

Bly opened the door and Bryan burst in, his gun drawn.
When he saw no one but Fontaine and Bly he put his gun
away and nodded and the mayor entered, a pale, pudgy little
man in a fancy suit and a derby.

"All right!" Bryan demanded of Fontaine. "Where the hell
is he?"

"Where the hell is who?" Fontaine replied mildly, not
moving.

"That goddam Injun, that's who! I know he's here some-
wheres. Bring 'im out! I seen two Injun ponies out back. Now
you bring 'im out or I start shootin'!"

"You can't do that," Fontaine replied. "It's illegal."

"It's also illegal fer an Injun to be in the city limits! Now,
Mr. Gunslick, you bring 'im out or I'll fill that back room with
slugs. He cain't get out, I got a man out back!"

"That's right," His Honor said in a squeaky voice. "Violates
an ordinance."

"Hand!" Fontaine called. "Come out. Bryan, start shooting
and you'll start an Indian war and half the town will get
killed."

"That's right," Hand said from the doorway. "You don't seem to realize what my friends in Washington would say if they'd hear about this."

"Maybe," the mayor said, "we might be a bit hasty."

"You don't understand, Your Honor," Bryan smirked. "It's for his own protection!"

"I don't think I'd try to detain him," Fontaine said.

Bryan whirled to Fontaine, his hand on his gun. "Who's gonna try to stop me?"

"Me," Fontaine nodded. "Now, Your Honor, come here. Pick up this hat, Mayor."

The mayor stared at Fontaine, then at Bryan, sweat popping out on his brow.

"Come on, God damn it!" Fontaine shouted. "Pick up the hat!"

The mayor sidled forward, making sure he was out of Bryan's line of fire, and gingerly picked up a huge straw hat, revealing the carbine pointed steadily at Bryan's belt.

"Call the other one in," Fontaine said to Bryan.

"Come in, Lucius!"

The storeroom door opened and a bearded man in buckskins entered, his gun hanging loosely. Hand quickly grabbed it and Fontaine went behind him, paused at the door and said:

"Bye. It's been a pleasure. I'll leave the gun out here."

With that he slammed the door and Hand pulled several boxes in the way and they ran out the back door, vaulted on their ponies, and raced down the back street. As they cleared the town and headed north Hand leaned close and said:

"Say, I meant to tell you. One of my braves saw Lucius near camp yesterday."

"Yeah, I figured. . . . Say, you got any friends in Washington?"

"Just a couple of crooked Indian Agents!"

At eight o'clock the town was ready. Every store was open, clean and neat, awaiting the governor's arrival. Bryan was everywhere, making sure the town was ready. Some of the local citizens saw the three wagons coming but, of course, no one told Bryan, they merely made sure their women were off the street. Fontaine and Hand pulled their wagon to a halt at the north end of the street and Fontaine jumped down.

From the interior of the wagon came a wild assortment of grunts, howls, barks, and an occasional grunt from an Indian.

"Wait for my signal," Fontaine said and Hand nodded.

Fontaine walked down the street, his eyes darting from side to side, but all he saw were local citizens, nodding pleasantly at him. Right on schedule the mayor and Estes appeared from the other end of the street. Estes had a firm grip on the little man's elbow. Estes stopped the mayor in front of the council office and the rest of the members of the council came outside and waited silently until Fontaine joined them. He exchanged nods with them and said to the mayor:

"Your Honor, it's time you resigned."

"What do you mean, sir? You defied us once, you won't get away with it again!"

"Listen, you fat little bastard!" Fontaine said, his patience gone. "You sign this or you're out of business! Estes, show him your paper."

"No!" the little man screamed. "Bryan! Bryan!"

"All right," Fontaine grinned, "we'll do it the hard way!"

He stepped to the center of the street and waved his hat, first to the north and Hand, then to the south and Gomez, then to the cross street to the west and Grimes, the blacksmith. Three covered wagons surrounded by Indians lumbered onto the main street. Then Fontaine waved his hat again and the three wagons were opened and a howling, barking stream of Indian dogs poured out onto the clean streets of Jason, Colorado, and the townspeople erupted with laughter.

They had never seen so many dogs in their lives! Big dogs, little dogs, skinny dogs, short dogs, tall dogs; all hungry and all anxious to lift their legs after having been given all the water that they could drink and then being confined in the wagon for many hours. The hairy stream ran up the street, to be met by another stream going south. The Indians took up places at the end of the street, and between buildings to keep their dogs on target. And the targets were every post in town. Everyone, including several usually stoic Indians, was laughing at the wonderful spectacle; all except the mayor. He was, for once, shocked into speechlessness.

Suddenly Bryan rushed out of his office. At first he couldn't believe what he saw but then he reached back into the office and pulled out a rifle and fired a couple of shots into the air. A few of the closer dogs scattered, but Bryan could see that it would do no good. Then he ran into the street, his face white with anger, and raised the gun to fire at a dog. Before he could lever another shell into the chamber, two Indians stepped out, one from the alley, one between two buildings, and pointed their rifles at him. Bryan lowered his rifle, and backed toward his office. As he paused on the boardwalk, a big dog started to raise his leg at Bryan's boot. Bryan yelled and kicked at the dog and ran into the office, put the rifle inside and came out, closed the door and sprinted up the street.

Fontaine watched him a moment and his eyes landed on the prisoner, the chains still around his ankles. He was leaning against his barrel, tears of laughter running down his cheeks. Then the doors opened and the women and children came out to watch the fun with their men. Bryan stopped in the middle of the street and turned in a circle. Everywhere he looked was a brave, holding a rifle. Then Bryan saw the butcher shop.

"Meat!" he said. "A nice big ham!"

He ran into the butcher's and came out in a moment, waving a ham above his head. "Here, doggy! Nice doggy. Come on, doggies!"

Fontaine turned to the pasty-faced mayor and said, "I understand the governor might give you a job today, depending, of course, on what he sees here."

"What do you want?" the mayor said, his shoulders sagging.

"At first we wanted you out," Estes said, opening the papers in his hand. "But we've decided to be kind to you. This rescinds all the laws you've passed. You'll still be mayor, of a sort, but you won't have anything to say. It also fires Bryan!"

"I . . . I can't do that! Bryan would kill me . . . no! I can't do it!"

"All right!" Fontaine shrugged. "Let the governor see this in an hour, the smell will run him out of town. Sign it and you'll still be mayor and we'll get the dogs out before the governor arrives, take your choice!"

The mayor stared at his shattered world and slowly nodded. One of the men came out of the building with a quill and the mayor signed all three copies at Estes's insistence.

"Now tell him he's fired," Fontaine said, indicating Bryan.

The mayor shook his head in fright. Fontaine looked over his shoulder at a brave with a bow and arrow. "Can he hit that ham?" Fontaine asked Hand.

"Easily."

Fontaine nodded and Hand nodded to the brave and the arrow neatly picked the ham from Bryan's hand and dropped it in the street. Bryan turned angrily to the group, his hands flexing in hate, and Fontaine shouted:

"You're fired, Bryan! Tell him, Mayor!"

"They . . . they forced me!" the mayor said.

"You son of a bitch!" Bryan said, coming toward the mayor. "You politicians are all alike! You needed a goat!"

Bryan came forward, stalking the mayor. Suddenly he darted to his left and grabbed old Gomez and spun him around, pulling his skinning knife and pushing the old man in front of him.

"Now, Your Honor!" Bryan yelled. "You and me are gonna leave together!"

Bryan's eyes darted to Fontaine's carbine for a moment and then he pushed the old man into Fontaine and ran toward the mayor. Fontaine caught the old man, but he dropped his rifle and, not daring to wait to pick it up, he lunged toward Bryan and caught his knife hand and they twisted into the street, their hands locked.

"I didn't think you had the guts!" Bryan said. "It'll be a pleasure to earn Lane's money."

"Fuck you!" Fontaine yelled, losing his temper.

A couple of braves started to come close but Hand waved them back. Despite his feelings, he didn't want to risk an Indian shooting a white man, no matter the reason. Besides, it was Fontaine's fight. In their desire to watch, the townspeople crowded forward, standing shoulder to shoulder with the Indians.

Bryan tripped his lighter adversary and they rolled over and over in the street, Fontaine keeping a tight grip on Bryan's wrist. They came to a halt with Bryan on the bottom and he managed to get his boots into Fontaine's groin and toss him over his head into the dirt. Fontaine was thrown free, on his back. He lay there a moment, fighting for breath, and saw Bryan roll over, get to his feet and charge. Fontaine got to one knee, waited a split second, and then he launched himself forward and under the bigger man, bringing one hand up into Bryan's crotch as he rolled away. They both landed heavily but Fontaine was on his feet as Bryan raised up. He hit the collector in the face with a right, then a long left, bringing Bryan fully erect. Bryan stood there a moment, fear on his face as Fontaine stalked forward, looking for an opening to grab the knife, but Bryan had had enough. He turned and ran up the street. Fontaine took a deep breath, his teeth still gritted in anger, and then he ran after Bryan. He was gaining with each step until a dog darted in front of him, tripping him heavily to the ground. Bryan looked over his shoulder and turned with a grin, and charged.

As Fontaine raised up, the prisoner shouted, "Hey!" and Fontaine turned his head for a moment to see the man toss his spade toward him. Fontaine scrambled for it, as Bryan launched himself through the air. Fontaine ducked, grabbed the spade with both hands, like a rifle, did a complete roll and came up on his knees to turn and face the next charge. Bryan's angered face showed that he had lost all instincts but one as he quickly threw himself forward again before Fontaine could raise the spade. But Fontaine didn't raise it. As Bryan charged, Fontaine ducked under the wild swipe with the knife and brought the spike up into Bryan's stomach.

Bryan screamed with pain and the impetus of his body pulled the handle from Fontaine's hands. Bryan landed on his back, clawing at the handle. Fontaine rolled to his feet and stared down at Bryan, breathing heavily. Bryan was trying to pull the spike from his body, still screaming. Fontaine stepped forward and said:

"Here, let me help you."

Bryan stared wide-eyed as Fontaine took hold of the wooden handle with both hands, and leaned close. Then Fontaine whispered, "Die, you bastard!" and instead of pulling the spike he twisted the handle like he was churning butter and Bryan stopped screaming. Then, just to make sure, Fontaine pulled the spike loose, held it high for a moment, then slammed it down into Bryan's chest.

He turned and walked away as the women gasped and the men stared and swallowed hard. One Indian nodded as Fontaine made his way through the crowd and John Hand came up to him, clapped him on the back, handed him his carbine, and grinned:

"You sure you're not a Cheyenne?"

"I'm sure. I haven't had a bath in two days!"

Then the two men grinned at each other while the white men tried to think of something to say.

"Nevertheless, Jonathan Fontaine," Hand said, "you are a brave man."

Fontaine grinned tightly and held up his shaking hand. "Not right now, I'm not."

Then Estes was there to clap him on the back and the rest of the men began to come forward to be able to tell their children that they were there to congratulate the legendary Jonathan Fontaine.

"All right," Fontaine said to Estes, "you got your goddam town back. Now, get that telegrapher and get him to open up."

Estes nodded and they began to force their way through the crowd as the townspeople began to help the Indians get the dogs back into the wagons. Fontaine sent a telegram to Beesley which read:

TELL MY FRIEND THAT THE TWO OF US ARE COMING BUT HE GOT A HEAD START STOP TELL HIM MEET ME AS PLANNED LEAVING NOW WILL WIRE FROM HOLBROOK BE READY

FONTAINE

Then he made the telegrapher stay on the wire to Colorado Springs while he got an answer to his question to the stationmaster. The reply came back in a few minutes; the next southbound through train left Colorado Springs at six P.M. He threw two silver dollars on the counter and sprinted back to the council building. The street was almost clean and Hand was standing by the councilmen.

"Gomez!" Fontaine shouted. "Go to the stable and get my saddlebags and take them to Hand's wagon!"

The little Mexican, eager to be of service, ran off and Fontaine turned to Estes and said, "Well, you ready? If you're going with me you're gonna have to ride like the goddam wind."

"Well, uh," Estes grinned. "As a matter of fact, sir, no. One, I don't think I'd want to work for your Mr. Lane and, two, I think I'll stay here. Thanks to you, we've got a pretty nice little town."

"All right," Fontaine grinned. "Can't say as I blame you, but be careful. Little bastards like the mayor got a way of easin' through life. Watch him."

"Don't you worry, sir," Estes grinned. "When the governor

leaves he will be handed a letter signed by the entire council, setting forth what happened here; that should finish the mayor in politics."

"Good! Well, I gotta get my ass in the saddle. It's been a pleasure, sort of!"

Fontaine shook hands with the council, Louis Estes, and then John Hand.

"How can we tell our thanks?" Hand said.

"Two ways, John Hand. First, I want to borrow four of your fastest ponies. I've got to be in Colorado Springs by six. . . ."

"But that's seventy odd miles!" Estes said.

"It certainly is," Fontaine grinned.

"I'll see to it!" Hand said. "Mr. Estes, write four notes that can be attached to bridles saying that the council will pay for the return of the horses. I'll supply the horses!"

Then Hand turned and shouted in Cheyenne to his braves as he and Fontaine started up the street. "And what's the other way, Jonathan Fontaine?"

Fontaine smiled and pointed to Gomez as he met them at the wagon and whispered to the Indian. Hand grinned and reached into the back of his wagon for a moment and then came out with a small, fuzzy puppy, which he gave to Gomez. The little Mexican hesitated, then took the puppy in his arms. He turned to Fontaine and looked at him and the tears ran down his cheeks as the puppy licked his face.

"Even a Cheyenne understands that," Hand said as they turned to the horses.

There were four ponies, each with a blanket and bridle, one tied to the other. Fontaine took his saddlebags from the back of the wagon, threw himself over the lead pony and leaned down to shake hands.

"You will be welcome," the Indian said.

"Thank you," Fontaine said. Then he shouted "Yaa!" to the ponies and galloped west.

Chapter Ten

Fontaine had bought a fine horse at Holbrook with some of the money that Estes refused but, good animal though it was, it was spent by the time Fontaine reached his ranch. As he topped the last rise he smiled when he saw Linus standing in what had once been his front yard with four fresh horses. Fontaine slid to the ground, turned the winded animal to the spring, which still had some brackish water in it, then turned to shake Gonzalez's hand.

"I wasn't sure you'd make it this time," Linus grinned. "And we don't have time to talk about it. However you convinced that crazy goddam Indian to come back, it worked only too well. But he did a stupid thing. He ran by Toby's front door and put a war arrow right in the middle of it!"

"Christ! Toby get him yet?"

"He's got 'im cornered. That Toby, he's a smart one. He got out every hand he had, some fifty men, and figured the Indian would run for the Rim. He sent forty men over the other side, they got fifty more who were willin' to ride for a day's wage, and they formed a rope and drove the Indian back to this side. They've got him holed up in some rocks, just below Lane City. You know, in that long, skinny meadow just below town?"

"Yes," Fontaine nodded, accepting a drink from Linus's canteen, "I know."

"Well, Lane's going to starve 'im out. The Indian has already killed two men, so this gives Lane a chance to hang him as an example."

Fontaine took a deep breath, another drink, then bent over, touching his boots to work the kinks out of his back. Then he stood up, took a paper from his pocket and said:

"You take the best two horses. Go to Lane City and follow these directions. There's some blanks in 'em 'cause I wrote them on the train. But where it's blank, put in the word 'meadow.' I'm going by Toby's to see if I can talk to Mary Kaye first. Think there's time?"

"Oh yes," Linus nodded. "I think Lane's planning on a few days. Been there since yesterday."

"Uh huh. Tell me about the meadow. If I recall, the rocks are maybe a half mile below the town and the meadow's only fifty, seventy yards wide, but long."

"That's the place," Linus nodded. "Toby's got it blocked above and below. In the bushes on each side are half the town, waiting for the Indian to come out."

"Good. Follow those directions, the bushes seem the best."

"I take it you're gonna ride in there, with Toby and his rifles. Will you be all right?"

"Me?" Fontaine grinned. "Sure. I'm no Indian. Get going!"

Linus nodded and picked a horse. Fontaine untied the two he indicated and watched his friend gallop off. Then he mounted and rode to Lane's ranch.

As he rode through the outbuildings he was aware of the quiet. The place was deserted, almost. He found Mary Kaye leading a horse out of the stable. When she saw him she dropped the reins and ran forward to cling to him as he dismounted.

"Toby's going to hang him! And it has to do with you, doesn't it?"

"Yes," he said, pushing her to arm's length. "I've got a thing to tell you. You know about my daughter? Well, think about it a bit. I was knocked out. . . . By who? Toby Lane."

"How do you know?" she said. "Are you sure?"

"Yes. I ran the Indian down, he admitted it. . . . Mary Kaye, your uncle's sick, he's got a trouble with his brain. He wanted my land for the railroad right-of-way. . . . Oh, he probably didn't intend for my daughter to get killed, he just wanted me burned out so I would sell. But the Mexican went crazy and Toby, who was on the other side of the house with the horses, came around and knocked me out and dragged me clear. Through some perverted sense of friendship he could never bring himself to kill me. But he knew I wouldn't give it up, and as soon as the railroad came through I'd figure it out and then I would've come lookin' for him.

"So he got me here with the Indian as bait and he sent me on one thing after another, hoping somebody would do the job for him. Finally he couldn't wait any longer. He set up the Indian, and me, and sent me to find him, with a local gunman to see that I never got back. . . . I . . . I just wanted you to know, I'm going up there."

The shock showed in her face but, to her credit, she swallowed a couple of times and then nodded. "I think I believe you. . . . But I think I love you. . . . Could I talk you out of it?"

He shook his head. "No, ma'am."

She sighed and wiped away her tears on the back of her hand. "All right. I've said things to you that even a goddam two-bit whore wouldn't say. I'll add one more thing: be careful."

Fontaine nodded, ran his hand down her cheek, and turned to his saddlebag. He took out a handful of bullets and put them in his shirt pocket, made sure his carbine was fully loaded, and, leaving his gear on the ground, he rolled onto the spare horse and galloped toward Lane City.

As he approached the lower end of the meadow he saw a string of men keeping the local citizens at a distance. Fontaine cocked the carbine with his left hand, keeping it at his side, ignored the challenge and rode through the guards who hesitated to call out the well-known Fontaine. Another fifty feet and Leroy Starrett was standing in the way, his hand near his gun.

"Jonathan," Leroy said as Fontaine pulled his horse to a walk, "I'll stop you if I have to."

"You'll have to, Leroy," Fontaine said, shaking his head. "And I don't want to shoot you, but flick a muscle and I'll do it."

Starrett shook his head in a corresponding sorrow and his right elbow quivered; the carbine came up smoothly and the bullet caught Starrett in the right side before his gun cleared its holster. The impact threw him on his back, the gun flying clear. Fontaine rode close and looked down at Starrett and the foreman looked up with a wide-eyed groan.

"I'm beholden to ya agin. Ya coulda killed me. I didn't know you wuz left-handed."

"I'm not, Leroy," Fontaine said flatly. "I go both ways."

Then he rode to the center of the meadow, to where Toby Lane was standing alone by his horse. Lane had his revolver pointed at Fontaine.

"I can get off at least one, Jonathan," Lane nodded calmly. "Yeah The Injun told me."

"It better be a good one, Toby. If I get a shot you're dead," Fontaine said in the same flat voice. "Though I'd rather cut your throat, like your Mexican did to my daughter."

"So help me God, Jonathan, I didn't intend that . . . the Mexican got out of hand and I was late. . . . Good thing, or he'd have killed you, too."

"You ordered it," Fontaine said.

"Only the burning, Jon, not the rest."

"Not the rest, my ass! You hired Charlie Moss to go through my notebook and you sent word all over hell about me being a killer so someone would try me, didn't you?"

"Yes."

"And Alfred! And you got out the poster! And Bryan!"

"Yes, yes! But I couldn't kill you myself . . . before." Then, cheerfully changing the subject, Toby suddenly smiled, "Hey! What about Bryan?"

"I gutted him."

"Uh huh," Toby nodded as though hearing some news about a neighbor's cow. Then, his eyes flicking to the carbine a moment, "That thing works pretty good."

"It works pretty good," Fontaine nodded once, deciding that if he killed Lane now his horse couldn't run fast enough to get him out of the meadow alive. "Tell you what, Toby. You try the Indian first and I'll take on the winner."

"Why you son of a bitch!" Lane grinned. "You're just like me, only not as greedy. You think you can get the Indian with that thing and I can't take 'im with a six-gun."

"That's right, Toby."

"Goddam!" Lane nodded. "You planned that and then learned to use the weapon?"

"Like I told you, I'm not much at a draw anyway." Then Fontaine saw a black hand wave once from a bush at the edge of the meadow and he nudged his horse to slowly ease that way. Then he stood in the stirrups, his eyes still on Lane, and shouted, "Iron Shirt! Would you try Lane and then me? If you win you go free. You have my word!"

"I accept your word, Fontaine! What about Lane? What good is his word?"

The Indian's voice echoed across the meadow so that everyone heard him.

"Damn!" Lane shouted, then grinned and lowered his voice so only Fontaine could hear. "You son of a bitch, now I've got to defend my honor, otherwise all those human sheep I was gonna use to make money won't listen. . . . And my word, Indian!"

"Fontaine!" the Indian shouted. "Get off your horse! Drop your weapon!"

"Tell you what, Jon," Toby holstered his gun and grinned at the prospects of ridding himself of both at once, "shuck that rifle. Soon as I get rid of the Injun I'll give ya a chance with a knife, or barehanded even, but get rid of that carbine!"

"All right," Fontaine nodded, tossing it into the bush. Then he dismounted and stood to one side while Lane climbed on his horse and held up his hand to the spectators.

"All right!" Lane shouted. "You heard it. Make it fair!" Then dropping his voice so only Fontaine could hear, "Fair, my ass! But don't worry, Jon, your turn's comin'!"

Lane twisted his horse and the Indian rode out of the rocks, a buffalo hide shield in front of him and a lance in his right hand. Fontaine was between them, but out of the way to the right as the Indian charged. Toby raised his gun, holding his animal steady with his knees, and aimed carefully at the shield, held high in front of the Indian's face. The bullet thudded off the tough hide and then Lane tried a shot in the chest. The Indian grunted, was almost unhorsed, but the chain mail held and the Indian came on. Then, using two hands on his gun, Lane tried to hit the arm holding the lance and again missed. The Indian was almost on him and Lane lowered his muzzle to shoot the horse; the crowd roared its displeasure and then the lance pierced Lane's stomach.

Without waiting to see what he knew was a death blow, the Indian spun his mount in a tight circle and ran for the rocks. Fontaine ran to Toby, and Starrett, now in a buggy, held up his hand and the rest held their places. Fontaine knelt by Lane and the big man opened his eyes and grinned faintly:

"Get the son of a bitch, Jon boy!"

Fontaine nodded and ran back toward the Indian, and Iron Shirt rode out with a second lance.

"Linus!" Fontaine shouted, and the carbine was tossed through the air. Fontaine caught it deftly, pulled the hammer back and dropped slightly.

The Indian pulled his horse around again and ran into the rocks. In a moment he appeared without lance or shield but with his rifle; death on a running pony. Fontaine waited as the

Indian charged, shooting wildly, the reins in his teeth. Then Fontaine began to shoot. His hands worked smoothly as he calmly held his place and began to pump slugs into the big chest. The first shot staggered the Indian and threw off his aim, but when he recovered and his rifle began to train on Fontaine the next three shots from the carbine punctured the chain mail and chest armor as though it weren't there. The Indian was thrown off his horse and as the frightened pony thundered past, Fontaine ran to the Indian, kicked the rifle clear of the right hand, and knelt by the red man.

The Indian raised up and looked at the holes in his chest and said, "The shirt is very old, it needs mending." Then the head fell back, the sightless eyes staring at the sky.

Fontaine stood erect and turned toward Starrett and the riflemen. There was a momentary silence and then half a dozen men started to raise their rifles and Fontaine raised his hand above this head and shouted:

"Reverend Manley!" The preacher stood up from the brush and levered a shell into his rifle.

"Lacey!" And Lacey stood up from the other side of the meadow and there was another click-click.

"Purdy!

"Roberts!

"O'Rooney!

"Abe!

"Isaacs!

"Gonzalez!"

In the momentary impasse, Toby Lane, still lying on his side in the grass, held one arm high to Leroy Starrett to stay his men from being killed.

"It's over, Leroy!" Fontaine shouted.

"It's over," Starrett nodded sadly and lowered his rifle.

Then Fontaine ran to Toby and forced his way through the gathering crowd and met Starrett, who was grimacing at the pain in his side as they knelt by the dying man. Lane's face was pale and there was a spreading stain from the lance, but his eyes were clear. He looked up at the two men and said in a whisper:

"Goddam, that was something, clean as a whistle. . . . Pull it out, Leroy."

Starrett got a grip on the lance with one hand and pulled the shaft free, and the blood pumped faster. Lane looked at the blood for a moment, then put a hand on each man's neck.

"I coulda done it with you two . . . I coulda run the whole Territory, if you two hadn't been so damned stubborn. . . ."

His body jerked convulsively once and then the hands fell to the ground.

Fontaine got to his feet, helped Starrett up and said, "Let's get to buryin'."

"We'll do it. We'll bury the Injun in them rocks, but Mr. Lane's gonna git a proper buryin'. . . . There's a hill behind the house . . . but not here!"

"All right, Leroy," Fontaine said, waving at his friends.

Fontaine left the TL men as they began to form a funeral cortege; he mounted his horse and rode to the trail leading away from Lane City and waited.

His friends came up to him one at a time, some mounted, some on foot, and all remained quiet. He nodded to each one and waited until they had all gathered. In the background Linus pointed down the hill. Mary Kaye had stopped at the wagon where they had put Lane's body. Fontaine nodded and Linus rode down to the girl. Then Fontaine turned to his silent friends and nudged his horse along the line while he shook each man's hand.

"You're all free to go or stay, as you choose. . . . And if you're wondering, yes; I used you. All of you. But I paid you well with Lane's money, and maybe you learned something, so you weren't cheated. If you stay, I'll be pleased to have any of you for neighbors."

He turned his horse and loped to where the road cut the edge of the meadow and stopped and waited. In a few moments he saw the girl and Gonzalez pull their horses away from the wagon and ride toward him. While he waited he took out his notebook and his pencil stub and made an entry.

Lane City will never be without a Toby Lane; bastard and dreamer, tyrant and sometimes friend. Lane City will be, as it is now, stillborn, because without a Toby Lane there'll be no one to get it through its growing pains. In a few years it'll be gone and no one will ever remember it. . . .

Fontaine was right.